BOYFRIEND MATERIAL

EVERNIGHT PUBLISHING ®

www.evernightpublishing.com

BOYFRIEND MATERIAL

DEDICATION

For the Club crew, who are always encouraging and supporting me.

BOYFRIEND MATERIAL

#

The Man Catalog, 2

Megan Morgan

Copyright © 2018

Chapter One

Grace Bennington slapped her checkbook shut, dropped it on her lap, and chewed on one of her gel-tipped nails. She abruptly stopped herself, because a gel manicure was expensive and she didn't want to screw her nails up before the trip. Such a bad habit. She tucked her hand under her thigh and stared down at the closed checkbook. Her bank account balance danced in front of her eyes, without even looking at it. Taunting her.

You can afford to do this, she told herself. *In fact, you can't afford* not *to do it.*

To appear as anything less than complete, anything less than absolutely unassailable in front of those petty, immaculate women would be a living nightmare. She had to look, act, and seem the part—that was, the part of a goddess, whose life hadn't fallen into utter shambles over the past year.

"Come on, come on," Grace muttered, and looked

at the time on her phone. "I don't have all day."

The office was warm and filled with sunlight, and the décor consisted of bright flowers, kitschy knick-knacks, and framed pictures of happy couples on the desk in front of her. She grimaced. Too much false chipper optimism and forced hominess, like a doctor's office where you'd soon be told you had inoperable cancer. She supposed most women who came in here were just as nervous as if that bomb was about to be dropped on them.

And apparently, they had to wait forever for the diagnosis.

Finally, a door behind the desk opened, and a pretty, middle-aged blond woman stepped out, carrying a stack of books. She smiled at Grace, with the same put-on cheeriness as the rest of the room.

"Mrs. Bennington?"

Grace quickly stuffed her checkbook in her designer bag—bought at an outlet store, but no one could tell, right?—and got to her feet. She held out her hand, sleek nails flashing in the sunlight.

"Grace Bennington, yes. Just call me Grace."

The woman shook her head. "I'm Monica Hunt." She had a kind face and gentle eyes, and somehow, the soft assuring tone of her voice made Grace's stomach stop doing flip-flops. This woman probably floated her way through life, drawing people to her like flies to honey with an aura like that. Grace often found herself disgruntled by such people. They made it look so ... easy.

She was the absolute opposite of the women Grace usually hung around.

"I'm the director of SASS." Monica chuckled. "I love saying that."

SASS—Social   Arrangement   Service

Specialists—was a silly acronym in Grace's opinion, and they manipulated it for even sillier advertising. "SASS-y Women Find Love in Unusual Places!" their marketing claimed. The business was, on the surface, a dating and matchmaking service. However, Grace was seeking them out for the more in-depth, specialty services they offered. She intended to hide her patronage, of course. The very thought of her friends finding out filled her with dread.

"Grace." Monica kept an easy smile on her face. "I'm happy to meet you."

"I need to get down to business," Grace informed her. "I'm on a tight schedule. My apologies."

"Of course, by all means." Monica motioned to Grace's chair.

They both sat. Grace smoothed a hand over her silk skirt. Despite her nerves, she'd made the solid decision a few days ago to forge ahead, and she wanted to get this over with so she could focus on more important things—like what outfits to pack for this weekend.

Monica remained unruffled, and Grace felt instantly embarrassed for being so abrupt. She seemed like a very nice woman. On top of that, she was about to provide Grace with a much needed service.

"I'm sorry," Grace said. "I'm on a time constraint, you see. It's making me really anxious. I don't mean to be rude."

Monica patted her pile of books on the desk. "I understand completely. It's somewhat nerve-wracking just being here, isn't it? Let me put your mind at ease."

Grace nodded.

"First, I trust you understand the services we offer here? You sounded like you were well informed on the phone, so I don't want to presume anything."

"Yes, I know you run a dating service as a front

for an escort business." Grace took her bag from the chair next to her and plopped it on the edge of the desk. "The wealthy women I'm friends with have gossiped about it many times. I get it. Now, I need someone beautiful, suave, and most importantly, able to put on a good show. It's imperative that everyone believe he's my boyfriend. I'm willing to tip him additionally if he can pull it off." She fished her checkbook out. Why she'd put it away, she wasn't sure. Maybe some insane part of her was terrified Monica would see through the cover.

Monica continued to hold a relaxed, friendly smile. "Our gentlemen are well versed in charm and social graces. You're looking for something short-term, I take it? Not one of our more long-term and dedicated packages?"

Grace raised her eyebrows. "Dedicated?"

"Some of our clients are looking for extended happiness and companionship. We have a high success rate of bringing people together for life. I'm rather proud of it."

For a moment, Grace wasn't sure what she meant, then she realized what Monica was saying and boggled. "You sell husbands too?"

One of the girls had mentioned you could buy a husband from SASS, but Grace thought she was joking. Surely such things didn't happen, in America, in this day and age. Right?

"We do." Monica nodded. "But that's not what you're here for, so I won't go into it."

Grace smirked bitterly. "Goodness. I wish I'd known that before. It would have saved me a lot of trouble."

"We provide male companions for discerning women, at least this division does. We also have a service for our gay and lesbian community. Our mission, overall, is helping single people find each other and discover lifelong happiness."

"Right." Grace crossed her legs and bobbed her Jimmy Choo heel. She'd gotten them at the same outlet store, and they complimented her outfit. "I'm not looking for another husband. I just need a man for the weekend. I'll be taking him to Barbados, so he needs to have a passport." She recalled the account balance in her checkbook again. It was burned into her retinas at this point. "I'll pay for his plane ticket and any expenses while he's there. We'll be staying at an all-inclusive resort, so there shouldn't be too many." He could eat at their atrocious buffets and she was definitely not paying for a spa package, unless everyone else did it and she had to bring him along.

"That sounds lovely." Monica shuffled through her stack of books and drew one out, a large soft-bound book with a red cover. "A weekend is three thousand dollars."

Grace flicked her nails, picking at them. "Fine," she said coolly. "I have it, no worries."

"These are our gentlemen who do short-term excursions." She held the book out to her, across the desk.

Grace eyed it. She'd heard rumors about this book, the fabled "man catalog." Could she really browse guys like she was at the produce section of Whole Foods?

"If you'd like to take this home," Monica said, "so you can peruse it at your leisure, there's a deposit. It's five-hundred—"

"I'm leaving tomorrow morning." Grace grabbed the book. "I'll purchase his ticket tonight. Let me just pick one out right now." She had wanted to do this earlier, so she wouldn't have to pay so much for a last-minute ticket for her companion, but she'd had to wait until a certain deposit finally went into her account. She'd made it, just barely.

Monica frowned, the first change in her breezy, confident expression. "You really are on a time constraint, aren't you? It's not an easy choice, trust me. Are you sure you don't want to take it home?"

"No, I'll choose one now, it's not an issue." Grace sat back. She stared down at the book for a moment, then opened it.

As she flipped through the broad, heavy pages, what she saw gave her pause. This was indeed a man catalog, and while she was currently an overwrought, distracted ball of anxiety, the offerings presented commanded all her attention.

Each page displayed a different man, accompanied by two pictures: one a headshot, the other a full body. The photographer was certainly skilled at catching their good sides. Printed below the pictures was a first name only and their age. Each entry also listed their occupation, ethnicity, interests and hobbies, and their availability. Some were labeled as "one encounter," while more were "multi-day" and "weekly." She realized her cheeks were getting warm, and she rarely blushed.

All the men were dangerously handsome, some intimidatingly so. Not the sort of men she imagined needed to sell themselves. All were dressed in suits and formal wear so they looked sophisticated and high-class. She hadn't expected there would be so many to choose from.

Monica folded her hands on the desk and watched her as she flipped through the pages. "What do you do for a living, Grace?"

Grace looked up at her and smiled. "I own several boutiques in Manhattan. Maybe you've heard of them—

Graceful Garments? They're quite popular amongst the stylish upper echelon." Pride swelled in her, but it was quickly deflated by painful memories and even more painful, probable prospects that lay ahead of her.

Not to mention she was lying about the "several" part. She'd *had* several boutiques, once, and that still counted, as far as she was concerned.

Monica perked. "Oh, yes. There's one on West 35th, isn't there? I bought a dress there a few months ago."

Grace's pride managed to struggle back up through the cracks. "You did?" She gazed at Monica in surprise. The one on West 35th was her last bastion. "Well ... thank you. I design the clothes myself, though I have a few girls who work with me too, adding insights. I hope you like it."

"I love it. It's a sweater dress though, and I'm waiting for fall to come back around so I can wear it again." Monica's smile had returned.

Grace resisted telling her it would surely be out of style by then. Some women didn't care about that. She ought to be grateful instead of critical.

"Business must be good." Monica's voice wrapped around her like a hug, a strange reaction for Grace to have to anyone these days. "Going to Barbados, to a resort. That sounds exciting, and expensive."

Grace tucked her hair behind her ear and played with an errant curl against her neck. "Yes, business is booming. I used to have a lot more stores, but you know, I downsized." She was paranoid now that Monica, being a customer, would discover the truth. "It's too much work, so I went down to just a few. I had no life of my own, I was running myself ragged. I needed some me-time." She gave a bright, false laugh.

"Many women who come to us are too busy to

pursue relationships. We live in a fast-paced world and that's why we feel our services are so important. No one should suffer just because they're struggling to build their own business or make their mark on the world."

Grace tugged at her hair. Yes, too busy for love. That was her excuse, wasn't it? And it was true, mostly.

She turned a page, and her breath caught.

Her toes curled in her overpriced shoes. The man she stared at was the opposite of what she'd intended to look for, and yet he was also perfect for so many reasons.

He had a dusky copper complexion, and thick, straight, jet-black hair, brushed back from his face and hanging past his collar. Long enough to be sexy but not unkempt and rebellious. He had a square jaw covered in dark scruff, and deep, soulful brown eyes beneath thick but well-groomed eyebrows. He also had lips that commanded attention. Just as it was unfair some guys had lashes a woman would kill for, this guy had a mouth that catwalk models in Milan would give up their sponsorships to obtain. They were full and pillowy and pale, and screamed *kiss me, suck on me.* Her heart pounded at that boyish, beautiful, yet rugged and boldly masculine face.

She tore her gaze from his picture and looked at his info.

His name was Tybalt, which almost made her laugh because it sounded so dramatic. He was twenty-eight. In both the head shot and full-length picture he wore a gray blazer and crisp white shirt with the top buttons undone, collar popped. In the head shot he was smiling, his teeth perfectly white and straight. In the full-length picture he had a smoldering, intense gaze.

He almost looked too much like a man one paid for, and yet...

His stats said he was Italian and Greek, which

explained the dark and handsome look. His occupation was "business owner," so they'd at least have something in common. She didn't bother reading his interests and hobbies. Most of those things were superficial and made up to get you to pick them, she assumed.

"Does he have a passport?" She turned the book around and held it out, to show her Tybalt's page. "Can he be at JFK by 10:00 AM tomorrow?"

Monica took the book from her and placed it on the desk, and turned to a computer next to her. "Many of our gentlemen have passports. They enjoy travel."

"Even more on someone else's dime, I'm sure." Grace glanced at the book. Hopefully, he was a good conversationalist. If not, he could just stand there and look pretty. He had enough edge he should induce envy amongst her catty friends, who all wished for something younger and hotter than their stuffy husbands.

Monica typed on the computer, and after a minute, spoke. "Yes, he has a passport, and he's currently available." She swiveled toward Grace. "I can call him. Would you like to meet for coffee this afternoon and see if you have chemistry? There's no commitment."

"No." Grace picked up her checkbook. "Just have him show up at JFK at 10:00 AM, and meet me at the American check-in. I need you to send me his information so I can purchase him a ticket, as soon as possible." She paused, trying to remember everything she needed to convey. "Tell him to bring resort-appropriate clothes, nothing too trashy, and at least one formal suit. Something designer, preferably. Calvin Klein, at the low end." She pulled out her own pen, a gold-plated Cartier limited edition. "Is it three thousand total, or are there taxes?"

Monica blinked a few times.

"Are you sure you don't want to meet him first?" Her tone was still light, but now held a touch of concern. Maybe she wasn't used to women who could make up their minds quickly. "Many of our clients would rather meet the gentleman first, in case they don't get along. You could still pick someone else. There's time."

"It doesn't matter if we get along, just how he looks." Grace clicked her pen. "Now, who do I make this out to?" She should have brought cash, in retrospect. She couldn't pay by debit card, as the amount was too much. But still, the charge might appear as something non-discreet in her account, and what would the bankers think? She had been reduced to paying for a man, and this was truly the low point of the entire year. Did it really matter anymore?

"Um," Monica said, "just make it out to Hunt Services."

The transaction took less than twenty minutes. Because it was such a large amount, Grace had to call and clear it with her bank, but everything went through. She wrote out her instructions detailing what Tybalt should bring, and exactly where and when he should meet her. Monica promised she would send his details along as soon as he gave permission to release them.

She and Monica shook hands again as Grace got up to leave.

"Enjoy your trip," Monica said. The woman never stopped smiling. "I'm sure your gentleman will only improve upon your good time."

Grace forced a smile in return. "I'm sure he will. Thank you for your help." At least she'd have something nice to look at this weekend.

Grace turned and headed toward the door but stopped short when Monica called after her.

"Grace?"

She looked back.

"That's a lovely bag." Monica nodded at it. "Burberry, isn't it? So chic. I absolutely love it."

Grace smiled and held it up on her arm. "Yes, it is. Thank you."

"You have impeccable taste, in both accessories and men."

Grace laughed. "Oh, darling. You wouldn't say that if you knew me." She turned and sauntered out the door.

* * * *

Grace's outfits were carefully chosen, including shoes for each, and complimentary accessories, all neat and tightly packed—now she just had to hope it was good enough.

She stood in front of her bedroom window, high above the city street, in a white silk bra and panties. No one could see her up here, but she wouldn't mind if they did—or at least that's what she told herself. She was fit and curvy, maybe she was some Peeping Tom's fantasy. She tried to go to the gym a few times a week, though she often had to wedge it into her schedule. She was careful not to eat too many carbs, counted every calorie, and took it easy on wine nights with the ladies. She'd managed to scrape together enough money to laser off every unsightly hair, manicure every nail, and moisturize every inch of skin so she didn't have any wrinkles, lines, blemishes, or discoloration. Heaven forbid.

She raked her fingers through the waves of her hair, which was long and full and well-hydrated. Maybe she should have re-colored it this week. Were the burgundy highlights in the deep brown too dull? Were her roots showing? She glanced over at the full-length mirror, suddenly nervous. If she had a single dry strand or split end, she would never hear the end of it.

You have to be bulletproof, girl. Hold your head up high in front of those broads. Show them you still belong. She tilted her chin up. *You're just as good as them, even better.*

She thrust her chest out and looked down. Her boobs weren't sagging, were they? She slumped and sighed. This was exhausting.

Grace walked to the bed, where her suitcase sat open, awaiting the last few items she would throw in there tomorrow morning. She picked up the information package she'd gotten from SASS and her phone, and sat down on the edge of the bed.

Tybalt's phone number was listed on the sheet, and Monica had already sent her all his pertinent information, so she could get his ticket. He was from *Bensonhurst*, good Lord. Maybe she should call him and meet with him tonight after all, just in case he was too ghetto for this. She could instruct him on all the things he was supposed to do and say this weekend. She had enough saved up to tip him an extra five hundred, if he behaved himself to the letter.

Her phone rang in her hand, startling her. Was he calling her first? She frowned at the screen, then sighed, even heavier than before. But she answered with a cheery, expectant voice.

"Amelia! How are you?" She got up and strolled over to the mirror.

"Just as excited as can be, darling," the other woman purred through the phone. "I was just calling to make sure you're ready."

"I am." Grace leaned toward the mirror and inspected her eyebrows. "God knows I need some fun in the sun. I've been so busy with the boutiques lately. They're all doing so well."

Amelia chuckled, but it was a derisive sound.

Grace wasn't sure she had worked a day in her life, and she didn't need to.

"I'm looking forward to the sun, that's for sure." Amelia's voice was a lazy drawl. Grace always pictured her sprawled on a chaise lounge, sipping wine, whenever she called. "It's been a long winter, and this spring is taking forever to bloom. Anyway, even in the summer I can only do tanning beds here in the city. I can't lay out with all the pollutants in the air." Her tone brightened. "Carl bought me a gold lamé bikini for the trip. Wait until you see it, you will just die. I look like a movie star in it. He said it cost six hundred dollars. I'm sure he just got it so he can look at the tits he bought me, too."

Grace twisted her lips. "That sounds beautiful. I'm sure you look lovely." She thought of her own bikini, one she had designed herself. It wasn't nearly so showy.

"We have to go shopping while we're there," Amelia said. "I hear the resort has a few high-end stores nearby. I bet you could find some rags at the local shops, too. Bring them back, fancy them up, and resell them at your boutique."

Grace wanted to explain that's not how it worked, she didn't repurpose clothes but instead took pride in making her own designs from scratch, but Amelia wouldn't understand. She hadn't worn anything without a designer label on it since she was a child, and probably not even then.

"Perhaps." Grace kept her tone light. "I'm all up for shopping, though." The balance in her bank account screamed otherwise.

"Oh, and we're finally going to meet your man, I hear?" Amelia chuckled. "I can't wait. I'm so glad you've finally moved on from Brent, you've spent far too much time stuck in the past. I was starting to worry about you."

19

Grace tugged at a strand of her hair and kept her voice neutral. "Oh no, don't worry. I'm not stuck in the past. I know when to cut my losses and move on."

"I'm glad to hear it. How embarrassing for you." She tittered. "You recovered like a pro though, darling. Don't let these men keep you down. Does your new beau know about Brent? I wouldn't tell him you have an ex-husband in prison if you can avoid it. That's not the sort of bomb you want to drop on a man you don't have fully wrapped around your finger yet."

Grace yanked her hair. "I tell him only what he needs to know, and you're right, that's not important. I'm moving toward the future, not dwelling in the past."

"That's the spirit. What's his name again? Did you tell me?"

Grace had made up a "boyfriend" over the past couple weeks but kept the details vague under the guise they weren't serious yet. Her friends rarely listened to her anyway. Still, she could no longer stand their side-eyeing at brunch when she explained she was far too busy to get heavily involved with someone. She'd been hoping she might meet someone before the trip, and barring that, at least find someone to playact with her before she had to go to the extreme of actually purchasing a man.

Maybe she was just as pathetic as they obviously, secretly thought she was—or not so secretly. She was sure behind closed doors they laughed at her.

"Tybalt." She turned from the mirror. "He owns a business, like me. We're both entrepreneurs. We have so much in common. I couldn't believe it when we first met, he's a perfect match."

"Ah, I see." Amelia sounded bored. "Well, I hope he has a good time. You know we can get a little crazy." She giggled. "He can hang out with the men and talk about boring business things. You can push him off on them so we can have our girl time."

Grace laughed. "Yes, those men get tedious, don't they? All that talk about money and investments. Not to mention golf. They can go on forever about golf."

"As long as Carl keeps buying me things, I don't care. Let him stay on the green or go to the office. The last thing I want is to go to a tedious job every day."

Grace laughed again, forcing it through the tight ache in her chest. Amelia seemed to possess not one ounce of self-awareness.

"Anyway, Gracie, I'll see you in Barbados. You and your man. Is he young and hot? Please say yes, we need some fresh meat to ogle."

"Of course he is." She plucked at her bra strap. "I deserve the best, after what I've been through."

"Indeed." She blew a kiss through the phone. "Bye, darling. See you tomorrow."

Grace blew her a kiss in return and hung up.

She tossed the phone on the bed, next to the sheet with Tybalt's information, and stood there a moment, trying to breathe. Then she turned and faced the mirror again. Her eyes were bright with unshed tears. She stepped up to the mirror and wiped delicately beneath them, trying not to smear her mascara.

"Stop it," she told herself. "You're still good enough. The past is over." She sniffed and lifted her chin. "You're going to keep your head up. That's what you do."

The past was far from over, though. It loomed in a huge stack of legal papers on her desk—a stack of papers she was sick of looking at, that she couldn't bring herself to pick up and read through one more time. Those papers represented so much money sucked away, from her business, from the equity in the penthouse, from her wardrobe, from the luxuries she'd gotten used to having but were now slipping through her fingers. Each thing she had to sell felt like another nail in the coffin.

She stared at the papers over her shoulder in the mirror, just sitting there, taunting her in the afternoon light. A big, fat pile of failure.

She burst into sobs.

Chapter Two

Ty Rossi jammed the last of his clothes in the suitcase and looked up at his sister, who leaned in the bedroom doorway, her arms crossed and lips pinched. That expression usually preceded a brow-beating, and he wasn't wrong.

"*Barbados?*" Luci's tone was incredulous and accusing. She sounded just like their mother when she did that. "For the entire weekend? Really, Ty? Right now?"

He sighed and slapped the lid of his suitcase shut. "It's three thousand dollars. You really want me to say no to that?" He started zipping it up.

Luci rolled her eyes. She favored their mother in looks too: brown eyes and long, curly dark hair. She was pretty, the kind of pretty that made an older brother anxious and protective. He'd been giving the guys who flocked around her the evil eye since high school. When their father passed, he'd tried to extend that shell of protection to his mother as well, in different ways, but he had a lot of respect for his old man—they were both a lot of woman to handle. How Ty managed was nothing short of a miracle.

Or maybe he didn't manage at all.

"You should stay here and run the store." Luci stalked toward him. "We have to do inventory and start figuring out what items to get rid of that don't sell. We're bleeding money. The books gotta be balanced."

"All the more reason for me to go make three thousand easy dollars, huh?"

"We need you around." She stopped next to the bed, hands on her hips.

"I have faith in you. Besides, you and Ma are better at that stuff than I am." He reached out and gripped her shoulder. "Even if I was here, you know I'd still leave all that balancing stuff up to you. You're the brains, I'm just the muscle, remember?" He winked.

She shrugged off his hand, scowling. "What about Becky? She's getting to the age she notices when you leave for days at a time. It's not good for her."

Ty raked his fingers through his hair. "I'm not gonna do this forever, okay? I'm doing it for her too, you know."

Luci stared him down. "Being a *putano* for your daughter. How precious."

"I'm not a whore." He finished yanking the zipper on his suitcase shut. "This is legal, and I won't be young and good-looking forever. Why shouldn't I rake in the cash while I can? We need it. And I want a future for Becky, one that doesn't involve her having to do inventory and balance the books for the rest of her damn life." He'd raised his voice and he instantly regretted it, but Luci seemed to realize he was serious when he turned passionate like that.

She backed off but shook her head. "I don't know why any girl would actually pay money to hang out with you." She turned and huffed toward the door.

Ty picked up a discarded t-shirt and flung it after her. "Bitch."

She turned and gave him the finger. "Man whore." She left the room.

Once he was fully packed, Ty wandered out of the bedroom and into the kitchen, where the smell of tomato sauce permeated the air. Even after a full year, it was still weird for him to be living back in the apartment above the store, with his family. Sometimes he felt like he'd gone back in time to when he was a teenager, when he couldn't wait to get the hell out, get the hell away from the "family business" and the tight-packed quarters.

But here he was. Back home, back in the business, deeper than ever. Fate had a way of knocking him off track.

His mother stood over the stove and she glowered at him as he walked in the kitchen. Had his sister already told on him, that he'd called her a bitch? He tried to remember he was *not*, in fact, a teenager anymore, he was a grown man who could talk any way he liked in his own house.

Unless, of course, his mother said not to.

"Ah." His mother's tone sounded exactly like his sister's ten minutes ago. "I see it's my son, the gigolo."

Luci sat at the table, her college homework spread out on it, and she smirked at him. Ty scowled and walked to the fridge.

"Ma, c'mon. Knock it off, you're not funny."

"Don't you sass me." She glared at him. She was a big, boisterous, powerhouse of an Italian woman, and the last thing he would ever presume to do was sass her. He'd taken too many slaps to the head in his youth.

"Ma, I didn't go on any jobs all winter, did I?" He yanked the fridge door open. "It's three thousand dollars. That's enough to put in Becky's savings fund *and* get stuff done around the store."

"You can make three thousand dollars the honest way."

"It is honest." He grabbed a bottle of water. "It's an actual job. And I'm not gonna make three thousand dollars in one weekend in the store. We can get the freezer fixed in the back room and patch up that hole in the corner. Maybe we can upgrade the register, too."

Luci looked up. "Oh man." Now she seemed interested. "That would be awesome. I'm tired of hitting it with a hammer when the drawer gets stuck."

His mother shook her head. "Your father is

rolling over in his grave." She crossed herself.

Since her back was to him, he rolled his eyes. "Dad wouldn't think I was stupid for getting paid to hang out with beautiful women." He opened his bottle of water and took a drink, to hide a grin.

His mother looked over her shoulder at him, eyes on fire.

"Sorry," he muttered.

She turned back to her pot. "And what about Cassie, God rest her soul? What would she say about this?"

Ty pointed at her around the bottle. "Don't." He spoke with a type of firmness and seriousness he rarely used with his mother, but she had crossed a line.

She knew it, too, and didn't persist. She continued her cooking, stone silent. Luci looked down at her notebook. He supposed he deserved it, for bringing up his father, but he wanted this discussion to go no further.

He flopped down in a chair at the table and looked over at what his sister was doing. "What's that?"

"Economics." She was writing. "I've got class at seven."

Of course she would open a business someday, a store probably, like everyone else in their family. She was taking classes at Kingsborough during the evenings so she could work in the store during the day. No one in this family ever seemed to want anything else. They never tried something different, something outside their norm. Something outside this sad, broken legacy.

That was why, despite the harassment, he kept dating women for money. When he'd signed up with the agency, his mother and sister thought he was joking at first, then they held him in a sort of contemptuous disbelief when they realized he wasn't. But the money was good, and the money was a way out, a way to do something different, if not for him, then for Becky.

"Daddy?" a little voice said from the doorway.

Ty turned in his chair and smiled. His sleepy-eyed daughter stood in the doorway, rubbing her face. Her light brown hair was pulled up in a ponytail on top her head and secured with a Hello Kitty bow. He stood and walked over to her.

"Did you have a good nap?" He scooped her up.

She nodded. "I'm hungry."

His mother blew a kiss to her. "Dinner will be ready soon. Ma-Ma is making your favorite, baked ziti with the cheese on top."

Becky sagged against him. She suddenly got a very serious look on her face, at least for a four-year-old. "Are you going bye-bye, Daddy? Aunt Luci said you was leaving."

Ty scowled at his sister. Luci shrugged.

"Just for the weekend, honey." Ty kissed her cheek. "You'll stay here with Aunt Luci and Ma-Ma, and I'll bring you back some presents."

Becky perked at that and nodded. "Okay."

Soon, he wouldn't be able to ease her anxiety with the promise of toys. He wouldn't be able to disappear overnight or for a few days, no matter how good the money was. He just needed to do this for another year or so, that was it. He'd have enough stashed away by then, enough to make sure Becky didn't have to follow in the rest of her family's footsteps. She'd never need to know, when she was older, how he got it.

The general mood for the rest of the night was tense and frosty, but he tried to ignore it. His mother always huffed and chastised, but she never said no when he paid for maintenance on the store or paid the bills up a few months in advance so they could breathe easier. His sister acted holier-than-thou, but she certainly didn't dislike the gifts he bought her, or how he paid her tuition every semester. Funny how that worked.

After tucking his daughter in that night and kissing her forehead, he stepped out in the hallway and found his sister just coming out of the bathroom in her robe, a towel wrapped around her head. They both paused, staring at each other.

"Be careful," she said softly. "I worry about you getting killed by some crazy broad with a meat cleaver." She stepped over and put her arms around him.

He hugged her back. "You got this?" He spoke quietly as well, since their mother was in bed. "I'll call you while I'm there to check in—I know it'll be a hell of a charge to make an international call, but I will. If anything goes wrong with the store, or anything else, I'll come right back here."

"You know I got it." She lifted her head and looked up at him. "I promise we won't burn the place down while you're gone."

"I sorta wouldn't mind if you did."

She slapped his side. "Our fucking apartment would burn down too, *stunad*." She slipped away from him. "Please just be careful, okay?"

"I always am."

"And don't catch a crotch disease."

"Never have, and not for lack of trying." He grinned.

She grimaced. "Ugh. Gross." She hustled toward her room.

The truth was, he rarely slept with the women he dated. The agency rules explicitly stated that the service was not prostitution, and he was not allowed to provide any physical services. Most women were lonely and just wanted his companionship, rather than his body. Every once in a while though, attraction flared, and it happened. After all, they were consenting adults, and the sex was considered outside the contract.

"I'll see you Monday." He headed toward his own room. "I love you, stupid."

She leaned out from the doorway of her room. "Love you too. Have tons of fun getting paid to screw rich women on a tropical island."

"It'll be tough, but I'll try."

* * * *

Ty opted for a sexy-causal outfit for the flight: the most expensive jeans he owned—and they did amazing things for his hips—a formfitting white t-shirt with a scoop neck, and a slim, tailored gray blazer. The look was stylish but also catwalk-model sexy, which seemed to be what his client wanted of him. He slipped on a watch and simple gold chain, boots, and spritzed himself with his designer cologne, the stuff he only wore for dates. Some of the money he made had to be invested, too.

He checked himself over in the mirror as he worked his hair into an equally stylish knot at the back of his head—the fabled man bun. "Way to look like a hipster," he murmured.

But the client was always right. He could take on any look they wanted.

On his way to the airport in the back of a cab, he psyched himself into the headspace he'd need to stay in all weekend. When he'd first started going on dates, he was anxious and nervous, and as a result he overcompensated. He'd learned quickly that what women wanted was a man who didn't seem phony, like he was just there to collect a check. He did his best to forget about himself and focus on making the woman feel comfortable, engage her in conversation, and listen.

Eventually, he'd figured out "the persona."

Part of the fantasy was making the women believe they were dealing with a suave, sophisticated man of the world, not a working-class grocery store owner from Bensonhurst. By the time the cab pulled up in front of Departures, he was in the mind of that guy, that cool, confident alter-ego he'd created for himself. He climbed out and closed the door on his real life, and stepped into the world of refinement, money, and luxury.

He'd only gone on one date-trip before, to Canada, and he'd had fun there. Mostly, he and his older but charming companion hung out in casinos and went sightseeing. She liked to dance and talked often about her late husband, especially when she drank champagne. He was looking forward to checking out the tropics this time, maybe having a little touristy fun in addition to playing his part.

He walked into the terminal, stopped inside the doors, and looked around. The place was filled with early morning travelers. He scanned the crowd for the woman Monica had described to him. Usually, they met beforehand, but she was in a hurry and apparently had just picked him out on the spot—*not* that he was silently gloating over that. He started toward the ticketing counter where he'd been instructed to meet her, keeping an eye out for a woman with a red suitcase.

As he approached, his gaze settled on a woman who matched the description. She stood next to a pillar, looking at her phone. At her feet sat a candy apple red hard vinyl suitcase. If this was really her, he was in for a nice weekend. Because, wow. *Wow.*

She had long brunette hair streaked with burgundy, filled with big, luscious curls. She wore a formfitting maroon dress that reached mid-thigh, and black sandals studded with jewels on the straps. She was cock-stirringly voluptuous, with curves for miles and long, sleek, tanned legs.

He gripped the handle of his suitcase, praying, and walked toward her. As he closed in, she looked up.

She was *fucking gorgeous*. He couldn't summon a better descriptor. She had high cheekbones and a heart-shaped face, and striking green eyes. Her lips were a plump bow, painted red, her makeup immaculate so she looked like a girl from a magazine. She wore a delicate silver chain around her neck with a teardrop diamond dangling from it, and matching earrings.

She stared at him, and he slowed, thinking he'd made a mistake. Then she gave him a saucy, sexy smile.

"You must be Tybalt." She lowered her phone. "Your picture doesn't do you justice." She swept him with an appraising look, and for the first time in ages, he felt inadequate.

He almost couldn't maintain a cool demeanor. "You can call me Ty." He smiled broadly. "Grace, is it?" He looked her over as well, from head to toe, and didn't hide the fact he was doing so. She had ample tits and wide, grab-able hips. This was the kind of girl he'd always hoped to go on a date with someday.

"Yes, Ty." She bent and picked up her bag, so he got a quick peek down her dress. She stood upright. "Is Tybalt really your name? It sounds like a stage name for an escort." She had a voice as silky and smooth as the rest of her.

He chuckled. "Yeah, it's real. My mom loves Romeo and Juliet."

No talking about family unless she asks. No thinking about real life. He locked that door firmly.

She extended the handle on her bag. "Well, are you ready to travel? Brought everything with you that I requested?"

He patted his blazer pocket where his passport was and lifted his bag. "Yes."

"Good." She turned, pulling her suitcase. "Let's get this underway."

She walked ahead of him toward the ticket counter, and he deliberately lingered a few feet behind, to watch the scintillating sway of her hips. Maybe this would be one of those times he provided a little more than companionship and conversation. Of course, he'd never slept with a woman like her, and he wasn't sure his skills as a lover were up to snuff. He didn't want her to ask for a refund.

"Have you ever been to Barbados?" she asked over her shoulder.

He fell in step beside her. "No, but it sounds like a nice destination. Have you ever been there?"

"Yes. This resort we're going to, it's upscale, and the fun is rather structured." She swung her hair over her shoulder, and the light caught the glossy highlights. "You might find it droll." They reached the line at the counter and stopped. "It could get tedious, despite the locale, and you'll want to look for something to occupy your time." She looked him over again, suggestively. Was she worried he would wander off and bang some island girl?

"I'm good at entertaining myself."

She flipped open her passport. "I'm sure you are."

He leaned toward her and lowered his voice. "I'm here to entertain you, though."

Her perfume wafted over him, light and floral. She looked, smelled, and sounded like money. He could appear the same, but it was all an act, and he hoped she didn't see through it.

"We have a long flight." She snapped the passport shut. Her nails gleamed, like everything else about her. "Plenty of time for you to learn everything I need you to do."

He raised his eyebrows. "Everything you need me to do?"

"I need you to play a role, Ty, a very important role." She fanned herself with the passport and stretched up to look at the counter. "I need you to act as I say, and do everything per my instructions. I'll tell you how to behave, and when, and how to answer any questions that are thrown your way. I need you to obey me and everything I tell you."

He grew uneasy. Was this some BDSM thing?

"I'm good at following a script." He spoke with forced confidence. "I've done this before."

"I need you to be the perfect boyfriend, Ty. So perfect my friends won't see through the ruse. I need you to impress them."

"I can manage that." He relaxed a little.

"To the letter." She continued fanning herself, which made her perfume billow across him in distracting blasts. "If you do a good job, to my specifications, I'll give you a handsome tip at the end."

That sounded like throwing a dog a treat, but he could always use the extra money.

"Of course, I'll be happy to do as you say."

She stopped fanning and folded her arms beneath her ample chest. He stole a glance at her cleavage. Her skin sparkled with a fine, glittery sheen.

"I'm going to be swimming with the sharks," she said. "We both are. I'm going to use you as bait."

He frowned. This sounded ominous. Maybe he should have insisted on meeting her beforehand.

She looked at him. Her gaze was guarded, and he realized for the first time the beautiful façade had some cracks in it. Strain showed through her expression, her shoulders tight with tension.

"That sounds … scary." He tried to keep his tone light and teasing. "I hope you don't mean literal sharks. I've never been in the ocean before."

The joke fell flat. She didn't laugh, or even smile.

"Worse than literal sharks, trust me. The kind of people who will chew up your mind instead of your body, and spit it out."

"What do you mean?" Worry crept into his voice.

"Oh, you'll see, Ty. You'll see."

She grabbed her suitcase handle as the line moved and strode ahead toward the counter. He stood there a moment looking after her, clutching his passport.

What the hell had he gotten into?

Chapter Three

"Stewardess, I'd like a vodka soda. Nothing cheap, Grey Goose if you have it." Grace hated to fly, though she wouldn't let her seat companion know that. She would be tense for the entire flight, listening to every sound and internally panicking every time the plane made a noticeable movement. Everyone drank on flights, right? Getting drunk on a plane was a normal thing. Her ex-husband certainly partook. But then again, they were usually on a smaller, more private plane.

The blond woman who stood next to her seat gave her a pinched look. "We'll be serving refreshments as soon as the flight takes off, ma'am." She walked away.

Grace wished she'd sprung for first class, but she didn't have the money after paying for this sure-to-be-miserable trip.

Ty leaned toward her. She'd given him the window seat. "I think they're called flight attendants now," he whispered.

She shot him a frosty look. She knew that, of course, and it stung to be called out on it. He dutifully sat back and stared straight ahead. He was damn lucky he was beautiful.

"Beautiful" wasn't quite the word, though. The pictures really *didn't* do him justice. His thick, shiny black hair was brushed back and settled against the shoulders of his smartly fashionable gray blazer. It was well-tailored and traced the lines of his lean, tight torso with ease and aplomb. The low cut of his clingy t-shirt showcased the thick graceful column of his dusky neck and provided a peek of dark hair on his chest. He smelled divine as well, like the men's cologne counter at Macy's. He fit the part she needed him to, visually. He also had an easy, laid-back confidence that would assuredly help him play the game. She'd dated an Italian boy once, when she was young and less uptight, and they'd had a lot of fun together. He brought back fond memories for her.

"I suppose we should get to know each other a bit." She crossed her ankles beneath the seat in front of her. She'd managed to choose a dress that was fashionable but not too restrictive for the trip. She wouldn't dream of sacrificing taste for comfort. "It says in your biography you're a business owner. What sort of business?" She was rusty at making small talk, but they had a long flight, and she had to put him at ease so he'd be more receptive to her demands.

He hummed in his throat. He had a deep, husky voice, cultured yet relaxed, like the rest of him. If it wasn't real, he was very good at faking it. Either way, it was a win for her.

"Yes, I own a small grocery store in Bensonhurst, at 18th and Bay Ridge. It's been in my family for generations. My grandpa bought it when he was a young man."

She'd been hoping for something a little more glamorous, but she could work with this. Maybe they could say it was an artisan or niche market. Maybe move it somewhere more glamourous in Brooklyn, like Park Slope.

"A family business, then." She glanced down the aisle, looking for the *flight attendant*. She wondered if she could bribe her into bringing her something, as she needed a drink in her before the plane took off. "That's nice."

"My grandpa passed when I was a teenager, then it became my father's. And then he passed…" He trailed off and looked out the window. "So now I run it." For a moment, his slick demeanor crumpled, like a mask falling away, but it was quickly replaced. "Entrepreneurship is the American dream, right? We all want to be our own boss."

"Indeed." She eased back against the seat. "I run a business myself, Graceful Garments. I have shops on West 35th in the Garment District in Manhattan and also one on 5th Avenue. Have you heard of them?" She looked eagerly at him. The one on 5th Avenue was the one she'd been forced to close late last year, and it still stuck in her heart, a nagging, festering despair that wouldn't go away.

He shook his head and gave her an apologetic smile. "No, but then, I don't get to Manhattan much."

She waved a hand. "No matter. They're quite popular, though. A lot of women wear my styles. Business is good."

"Seems like it." He glanced around. "This is quite a trip we're going on." He smiled again, but there was something false about it. He would have to get better at acting.

"What about your store?" Maybe he was much wealthier than her. Maybe he was judging her right now for not springing for first class. The thought made her stomach clench. "Are profits high? Do you do good business?"

"I pay the bills." He smoothed his jacket. "You know how it is though, being a business owner yourself. It's not all rolling in money and living the high life. A business is hard work and it takes away from the rest of your life. Somedays I feel like I never leave the store."

She clicked her nails together. "Yes, I know that feeling." She side-eyed him. "So, you just do this on the side for fun? What's the motivation?"

He rolled his head against the seat and looked at her. He smiled, this time for real. He had a wide, bright, charming smile that made him look adorably boyish. "I get paid to go on amazing trips with beautiful woman. Why *wouldn't* I want to do this on the side?"

She smirked. "How long have you been a man for hire?" For the first time, she was genuinely curious about him instead of trying to figure out how to best present him.

"Hmm." He gazed forward. "A little over a year, I think. Though I don't go on dates every week or anything like that. I'm not in terribly high demand."

She arched an eyebrow. "Really? I would think you'd have women taking a number."

He laughed, flashing that brilliant smile again. "No, not really. I think women these days want someone a little more clean-cut. And maybe a little more all-American, if you catch my drift."

She was surprised to hear that. She'd always preferred the edgy, wild-looking boys. And she'd dated men of many ethnicities. Sometimes she still boggled at how Brent, who was exactly the type of man he was describing, had charmed her into marriage. But then, he was very slick and very deceptive, and he opened a door to a lush, rich world she had never known before. A world that sucked her in and now had her trapped.

"That sounds silly and shortsighted to me." She shrugged. "All the better, though. It means you were free for me."

He smiled and patted her hand on the armrest between them. His skin was soft, his fingernails manicured and shiny. She expected rougher hands, being a working man. Then again, she was a working woman and she knew how to hide those blemishes as well.

"I'm at your service." He stroked his fingertips across the back of her hand, and that light touch made tingles rush up her arm. "Whatever you need."

What she needed. That was an extensive list, and it only got more and more complicated as she went down it. He couldn't give her what she truly needed. No one could.

The flight attendant didn't bring her a drink before takeoff. Rules or something, about not having liquids out in the cabin. She squeezed her eyes shut and clutched the seat rests, unable to help herself. The speed made her hold her breath and she let it out shakily as they lifted off the ground, the sudden lightweight sensation making her stomach do a flip.

Ty chuckled and rubbed her forearm. "You okay? You scared of flying?"

She cracked one eye open and peeked at him. "A little."

"Don't worry, it's actually a really safe way to travel. You know, they say more people die in car accidents than in plane crashes, it's a statistical fact."

She made herself breathe. "That's because more people drive than fly, it's simply a numbers game. There's more car accidents than plane crashes. However, you have a much higher chance of surviving a car crash than a plane crash."

Ty frowned. "I never thought about it like that."

"I think about it every time I'm on a plane, trust me."

When they reached cruising altitude and leveled off, she finally managed to relax a bit. The "fasten seat belt" sign turned off. People started moving around. She tried to focus on the days ahead to keep her mind off the sound of the engines.

"We met at a bar in Hell's Kitchen," she said.

Ty was gazing out the window. He looked at her. "Pardon?"

"We met at a cocktail party in a swanky bar in

Hell's Kitchen." She sat forward and pulled her purse from under the seat in front of her. "A place called The Skylark." She fished around in her purse, pulled out a business card, and held it out to him. "It's an upscale place where a lot of young professionals hang out. Beautiful view of Midtown from the rooftop. We were there for a business owner's soiree. Lots of mingling and martinis and tapas."

She had only been there once, with Brent and some of his business clients. She'd dug through his old things to find the card when she decided it was where she and Ty met. None of the others went there regularly, at least not that she was aware of.

He took the card and looked at it, then smirked. "You were wearing a slinky black dress and sinfully high heels. You caught my eye immediately. Especially those legs."

She smiled widely. "And you had on a Fendi blazer with no tie. You were the suavest man in the room. Drinking a Macallan on the rocks."

He wrinkled his nose. "I hate scotch."

"Scotch is a sophisticated man's drink."

"I don't know about that." He turned the card over between his long fingers. "My grandpa drank scotch he got from the liquor store down the street, it was eight dollars a bottle. I don't think it was very sophisticated. It smelled like an old Band-Aid."

"You were drinking good scotch." She looked around for the flight attendant. "We've been casually seeing each other for six weeks now."

"How come I haven't met your friends yet?"

She looked at him and blinked.

He shrugged. "You want me to say all these things, I'm sure it's going to come up why I haven't met your friends before now, why you haven't brought me around. I mean six weeks is a while. Even if you're just sorta seeing each other."

She pressed her lips together. "They're not so much 'friends' as people I'm obliged to be around."

"Why are you obliged to be around them?"

She ignored the question. "You've been very busy with work, we both have, and we've only been dating casually, so we weren't sure. Meeting friends is a big step. It's an implied commitment."

"All right. When do I get to meet your parents?"

She glared at him.

He laughed. "I'm joking, lighten up." He patted her hand. "Yes, I'm a very busy man, and we weren't sure we really wanted to date, but now we're falling in love and I'm happy to come along on this trip and finally meet them."

"Falling in love?"

"Well, yeah." He shrugged. "Otherwise, why would I go all the way to Barbados with you? Especially when I have a store to run?"

He had a point.

She spoke reluctantly. "Could we change what sort of store you own?"

His frown was not nearly as pleasant as his smile. "Why?"

"It can still be family-owned. Maybe just something a little more hip. An artisanal bakery, perhaps. Or a small organic market? We could move it a little bit north, but still in Brooklyn."

"Is there something wrong with owning a simple grocery store in Bensonhurst?" His voice turned gruff.

She sighed. "The people we're about to spend the weekend with are very rich and self-centered. They only like the finer things in life. They're going to judge you, terribly. I just want you to be comfortable." She wanted *herself* to be comfortable, really, but she knew they would chew him up too, at the first sign of weakness.

"They're going to judge me, are they?" He spoke wryly. "I can't imagine what that's like."

She frowned. Was he making a jab at her?

"I paid you for your company this weekend," she reminded him. "A nice bit of money, I might add. I don't need you to be genuine, I need you to do as I ask. Play a role. If you can't do that, you should have said so from the start."

He held up his hands. "Fine. Like I said, I'm at your service."

"I think an artisanal bakery sounds nice. Don't worry, they won't try to come visit it. Most of them don't set foot off Carnegie Hill if they can avoid it."

"What does artisanal mean, anyway?" He picked up his phone from his lap, as if to Google it. "I take it you don't just get donuts and bagels there?"

"You won't get service up here. Artisanal means it was made by hand, with good, wholesome ingredients. You're an artisan at making baked goods."

He looked up from his phone. "Okay, I guess that's not so bad. Sounds kind of cool, actually."

"You can say it's in Park Slope. I doubt they'll ask many questions. They'll be too busy talking about themselves for that."

He lowered the phone. "The way you talk about these people, they sound awful. Why are you going to hang out with them on an island?"

She wished she had an adequate answer for that. Mostly, it was so she didn't lose more face than she already had. Pretty soon she was going to be down to her skull.

"It's complicated." She shoved her purse back under the seat. "You should probably go by Tybalt instead of Ty, it sounds more sophisticated."

He slipped his phone into the breast pocket of his blazer. "The only person who calls me Tybalt is my grandmother, on my mother's side."

"Well, for the next two days you'll be making your grandmother happy." She swiveled in her seat, irritated. "Where is that stew—flight attendant? Really, how long does it take to get a drink?"

Ty spoke, in a stilted tone. "Hello, I'm Tybalt. I own an artisanal bakery in Park Slope and I drink scotch." He paused. "Anything else? Should I make myself younger than I am, or older? Which is more sophisticated?"

She whipped back around to glare at him. "I'd like to know why you're being so sarcastic when I've paid you three thousand dollars, and I'm paying all your expenses as well. I'm not asking you to go on a crime spree with me. I'm asking you to tell a few white lies to some finicky, over-wealthy people." Her voice took on a sharp, stressed-out edge she hadn't meant it to. "Think of it as playing a role on a TV show. Is it so hard to play a bit part for a few days? You're literally getting the best end of this deal. A trip and money, and all you have to do is pretend you make goddamn fancy bread!"

He stared at her. Her hands were clenched into fists on her lap. His scowl fell away and his face softened. She hadn't meant to lose her temper and act so crazy, but her nerves were at their breaking point.

"I'm sorry." He leaned toward her. "You're right, it's not hard. I don't mind playing a part, especially when that's literally what you're paying me to do. I truly apologize."

She took a deep breath. Her shoulders were so tense she thought they might snap up and break her neck. "It's fine. Don't worry, we won't be around them all the time. I couldn't stand it if we were. I'd go mad."

He touched her arm and lowered his voice. "Should we work out where we had our first kiss?" His cologne filled her nostrils. Fragrant, suave, and yet— very him, not false. It fit his dark hair and dark eyes and coppery skin, musky and spicy at the same time.

She let herself relax a little. "You kissed me that night, of course. Bold as you are. Right there on the rooftop in front of everyone."

"Sounds like me."

"You were drunk and boisterous."

"Sounds like me, too." He smirked.

The flight attendant finally came with her drink. She took it, and then looked at Ty. "Would you like one too? Do you like vodka, at least?"

He nodded. "That's more my poison."

She looked up at the flight attendant and smiled. "Could we please get another? Thank you so much." She would try to be a little nicer for the rest of the trip. Something about Ty's obvious disapproval of her rudeness made her want to behave herself. Also, he seemed a lot more wholesome and kind than most people currently in her life.

That was worth acting right for.

* * * *

By the time they landed in Florida, where they would make their connecting flight, Grace was slightly tipsy, infinitely more relaxed, and they were laughing and chatting like old friends. She found she could commiserate quite easily with him over the woes of running one's own business. She almost told him about the closures, but ultimately held back. She didn't know him well enough yet to share her secrets. As they collected their carry-ons to get off the plane, they were still laughing and joking.

"There was this guy who used to pass out in the doorway of the store every night after we closed." Ty eased out of the seat row behind her. "He wasn't homeless, just a drunk who always chose to pass out in my doorway, of all places. We didn't even sell him the damn liquor that got him that way."

She slung her purse over her shoulder. "That sounds like my uncle. He used to get drunk and pass out on our front lawn. He and my aunt lived down the street and he could never seem to make it that far. My mother would get so mad when she woke up and found him out there. She used to call my aunt and scream at her, tell her to keep her deadbeats on her own lawn."

Ty chuckled. "Well, this guy,"—he slid in behind her as they stood in line, waiting to deplane—"if us or the police didn't get him out of there during the night, he would wake up in the morning and tell my customers waiting outside that he owned the place and there was a cover charge to get in. Sometimes it was ten dollars, sometimes twenty."

Grace threw her head back and laughed. "It was an exclusive club, was it?"

"Apparently so." He slipped his hand onto her waist. He stood close enough behind her they were nearly pressed together.

"You should have told him you would take a seventy-five percent cut of all money collected, like any club would. That might change his mind." She looked over her shoulder at him.

Maybe it was the vodka sparkling through her veins, but he looked even more handsome now, brown eyes gleaming, an easy smile on his rugged face. His hand felt good, heavy and protective on her waist. She didn't mind it there.

"I don't have much trouble with vagrants where

I'm located." She looked forward again. "But there's this strange and eccentric woman who comes in at least once a month and insists that someone up the street is stealing my designs and selling them from their storefront. I've been to this store and they don't even sell clothes, they're a jeweler."

He squeezed her hip. "Maybe they're selling them out of a van out back. They think your designs are just that good. I'd like to see some of them, if you don't mind."

Warmth filled her chest, and it wasn't just the vodka. "I talked to the woman who owns the jeweler and she said the same woman comes in there and tells her people are reselling her jewelry at another store. There must be a whole black market of redistributed goods in the Garment District I don't know about. Seems unnecessarily convoluted and expensive."

"The joys of business ownership, huh? Dealing with the public is an unavoidable part—and unfortunately, you have to deal with *everyone* in the public."

She sighed and leaned back, so she rested against him. His hand seemed to suggest it was all right to do so. He was a solid, sturdy man. "I wish this would hurry up."

"I don't," he murmured next to her ear.

She grinned and leaned a little more heavily against him.

In the airport, they had time to grab something to eat before they got on the second flight. She hated waiting around in airports as much as she hated to fly, but being with him made the time much better. They talked more about their lives—though she was careful to avoid certain subjects—and she showed him some of her designs on her phone.

"These are really nice." He scrolled through her

gallery as they grazed on an appetizer in a bar near their gate. "Do you ever wear any of these? I bet you look really sexy."

She sipped her drink—she'd switched to soda water so she would mind her tongue and not start babbling about things she'd rather not reveal—and found her cheeks warming. She heard sincere compliments all the time, but coming from him it seemed even more genuine.

"I do, from time to time." She took her phone back and found a picture of herself in one of her favorite items, a slinky black dress. "For example, the dress I was wearing the night we met." She turned the phone around and showed him.

He whistled. "Yeah, I definitely noticed you in that."

She winked. "You haven't seen the bra and panty set I had on underneath yet."

"Did you design those, too?"

She shook her head. "I know a woman who designs lingerie, though. Quite sexy stuff."

"Well, we have the whole weekend." He took a sip from his drink, eyeing her over the glass. "Did you bring them with you?"

She laughed. "Something similar, yes."

"How did you get into designing clothes?"

She picked at some garnish on the plate. "I always had an interest, I think. I used to cut up my Barbie doll's clothes and glue them back together to make different outfits. I only had a few dolls but I begged my mother to buy me tons of clothes for them."

"That's cute."

"I attended design school." Her thoughts went back to another time, another place, when she was a different person. "I won a few awards for my designs, just small honors really. But it gave me a boost of confidence. I always feel good when I'm creating. When I feel the fabric between my hands. When I can picture the finished outfit in my mind's eye."

"So, you opened your own boutiques after you finished school?"

She had to skip over a lot of changes in her life from graduation to that point, but she nodded. "Yes."

He played with the straw in his drink. "It's a good thing, to do something you love."

"What about you, do you like running a grocery store?"

He was smiling, but it didn't look like a happy smile, almost like a grimace. "It was expected of me, that's all I can say. And I know how to do it, so I guess that's a good thing. I'm capable." She wanted him to elaborate, but he leaned toward her and put a hand on her knee. "This weekend isn't about me, or my life." He looked into her eyes. "I own an artisanal bakery and we're here to have fun, celebrating our new relationship. And I want to see you model that bra and panty set."

She grinned. "Play your cards right and you just may." She took a sip of her soda and winked. She didn't push his hand off her knee.

By the time they stood in line at their gate to get on the plane, they were holding hands. She wasn't even sure how it happened, but his hand was warm and strong and felt good holding hers. She wondered how it would feel on other parts of her body, not just her knee or her waist. Why had he taken her hand to begin with? Just practicing for the trip? She didn't mind, or care.

When they stepped up to the agent, she smiled at them. "You're a beautiful couple." She scanned the passes.

They looked at each other and grinned. She

would have to take a selfie of them to check this out for herself.

"Have a great trip." The agent handed them back their passes with a broad smile.

They walked down the jetway to the plane, and Grace squeezed his hand. "I think we're going to make a good impression on everyone."

"I aim to please."

She smiled slyly at him. "You certainly do."

Chapter Four

When Ty was a kid, his grandfather would tell him about the Greek Islands. His grandfather had spent most of his childhood there, before immigrating with his parents to America. He liked America and said he'd never think of going back permanently, but he often spoke fondly of the sprawling beaches of Mykonos and the sun-bleached cliffs of Zakynthos. When Ty imaged those white sand beaches and clear blue waters, he imagined a place like this.

The resort was flanked by the Atlantic Ocean, the water as vibrant and crystalline as the water in the pictures his grandfather showed him. The sky was its equal, the sun blazing brilliant on the pink walls and white patios. Despite the beach being within throwing distance, there were several pools, all of them large and crowded. Ty couldn't help but be confused at this. He supposed it was safer, though. Less chance of being dragged out to sea or having an encounter with a curious jellyfish. Or most probably, being made icky with saltwater.

"I'm sorry there's only one bed," Grace said. "I want to maintain the illusion in case any of them come into our room."

Their "room" was nearly bigger than the apartment he and his family lived in. It consisted of a main room with huge windows looking out on the ocean, a bedroom with a king-size bed and a balcony with an identical view, a bathroom with both a shower and a tub that doubled as a jacuzzi, and even a small kitchen. They also had a small tiled room just inside the main door, which contained a footbath with a hose. He assumed this was for changing out of swimwear and cleaning sand off.

"I don't mind at all," he said. "Plenty of room for

both of us." He grinned and walked to the French doors that opened onto the balcony. Several loungers, a glass table, and an assortment of wicker furniture had been placed out there. Palm fronds scraped the balustrade, as they were on the fifth floor.

"This place is all-inclusive," Grace called out to him. She sorted through her bag on the bed. "Food, drinks, I think some activities like golf and tennis, maybe jet-skiing. I'm sure they find plenty of things to charge you for, though. If you want decent or gourmet food, you'll have to go off the resort. In places like this it's mostly buffets and room service."

The air was warm and humid, but the breeze off the water kept it from being oppressive. He'd never been anywhere tropical, but he'd always wanted to. Maybe he'd return even more tan than usual. That would make his sister jealous. He slipped his phone out and took a few pictures. He was supposed to be paying attention to Grace, but he had to get some photos of this.

"They have boat excursions, too," she said. "Around the island. Perhaps we can do that, if it gets too unbearable being around them."

Her phone rang. Ty looked into the room. She picked it up and her voice went high and false as she answered.

"Hello, Amelia darling! Yes, we're here. I can't wait to see you." She grabbed some clothes and headed toward the bathroom. "Oh yes, he's dying to meet you." She stepped inside and closed the door.

Ty walked back into the room. Her voice drifted faintly through the door, but not enough to make out what she was saying. He was a little apprehensive. He'd dealt with a lot of jerks in his life, but they were usually on his level. Rich jerks were a whole different animal.

He wandered over to the bed and checked out her

clothes scattered across the plush purple bedspread. A lot of thin, wispy, silky things. He picked a dress, held it up, and smirked. The material was sleek green satin, and it had thin spaghetti straps and what appeared to be a scandalously short skirt. Once she stuffed those curves of hers into it, he could imagine it riding all the way up her thighs.

He already liked the tropics.

He placed the dress carefully back on the bed and peeked in her suitcase. Lots of lace and frills. Bras and panties, and stockings. He wanted to check those out, too, but resisted. He wasn't a pervert. Well, not much of one. Besides, if he played his cards right, maybe she would show him of her own volition.

He went to where his own suitcase sat on a chair and opened it. He'd brought his designer and most expensive clothes, as instructed. That wasn't saying much, though. Hopefully no one would be checking labels. About ten minutes later Grace emerged from the bathroom, no longer on her phone. Ty paused pulling things out of his suitcase and stared at her, openly and unabashed.

She'd changed—into very little, God bless the warm weather. She wore a red bikini top that tied around her neck and was only precariously restraining the great, glorious swell of her ample breasts. She had a tight, flat stomach. Around her waist she wore a flowered sarong that covered her to the knees, so he regretfully couldn't check out the rest of the bikini. Her skin was creamy and pale, and his fingers itched to touch it and discover if it was as soft and smooth as it looked.

"We have to meet everyone for cocktails." She started pulling her loose burgundy-streaked curls on top her head. "They all just got here a bit ago as well. We're going to say hello and mingle for a while." She walked over to the vanity, which had a huge mirror. Her hips swayed enticingly beneath the sarong.

He couldn't quit staring at her. "So, I guess I should dress down, huh?"

She stared into the mirror, fussing with her hair. "Just put on some swim trunks and a shirt. We'll probably take a dip in the pool after."

He glanced out the balcony doors. "There's a big ocean right there."

She turned and walked to the bed, where she snatched up her makeup bag. "Saltwater does terrible things to your hair and skin." She wrinkled her nose. "Go on, get dressed. But don't look too casual."

He frowned, confused.

She gestured at him. "Swim trunks, but not too casual on top. That's what I mean. Look like the playboy you are."

"Okay. Sure." He was still lost.

He took some clothes to the bathroom. Changing wasn't easy though, as he was now at half-mast. He had to fight it down before he emerged into the room.

Grace made him change twice before she was satisfied with his outfit. He put on his swim trunks, which were tight navy-blue shorts, and ultimately a white button-down, entirely unbuttoned, with the sleeves rolled up to his elbows. He looked every bit a man whore, or an obnoxious frat boy tourist.

"I wonder, should we pull your hair back?" They stood in front of the vanity and she raked her fingers through his hair. She pulled it up and studied him. Her nails across his scalp did nothing to squelch the erection that was threatening to return. "Yes, I think I like that."

She wound his hair into a knot at the back of his head.

"I look like a hipster," he complained, frowning

at himself in the mirror. He liked his hair down. When it got hot in the summer he'd put it in a ponytail, but that was it. He never did anything fancy with it, despite his sister telling him regularly how much he looked like a bum.

"It's sexy." Grace straightened his collar and looked over his shoulder into the mirror with a saucy smirk. "We're going to have to get you a Speedo while we're here. Too much cloth on those shorts."

He cringed. "I'm not sure I have the cheeks for that. Afraid I'm going to have to draw the line there."

"Too bad." She pouted.

He felt like a doll she was dressing up, one of those Barbies she used to play with. *Three thousand dollars, a sweet vacation, and a hot woman,* he reminded himself.

The cocktail get-together was held in a bar downstairs. Like the rest of the place, the bar was lush and open. The sea breeze flowed through, sand on the tiles, and big tropical plants stood everywhere. Ty felt like he'd been transported from chilly spring back home right into immediate summer, as everyone wore bathing suits, sarongs, sandals, and light fabrics. Beyond the open doors looking out on a deck, the sea shimmered sapphire and enticing. He was going to jump in there before this trip was over, saltwater be damned. He started heading toward the long wooden bar that ran along one side of the room to order drinks, but Grace grabbed his arm.

"Hello!" She waved wildly and gripped him tighter, pulling him closer. "Oh my God, it's so good to see you!" Her voice sounded the way it had on the phone.

Two women hurried toward them, giant cocktails with umbrellas and overflowing fruit in hand. They were both toned and tan and beautiful, and wearing very little clothing. One was blond and the other brunette, the blond wearing a gold bikini. Ty pointedly looked away so he wouldn't stare at them. Not that they were prettier than Grace, but so much luscious female flesh was difficult to ignore.

The women exchanged hugs and cheek kisses with Grace. Lots of affected fussing and squealing took place. Then, they turned their attention on him. He tried to play it cool.

"So, this is him, huh?" The blond looked him over appraisingly. "Damn, Grace. You weren't kidding when you said he was good-looking."

Grace gripped his arm even tighter. Ty smiled politely and tried not to wince.

"Tybalt, this is Amelia and Roxanne, two of my dearest friends." Grace rubbed his arm. "Girls, this is Tybalt."

"Tybalt." The brunette—Roxanne—also looked him up and down as she sipped from her straw. "It's good to see Grace with a man again. I mean, we all think she works too hard. We thought she'd never get a social life."

They chuckled derisively. Grace tittered. Ty rubbed her forearm in return.

"Yes, well," he said. "I like a hardworking woman. It shows her character."

The two women exchanged bemused glances. Grace tensed against his side.

"Speaking of hard workers." Amelia jerked her head toward a group of people nearby. "Come meet our hubbies, Tybalt."

Their "hubbies" were everything Ty expected: clean-cut, professional, well-dressed in their designer shorts and linen shirts, generically handsome and strong-jawed, all drinking from martinis or tumblers of scotch. Ty shook hands and the women looked him up and down, some with obvious hunger, so he felt like a piece of meat. The men seemed to be assessing him as well, for different reasons. He struggled to remember anyone's name.

"Tybalt, what do you do for a living?" A man with a booming voice who he thought might be named Craig stared him down. Or was it Carl? He was a few inches taller and had shoulders like a linebacker.

"I'm a business owner." He reluctantly let Grace go, so she could mingle with the women. "I own an artisanal bakery in Park Slope, in Brooklyn."

Grace glanced over her shoulder at him. She stood a few feet away, within hearing distance.

"Oh, really?" Craig chuckled and elbowed one of his buddies. "Maybe I need to change where I get my baguettes. I could stop by when I meet with my clients across the river. What's the place called? Is it near Prospect Park?"

Ty froze. They hadn't hashed this out. Grace said they wouldn't come there.

"Uh, yeah, in that area. It's just called Tybalt's." He hoped the panic wasn't evident in his voice.

Craig chuckled again. "Simple and self-serving, I like it."

Craig's buddy, a man with his shirt unbuttoned and an uneven tan, narrowed his eyes at Ty. "Tybalt, is that Italian? You look kinda ethnic."

Ty tried not to grit his teeth and nodded. "My mother's family is Italian, but my father is Greek. My last name is Rossi."

"It's good to see they're diversifying that neighborhood a bit," Craig's buddy said. "You Italians sure know how to cook, I can say that for you."

Ty wondered what else, exactly, he would say for them.

Craig grinned slyly. "You're not part of the Mafia, are you?"

Ty forced a smile. "No, I'm just in a regular old street gang."

They got a good chortle out of that, thankfully, but Ty had a feeling they at least believed it to be partially true.

Craig looked over at Grace. "In any case, I'm glad to see she's finally met someone." He grinned lecherously. "I was afraid I was going to have to set her up myself with one of my college buddies. She's been single too damn long, didn't want a body like that to go to waste. Now she and Amelia can dish about us." He sipped his martini.

Ty really needed a drink. "Would you excuse me?" He walked over to Grace and tapped her shoulder. "Would you like a drink?"

She turned to him, and the look in her eyes was desperate, pleading. Her smile was painfully fake.

"Of course, darling." She kissed his cheek. "Get me something fun, you know me."

He glanced at the festive pink drinks the other girls were holding. "One of those?"

"Please."

The women were still obviously appraising him as he walked toward the bar. Normally, he liked when women looked at him, so why the hell did this feel so damn creepy?

He ordered Grace one of the drinks, which was essentially a Hurricane made with rum and fruit juice. He ordered himself a gin martini. Not because he liked martinis, but because he wanted to fit in with the guys for Grace's sake.

As he returned to the group, he noted the juxtaposition of Grace standing amidst the women, the men on the other side of the cocktail tables the girls inhabited. Indeed, she looked like she was surrounded by sharks—hungry, predatory sharks with glistening skin, sparkling accessories, and perfect highlights. She looked out of place, like someone had placed her there and told her to "just be herself" when it was the worst possible thing she could be. She hadn't been kidding about them.

So why the hell was she here on vacation with these people? Why was she calling them her "dearest friends?" Surely someone as confident, beautiful, and hardworking as Grace could find better people to hang out with than this.

"Here you are." He handed her the drink and flashed a smile.

She took it, her eyes shining, the panic still evident. "Thank you, love. Are you having fun with the boys?"

Ty glanced at "the boys," who were laughing and talking boisterously. "Sure. I was just telling Craig about my business."

She stared at him, then blinked. "Craig?"

"Yeah, um. I think Amelia's husband?"

She looked over her shoulder, then back at him, widening her eyes. "Carl," she whispered.

"Oh … yeah, Carl." He was going to have to remember names better.

Her mouth twitched. "Well, have fun. I'm just gossiping with the girls."

"Sure thing."

The rest of the time was agonizing, as Ty expected, but he just gritted his teeth and tried to bear it. The men talked about their stock portfolios, profit and loss, fiscal quarters, and eventually, sports. Ty rarely watched any sport, as he had neither the time nor interest. He did a lot of smiling and nodding and humming in agreement. They also spoke quite openly about "hot broads" they'd seen around the resort already, well within earshot of their chattering wives. Ty sipped his martini, which was far too dry, and kept nodding.

"So, Tybalt, you turn a profit in your bakery?" Carl asked him. "A lot of young people over there. A lot of money must flow your way, I'm guessing. They'll buy anything with the word 'artisanal' in front of it. The marketing gimmick of the zeitgeist."

"Yeah, I do okay. I mean, I pay the bills. It's comfortable."

Carl looked over at Grace. "You'll need some cash flow with that one. She's got expensive tastes, since she got spoiled. Always did enjoy having her around though, she's a breath of fresh air. The rest of these broads try my patience."

Ty wasn't sure how to respond. Carl was lumping his own wife in that group.

"Amelia hasn't done a day of work in her life, except yelling at the pool boy." Carl chuckled. "Grace likes to work. She comes from a different background, much lower class, you know. It's a good quality, though. Good for a woman to keep busy and support herself."

Ty tried to keep his tone neutral. "I agree."

Grace came from a "lower class?"

Carl leaned toward him and lowered his voice. "A woman has to have a little fun now and then, though. You gotta relax. If you ever need any help with her, just let me know." He winked. "I got your back, my man." He slapped Ty's arm.

Ty just stared at him. Grace looked over, brow knitted.

Ty cleared his throat. "Uh, thanks. So how do you

guys know each other? I mean, how long have you been friends? She doesn't talk much about you. Of course, we haven't been together that long."

Carl took a swig of his martini and smacked his lips. "Her husband, of course, that wily son of a bitch." He shook his head, but the words were spoken with fondness.

Husband?

"He won't be in prison that long. White-collar crime comes with a light sentence. Or at least, you can find ways to make it lighter." He arched a knowing eyebrow.

Prison?

"I, uh…" Ty tried to find some words. "Yeah, I guess so. You can hire good lawyers and stuff."

"I feel bad for him. Those people weren't even worth fleecing. I told him, go higher up the food chain. The more money an investor has, the less likely they are to miss some. They were small fries." He sighed. "But Brent always did like a challenge."

Ty silently boggled. Was Carl casually discussing embezzlement?

"Don't fret, Tybalt." He clapped him on the shoulder. Ty really wished he would stop touching him. "We have a spot open for you in his absence. You can come to our poker nights, if you want. We go golfing on the weekends, too. Not always in the city. You ever been to Martha's Vineyard?"

Ty was okay at poker, but he'd never golfed in his life. "Uh, no."

"Nice place, great scenery. Some of the best courses I've played on."

He suddenly had a lot of questions, but he wasn't sure if he had the right to ask them. After all, he barely knew Grace and she was paying him to be here with her.

It wasn't like they were actually a couple, or even friends.

As Grace predicted, the party moved out to the nearest pool. Ty slid his sunglasses on as they walked out. Grace sidled up beside him and took his arm. She'd barely touched her drink.

"What were you boys talking about?" Her tone was light, but it didn't fool him. "You seem to be getting along."

"They invited me to poker night." He tried to sound casual as well. "And a few rounds of golf in Martha's Vineyard."

She snorted. "Maybe I'll have to keep hiring you to maintain the illusion."

"You're gonna pay for me to go to Martha's Vineyard? Really?"

She glanced at him but said nothing. He would never expect such a trip, and he wouldn't go anyway, because he didn't even know how to hold a golf club. He plunked his martini on a table on the deck as they passed by. He couldn't drink any more.

"They think it's great there's an 'ethnic' person running a bakery in Park Slope." They were out of earshot of the others, so he spoke freely. "Really gives the neighborhood a little color, you know?"

She sighed. "I'm sorry. I don't think any of them have ever spoken to a non-Caucasian person except to order dinner. Just smile and nod. We don't have to hang out with them the entire time."

"It's a little insulting. More than a little, really."

Her eyes were hidden behind sunglasses now, but the rest of her face continued to convey her distress. "I know." Her tone softened. She squeezed his arm. "I'm truly sorry."

She sounded it, and so he tried to push some of

his offense to the side. He really wanted to ask her about her husband, though. Did he need to be looking over his shoulder as well, waiting for an angry spouse fresh out of the slammer to kick down the door and beat him to a pulp?

"I'll feign being tired from the trip later," she said. "We can have dinner alone, maybe just order room service. I already need a break from them as well."

Carl leered at Grace as they walked down the stairs to the pool. Ty drew her a little closer against his side. "Sounds good to me."

Chapter Five

"My, my, Grace, he's quite the specimen. You weren't kidding."

Amelia's words barely registered in her brain. Grace stood beneath the furiously hot sun, holding her disgusting pink cocktail in its sweaty slick glass and trying not to drop it. She simultaneously sucked in her stomach and attempted to look casual and unbothered while she did all of this, as if she hadn't a care in the world. All eyes were on her, sizing her up, scrutinizing every inch of her for a crack, a fault, anything they could dig their talons into and rip her apart over.

"Hmm?" She looked around the pool patio, the world dimmed by her huge designer sunglasses. "Oh, you mean Ty... balt?" She'd almost said *Ty*. "Yes, he's quite the looker, isn't he?"

Amelia threw her towel over a nearby lounge chair. Ready to get her sun. She was already bronzed to perfection, evenly and without a spot or streak. Grace suspected a spray tan, because it was just too perfect.

The pool was gigantic, the patio around it white granite, populated with chairs and tables with blue umbrellas. The men congregated on the other side of the pool, around several tables, and broke out cigars. A young blond cocktail waitress in a bikini brought out more drinks.

"You need to tell us what the rest of him looks like, Grace." Amelia reached behind her and started untying her bikini top.

Amelia was a tall, sculpted, slender goddess of a woman. Her honey-colored hair fell in a perfect curtain down her back, not a hint of frizz despite the humidity. Her stomach was tight, her legs so waxed and toned they looked like they were made of plastic. She whipped her top off as if they were alone out there, and Grace glanced away.

They both had the same cup size since Amelia got her upgrade, but Amelia wouldn't have to deal with sagging like Grace would as she aged. Having it naturally just wasn't worth it.

"Yeah, Grace." Roxanne tossed her towel on another chair, next to Amelia's. "How does he measure up?" She held up her fingers, indicating a generous length, her grin salacious.

Roxanne's dark hair tumbled over her shoulders in salon-perfect waves. She also had a stunning model-esque body. The two of them were forever asking Grace to come to Pilates and yoga, but Grace couldn't skip out in the middle of a business day to go exercise. Instead, she worked out at the end of the day, when she was exhausted and depleted, no matter how late, and no matter how drained she felt. Thank God for twenty-four-hour gyms.

Amelia laid down on her stomach, facing the pool, and dragged her hair over her shoulder to expose her bare back to the sun. "Come on, Gracie, how many inches are we talking here?"

Grace tittered and took a sip of her drink. The thing was awful. She hated the cloying taste of rum, and mixed with all the other sugary crap in there, it was like ingesting the essence of diabetes itself.

Roxanne started pulling her top off as well. "If you're not willing to brag, Grace, that must mean it's small."

"I didn't say I wasn't going to brag, now did I?" She set her glass down on a table next to the lounge chair she intended to take. If she didn't put it down soon, it was going to slip through her fingers. "We've all been catching up so much I didn't have a chance to talk about it."

She looked across the pool. Ty stood with the other men, as attractive as could be, but it was clear he didn't fit in that school of piranhas. He stuck out so obviously it twisted her gut. A pang of guilt seized her—what right did she have to subject another person to these people? Maybe she should have chosen someone different, someone more like them. Some slick, older investment banker who could talk shop and drink scotch with the best of them. But that wouldn't have been fun for her, and it might make this even more unbearable. Plus, Amelia and Roxanne wouldn't be envious.

"So?" Roxanne tossed her top aside. She was natural still, and much smaller. "What's the number?"

Grace sat down on her chair as Roxanne flopped onto hers and rolled onto her stomach.

"I haven't measured it, for goodness sake." Grace laughed. "It's more than adequate though, and it gets the job done." She winked.

"A jawbreaker?" Amelia mimed giving a blowjob, her tongue poking out her cheek.

"Absolutely."

"Mmm, I thought so." Amelia rested her chin on her hands and gazed across the pool. Grace had a feeling she was looking at Ty and jealousy bubbled up inside her.

How silly. He wasn't her boyfriend.

"Where did you meet him?" Roxanne slathered lotion on her arms. "You said he lives in Park Slope ... what was he doing in Manhattan?"

Grace boggled. Did she think people weren't allowed to travel between boroughs?

"We met at The Skylark, in Hell's Kitchen." Grace sat back on her hands, perched at the edge of her chair. "They were hosting a cocktail hour for young professionals. I saw him on the other side of the room and I just—" She gazed across the pool and made a growling noise. "So yummy."

"The Skylark" Amelia lifted her head and squinted over her sunglasses. "That place overlooking Midtown? On West 39th?"

Grace cringed that she knew it. "Yes, it's very nice. Quite swank. Lovely view."

"I think Carl took a client there one time and they got food poisoning." She wrinkled her nose. "Clams or something. That's why I hate going to places below five-star. You never know how disgusting the kitchen is."

Grace clenched her jaw. Could they find something wrong with absolutely everything in the world? Anything that wasn't entirely upper-class and haute?

"We didn't eat there." Grace maintained a cool outward demeanor. "I only went because I knew some important business owners would be there and I wanted to make connections. Then I met Ty and I was very glad I did go."

"*Ty*." Roxanne set her bottle of lotion on the ground next to her chair. "Aw, that's cute."

Grace gritted her teeth. She was going to have to call him Tybalt even in private, so she didn't slip up.

"I like that better than *Tybalt*," Amelia said. "It sounds so pretentious and Ivy school."

Grace couldn't win. Despair started to settle over her, like a wet, heavy, disgusting blanket. Her guts were in knots of panic. Should she take her top off, too, so they didn't think she was a prude? She didn't want to, though. Some of the guys were already leering at them, including Carl. She had a thick layer of sunscreen on her pale skin to make sure she didn't crisp, and she would have to slather it on her boobs, too. That would be quite the show.

Torn between fitting in and modesty, she decided to sit back, legs stretched out and facing the pool, and mull it over for a bit. Or until the girls started mocking her for staying clothed. The other women sat nearby at some tables, chattering and ordering more drinks. She really wanted a vodka.

A few minutes later, Carl strolled their way, cigar between his teeth, martini in hand. She tensed.

"You ladies toasting your white fannies?" He stopped in front of them, smoke curling around his face, dark glasses hiding his eyes. "Better get those bottoms off, too."

Amelia lifted her head and scowled. She waved a hand. "Get that thing out of here, Carl. You know I hate smoking."

He plucked the cigar out of his mouth and blew a puff of smoke at her, then smiled a wide, toothy, and malicious smile.

Amelia waved her hand harder and coughed. "Shithead! Why don't you go play poker or something? I came on this vacation to escape your bullshit for a while."

"You didn't care about my cigars when I was paying for those tits, Muffin. You ought to act a little more grateful."

Amelia put her head back down, still scowling.

For as long as Grace had known the two of them, they had been hateful and cold toward each other. She couldn't imagine what the advantage was in being married—except, of course, that they both came from money, and together they had even more money. Carl also worked for Amelia's father.

Carl eased over to Grace's chair. She smiled, though inside she was shrieking. She shifted her legs aside as he sat down, next to her knees.

"It's good to see you again, Gracie." He sipped from his dwindling martini. "You're looking foxy as ever."

She kept her smile plastered on and played with a loose curl that had tumbled onto her shoulder. "Thank you, Carl."

"I keep hoping you'll show up for dinner. I tell Amelia to invite you."

Amelia *had* invited her, on multiple occasions. If Grace wasn't busy, she found a reason to be busy.

"I'm sorry, I just have so much going on." She adjusted her glasses. "Business is booming, and I have to be at the boutiques. You know how it is. I promise I'll try to make it sometime next month. Your chef is to die for, I miss those courses."

She'd gone to many a dinner at Carl and Amelia's house, when she and Brent were together. The food was magnificent, mostly because they employed their own Certified Master Chef.

Carl flicked his ash on the ground, holding his cigar in the same hand as his martini. "I talked to Brent a couple weeks ago." His tone was light, almost mocking.

She stiffened. "Oh?"

"Yes, I went to visit him."

She blinked a few times. "You went to see him in prison?"

He nodded. "We're working on a business deal, for when he gets out. He always was one hell of a shrewd investor. He's only got eighteen months to go, less if he behaves himself. He'll need something when he comes out."

The dissonance that rang through this group deafened her. They all knew her ex-husband had lied, cheated his clients, stole money from his own corporation, and certainly belonged in prison. They also knew about her struggles with him, that he had swindled her as well and left her high and dry. The divorce was easy, seeing as how he was incarcerated, but getting any of the money that belonged to her in the aftermath wasn't, since all his assets were tied up by the government.

At least they'd cleared her of any implication in his crimes almost immediately. She'd been left in the dark, like always, clueless to what he'd been up to. But she felt half the money in their joint bank account—much of which had come from her boutiques—was due to her. Brent had convinced her repeatedly not to put it in her own separate account, she knew now because he wanted access to it and ownership over it.

"Don't look so grim-faced, Gracie." Carl patted her thigh, and her cringing intensified. "I know what he did took you by surprise, but I don't think he ever meant to hurt you." He chuckled amicably. "He just loves money. I'm sure he loved you, too. How could he not? You're a hot broad." He didn't remove his hand.

She kept smiling, though she wanted to pull away from him. "I suppose he did. We had three wonderful years together, after all. And he lavished so much on me." He had, and her head still spun from it. That's why she couldn't let this life go. "I suppose you think badly of me for divorcing him."

Carl chuckled again and rubbed her thigh. His hand was dangerously high. Her skin crawled.

"No, I think he deserved it." He took a sip from his martini. "He could have at least cut you in." He smirked. "You can't sit around waiting for him, rotting away. You deserve to move on."

Amelia had her head turned toward them, her cheek on her hands. She never stepped in to stop her husband's inappropriate behavior, ever. Grace looked away.

"Don't worry." Carl leaned toward her and lowered his voice. "I think you have every right to ask for that money, too."

She looked back at him, her heart jumping into her throat. She hadn't told any of them about the lawsuit. But of course, if he had been visiting Brent in prison, Brent would have told him.

Carl winked over his glasses. "I won't say a word. And for what it's worth, he thinks you deserve it, too. You made that money together. But his hands are tied, he can't make the bastards hand it over." He shrugged and finally removed his hand.

She took the opportunity to subtly move away. Those "bastards" had every right to keep a stranglehold on Brent's money, but there was no use arguing that. As soon as Brent got out, he would be right back to a life of ease. Carl would make sure of that. He would never know the same hell he'd put her through. That twisted in her heart like a dull knife.

Ty walked toward them from the other side of the pool. He had a glass of scotch in hand, his sunglasses on top his head. He was focused on Carl. She shifted a bit farther away.

"Ah, here comes your young man." Carl didn't budge. "It's nice to see you back in the game, sweetheart. Don't worry, I won't tell Brent."

She didn't care if he did. In fact, she wished he would.

"As you said, I can't sit and rot." She picked up her drink and took a sip from it. The repulsive syrupy concoction was even worse watered down, as the ice cubes had melted considerably.

Amelia lifted her head and smiled up at Ty as he

joined them. "Having fun, Tybalt?"

Ty stood at the end of Grace's chair. He nodded. "Yeah, it's nice here."

Carl chewed on the end of his cigar. "We ought to see if we can get some golf in tomorrow morning. You can come with us if you like, Tybalt. You don't want to stay here and hang out with the women all day."

"It's not so bad," Ty said.

Amelia waved Carl off. "Why don't you run and play? Maybe Tybalt doesn't want to hang out with you boring bastards either."

Carl got to his feet. Grace drew an inward sigh of relief and relaxed against the chair. He bent and gave his wife a sharp slap on the ass. She yelped.

"Fuck off, Carl!" she snarled at him. "Go creep on the waitress or something."

"You get them titties tanned for me." He turned and clapped Ty on the shoulder. "Don't let these broads suck you in. All they do is gossip and shop."

Ty just gave him a tight smile and a nod.

Carl shuffled off, and Grace felt like she could breathe again. Amelia grumbled and shifted around, and reached behind her to tug her bikini bottom back over her cheeks.

"Don't go golfing with them, Tybalt," Roxanne said. "You'll be braindead by the time you come back. We have a lot more fun, trust me." She gave him a knowing smirk.

Grace tried not to prickle with more jealousy. She reminded herself that Ty wasn't really her boyfriend, and besides, she was paying him, so he wasn't going to leave her side. Indeed, he sat down on the edge of her chair, on the opposite side Carl had. She felt no need to pull away—quite the opposite, actually.

"Are you enjoying yourself?" She sipped her

drink again, tried not to grimace, and set it aside. "Are the boys boring you?"

As much as she liked him sitting there with her, she wanted him to try to fit in with the men. She considered dropping a subtle hint that he should leave her and go back to them.

"I just wanted to see what you were up to." He eyed her. "You looked like *you* were bored over here. I thought I would keep you company."

Her chest tightened. He hadn't come over because she looked bored, and she knew that. He'd come over because Carl was harassing her. She'd realized it the second she saw the look on Ty's face when he approached. She wasn't paying him to be protective, but maybe he thought it was a nice touch to act like a jealous boyfriend. Either way, it warmed her cold insides.

"I'm not bored, sweetheart." She gripped his knee and rubbed it. "I'm having fun with my girlfriends." She gestured to the other women, who had barely taken note of her since they stretched out.

Ty looked over his shoulder. "Not getting a tan with them?" He smirked.

"I will later. Too much sun and my fair skin will pay the price. I don't want to age it."

Amelia lifted her head. She slipped her sunglasses down her nose, looking at Ty. "We should hop in the pool. What do you say?"

Ty arched an eyebrow.

"Roxanne." Amelia turned to the other woman. She was propped up on her elbows now, and they were getting a peek of her acquired assets. "Why don't we get in the pool? Tybalt isn't having a good time with those assholes. Why don't we show him we actually know how to have fun? We must be nice to our guest."

Another frisson of jealousy shot through Grace,

stronger than before. She tried to stomp it out. She wanted him to be part of the group, after all.

Roxanne lifted her head, frowning. "I just got all oiled up."

"He can oil us back up, no worries." Amelia sat up, smiling. She seemed absolutely unabashed in her nudity. "Come on, let's have some fun."

Ty looked away, keeping his back to Amelia. Grace tried not to stare and be envious. It really was a nice boob job.

"We have plenty of time to lay in the sun." Amelia grabbed her top and started stuffing herself back in it. "Let's go splash around in the water." She stood. "Come on, Tybalt." She focused on Grace. "You don't mind if we steal him away, do you?"

Grace smiled. "Not at all, of course."

Ty glanced at her, frowned, and reluctantly got to his feet. He turned toward Amelia, but kept his gaze averted from her chest. However, she sauntered right up to him and turned.

"Can you tie me up, Lovely?" She pulled her long golden hair over her shoulder, out of the way.

Grace gritted her teeth but didn't react. Once again, she reminded herself *she'd* paid for him.

Ty laced up the ties on Amelia's top, at the back of her neck and below her shoulder blades. His expression was blank. Roxanne at least had the modesty to turn her back to them as she put her top back on. Hers was elastic and didn't have ties.

"Thank you, Tybalt." Amelia looked over her shoulder, her voice as smooth as honey. "I'm going to have to find one just like him, Grace. Carl needs to be replaced."

Grace let out a stilted laugh. "We'll have to hit the nightclubs together."

Amelia bent and snatched up her towel, her shapely bottom pointed directly at Ty. "Gonna swim with us, Gracie?" She turned and walked toward the pool, hips swaying.

"I'll be right over. I'll just dip my feet, I think."

Ty looked at Grace and spread his hands, as if asking *what do I do?* She waved him toward the pool, though she wanted him to sit back down on the chair with her.

Roxanne headed toward the pool as well. Amelia was sliding in, down one of the metal ladders.

"Come on, Tybalt!" she called. "The water feels wonderful." She splashed it up on the patio.

Ty scowled, plunked his glass down next to Grace's, and peeled his shirt off. He was gorgeous beneath, with tight abs and a broad chest that begged to be touched and caressed, maybe even licked. She could imagine Amelia doing just that and her insides went cold again.

"I thought I was here to entertain you," he murmured, and tossed his shirt on the chair at her feet.

"You're here to be convincing." She spoke lowly as well. "Try to have some fun."

"Yes, ma'am." He turned and headed toward the pool, where the girls were both in the water now and beckoning to him.

On the other side of the patio, Carl was sprawled in a chair beneath an umbrella. He grinned and lifted his glass to her.

She smiled and waved back. Inside, she was screaming.

Chapter Six

The last thing Ty wanted to do was get in the water and cavort around with other men's wives, but he apparently had no choice. This was, somehow, what he was being paid to do.

"Come on." Roxanne grabbed his arm and pulled him in deeper. "You have to get wet with us."

The water was cool, but it felt good in contrast to the heat and humidity. He might have fun in it under different circumstances.

"We want to get to know you better." Amelia gripped his other arm. Her lips were plump and shiny pink, her eyes hidden behind sunglasses. "You're the best-looking man here. I bet you're the smartest, too."

"I don't know about that." Ty tried to keep his demeanor casual, so as not to betray the panic he felt inside. He didn't know if he could keep up the charade if they started asking him a bunch of invasive, leading questions.

Grace had walked over to the pool and sat down on the edge. Her legs were in the water, but she showed no sign of joining them. She watched instead, her lips pressed in a tight line. The more he got acquainted with these people, the worse he felt for her. Obviously, that Carl guy was a massive creep and a predator, and maybe Ty had overstepped his boundaries by intervening in their conversation, but he couldn't sit casually by and watch him get his slime all over her. Besides, wasn't he here to be attentive and responsive? Wasn't *that* what he was getting paid for?

He could almost convince himself he was still just doing a "job."

They moved out into the water until it lapped

beneath their chests. Ty got the impression they stopped there so that Amelia's boobs could float enticingly on the surface. He carefully kept his gaze averted. Not that they weren't nice, but she was too obvious, and he wasn't interested in her anyway. Even if he had the freedom to do as he wanted, he would be put off by her behavior.

"How do you like Barbados so far?" Amelia drifted closer to him.

He looked over at Grace. She stared down at the water, idly kicking her feet below the surface.

"I haven't seen much of it." Ty shrugged. "Just a resort, so far."

"You don't want to go off the resort, trust us." Roxanne reached up and wound her hair on top her head. She was at least a little more tactful than Amelia. "It's nowhere near as luxurious, even the touristy spots. There's some good restaurants and decent shopping, but the locals are far too pushy and in your face."

Ty refrained from pointing out the irony.

Amelia smiled. "The resort is far superior. Don't worry, there's lots of fun to be had here. You never need to go out *there*." She said this as if it were some kind of apocalyptic wasteland beyond these white stone walls.

The men must have noticed him in the water then, as they started jeering from poolside. Apparently, swimming with beautiful women instead of hanging out with the bros was considered gay.

"Better be careful, Tybalt," Carl called to him. "The Kraken will wrap you up in her tentacles!" This was followed by collective laughter.

Amelia scowled. "Just ignore them. Carl's a bastard. The only thing I can still stand about that man is his platinum card."

Ty just nodded. He tried to subtly move toward Grace, but the girls quickly hemmed him in.

"So, Tybalt." Amelia moved in so close they were almost touching. She squeezed her shoulders together so her boobs pushed out, nearly spilling from her gold bikini top. "Where are you from?"

Ty stared at her. "Uh, Park Slope. Brooklyn." Perhaps Grace hadn't filled them in yet.

Roxanne blocked him on his right side, in the direction Grace sat. She was showing off her boobs, too, though they were smaller. "No, she means where are you from *originally?*"

Ah, of course. He forced a smile, though the corner of his mouth twitched. "My grandfather on my dad's side was born in Santorini, Greece. My mother's family is from Naples, Italy. I was born in the US, though."

"So exotic," Amelia purred. "Can you speak Greek? I bet it's a romantic language."

"Or Italian?" Roxanne added. "I've got some Italian in me, too." She smirked.

"I can speak a little of both. Not enough to hold a conversation, though. My parents both spoke English while I was growing up. They were both born here."

"Where did you go to college?" Amelia played with a strand of her hair. Though she hadn't pulled hers up, she seemed to be making sure not to get it wet.

Ty's panic intensified. They hadn't worked this part out. He couldn't immediately think of an adequate school they would approve of.

"I didn't go to college, actually." He stole a nervous glance at Grace. "I'm kind of a self-made man, you know. So was my dad. Lots of business owners in my family."

"Self-made." Roxanne smirked at Amelia. "Sounds like our darling husbands." She looked at Ty. "You own a bakery, right?"

He nodded. "Artisanal bakery."

Amelia shrugged. "Isn't that just a fancy word for making stuff by hand?"

Ty almost laughed. Maybe they should have come up with something a little more sophisticated.

Amelia bobbed dangerously close to Ty once more. "So how did you meet Grace again? She said you met at The Skylark. Was she throwing herself at you? She's been so long without a man."

"No ... I went up to her and talked to her first, actually." He glanced in Grace's direction again. She was looking away, across the pool. "She was the hottest girl there. I could barely speak, I was so nervous. If anything, *I* threw myself at *her*."

Amelia huffed. "At The Skylark? She was the hottest girl there?"

"She was wearing this slinky black dress." He smiled. "She made it herself, I found out later. She looked so good in it. Curves for days, she was just so gorgeous, I was head over heels instantly. I had to get to know her."

He hoped Grace could hear him. She looked over at them, so maybe she had.

Amelia reached up and toyed with the silly knot Grace had put in his hair. He frowned. "Well, now that you've met her friends, do you still think she's the hottest girl you've ever laid eyes on?"

Dear God. Grace wanted him to do this, so he had to remain polite.

"Um..."

Amelia bit her lip, smiling coyly. Her teeth were obviously capped, too perfect and straight. She kept playing with his hair. "Admit it, she's got some pretty sexy girlfriends, huh?"

Ty felt like he was the one surrounded by sharks

now, literally chum in the water.

"You are beautiful." He spoke diplomatically. "I appreciate feminine beauty in many forms. I wouldn't kick you out of bed."

Both girls giggled.

Grace drew her legs out of the pool and stood. She grabbed her towel, which she'd been sitting on.

"If you'll excuse me, ladies." Ty eased out of their trap. "I think I'm gonna grab another drink with the guys, if you don't mind. I'm not much of a swimmer."

Amelia tried to catch his arm under the water, but he slipped away. "Oh, come on." She pouted. "They're so old and boring. Don't you want to have fun with us girls? We're much more interesting than stock portfolios and golf."

Grace was walking away from the pool.

"I don't doubt that." He tried to remain polite. "But trust me, I think I'll have a better view of you two from up there." He flicked down his glasses and winked. They both smirked, chests still bobbing above the water.

"Don't feel like you have to be a stranger," Amelia said. "When you get bored, we'll be around."

She swam at him, and he felt a sharp pinch on his bottom. She'd grabbed his ass.

"And I'll be alone most of this trip," she whispered near his ear. "While Carl is busy with his friends."

He quickly swam away before she could get her hands on him again. What the hell was with these people?

He climbed out of the pool, horribly self-conscious that Amelia and Roxanne were checking him out. The guys teased him some more as he grabbed his towel. He just smiled and waved. They all deserved each other.

Instead of going for more scotch, he made a beeline for the cabana bar, which was in the same direction Grace had took off in. He didn't see her there and had no idea where she might have gone, so he decided to just get another drink and wait. He hoped she didn't give him hell or ask him to leave. As he stood in line to order, someone grabbed his arm. He cringed, thinking Amelia had followed him, but it was Grace.

"Looks like you're getting on well with everyone, darling." Her voice was clipped. "You seem to be having fun."

Ty looked over his shoulder. They were far enough away from the others they wouldn't be heard. "If this is your idea of fun, I'd hate to see what you think a bad time is. You weren't kidding when you said your friends were—difficult."

"The girls seem to like you."

"Yeah, they sure do."

She pulled him roughly out of line.

"Hey!" He stumbled after her as she dragged him around the side of the cabana. There were huts for changing into swimwear back there, and they were alone. She pushed him up against the wall of one of the huts and he gaped at her.

"I paid for you." She lifted her sunglasses and put them on top her head. Her sea green eyes were sparkling and fierce in the sunlight. "I didn't pay you to come here and flirt with my friends. I paid you to give me all the attention. Now, you don't want me to have to ask for a refund, do you?"

He gaped at her some more. "In case you didn't notice, I wasn't flirting with your friends. They—"

She placed a hand on his chest. "You're here for me, no one else. I thought that was implied in your contract."

Anger rose up in him. He'd had enough of this. "You *made* me get in the pool! I didn't want to, but you told me to. I'm starting to get whiplash trying to follow all your damn orders."

"You shouldn't have come over to us to begin with." She bared her teeth. "You should have stayed over on the other side of the pool with the guys."

"That Carl guy was creeping on you." He grabbed her hand on his chest. "He was feeling you up. What, was I just supposed to stay over there and let the dickhead manhandle my girlfriend? I know everyone else around here seems to have no problem schmoozing all over each other, but I thought you told me to be attentive. I was being fucking attentive!"

"I can handle Carl."

"You didn't look like you were handling him."

She visibly fumed. "This is a delicate situation. I have to be careful of what I say and do, and so do you. That means staying out of things, no matter what you see or hear. Nod and smile, and just look pretty. That's all I want you to do. And stay the hell away from Amelia."

"I was *trying* to stay the hell away from Amelia." He flung her hand away. "You told me to get in the pool. But frankly, I'm tired of taking these insane orders from you, money or no money. This is ridiculous and I'm feeling more than a little insulted."

"You're going to continue taking orders from me, like it or not."

"I'm not a fucking pet, I'm a person."

"You're a gigolo."

He opened his mouth to protest, but she suddenly lurched forward and smashed her lips against his. They were satiny soft and tasted like rum. He was so taken off guard he didn't try to get away. She kissed him with force, and it wasn't particularly pleasant.

He put his hand on her shoulder and pushed her back.

She glared at him. "What, do I have to pay extra for physical affection? Or would you rather give it to those sluts for free?"

He wasn't one to lose his temper, but this was completely ridiculous. He grabbed her by the wrists and whipped her around, so their positions were switched. He pushed her up against the wall—not hard, but firmly—and pinned her hands next to her shoulders. She gasped, and the ferocity in her eyes retreated. Her lashes fluttered.

"Listen to me." He spoke in her face. "I know who paid me, and what I'm here for. Those women are nothing but predators—rich, self-entitled harpies who are used to getting what they want without question. I've known girls like that before. Do you think I want to be trapped by them? I got in the pool at your insistence, and you're acting completely irrational and insane right now. I think you know that, too."

She was breathing hard. They were so close he could feel the heat of her body, even under the glare of the tropical sun.

He continued. "These are awful people, if you don't mind me saying, and I don't think you do. Stop trying to act like one of them, because you're not. And that's a good thing. A damn good thing."

She flicked her gaze over his face, then met his eyes again. She swallowed. "It's complicated." Her voice came out small and tight. "I told you, it's a delicate situation."

"I'm sure it is." He loosened his grip on her wrists, but still held them. She arched her back a little, so her chest brushed his. "But you don't need to act like this. Stop it. You're gorgeous, and I'm glad I'm here with you."

Her lashes fluttered again.

He let go of her with one hand and stroked the creamy slope of her cheek. "You're prettier than any of them, because you're not fake like they are. And your teeth aren't as sharp." He moved his hand to her chin and caressed his thumb beneath her lower lip, where her lip gloss was smeared. "Knock this off and stop treating me like a dog. I know who I'm here with, and I'm happy to do as you say if you don't turn it into abuse. Cut me some slack, and I'll do my job like I'm supposed to."

He probably shouldn't drop character this much, but he had no choice. He wouldn't be mistreated, and he wasn't going to let insecurity and jealousy ruin what could be an otherwise amazing trip.

She gripped his shoulder and pulled him toward her. This time, they shared a mutual kiss, deep and firm, but not forced this time. Behind the taste of rum on her lips it was all wet, warm sweetness.

He let himself indulge. He moved his hand to her waist and pressed against her. She was soft all over, her skin as hot as her mouth. The scent of her perfume and sunscreen filled his nose, a heady and enticing combination. Her breasts pushed against his chest, full and high and just as big as Amelia's, but real.

He wanted to make out with her forever, but his cock was perking up at all her lush sexy sensuality and he didn't want to make this awkward. He drew back and caught his breath. Her cheeks were pink, her eyes bright.

"Do you mean all that?" she asked quietly. "You're not just saying it because I paid you?"

"I mean it." He caressed the swell of her hip. He wanted to tuck his fingers beneath the skimpy fabric of her bikini bottom. His mind filled with tantalizing questions—was she bare down there? Was there a little strip of hair? Was she soft and velvety inside as well?

"Thank you." She looked down, her lashes shielding her eyes, and stroked her hand down his stomach. He didn't get to the gym as much as he used to, but he was still a pretty solid specimen, if he did say so himself. They needed to stop this, or he was going to pop a huge boner and wouldn't be able to walk back to the pool.

She looked up, and a tiny smile touched her lips. They were swollen and glistening now, and her lip gloss was nearly gone. "I don't mean to act so crazy or treat you so badly. This just isn't a very fun time so far. I'm truly sorry."

He snorted. "That's an understatement. So far, I've been pawed, mocked, teased, and had all sorts of low-key racist comments tossed my way. I feel like I'm back in high school."

"I'm sorry this is happening." She heaved a sigh. "Maybe I shouldn't have brought you here and subjected you to this. Maybe I should have chosen a man—more like them."

That stung a little, but he understood her point. And he was glad to not be like them.

"I wouldn't have had much fun with a man like that, though." She titled her head. "I'm happy I chose you. I just hope it doesn't become completely unbearable for you."

"I've got a pretty thick skin, don't worry."

"I thought I did, too."

"Just please stop jerking me around, okay? I can deal with them, but I need you to be clear with what you want."

She nodded. "I'll be nicer. I really am sorry, I don't know what I was thinking."

"I forgive you." He let go of her wrist where he

still had it pinned against the wall. "I can't drink any more scotch. I have to get something else, or I'm going to puke. I hope you don't mind."

She grimaced. "Don't worry, I can't stand any more rum either. Let's get some vodka."

He gazed at her a moment. She gazed back at him and licked her lips. He leaned in and kissed her again, briefly, and drew away.

She smiled. "We'll continue this later, hmm?"

She stepped away from the wall, tugged at her bikini top—making her boobs jiggle—and took his hand. "I'm afraid I have some bad news, though."

He walked with her back toward the cabana. "Oh? Just what I was hoping for." He tried to subtly adjust himself.

"We have to attend a party tonight, like it or not. I've been informed." She drew her sunglasses back down over her eyes. "I'm sorry. I would very much rather not, but if we don't, it's going to look suspect and I'll never hear the end of it."

He sighed. "It's all right, I'll practice my internal screaming."

"I have that down to an art." She smirked at him. "We'll have some fun tomorrow on our own, I promise. You don't have to go golfing with the men."

He squeezed her hand. "That's a good thing. I couldn't hit a golf ball if my life depended on it."

Chapter Seven

Grace stood in front of the vanity mirror and studied herself, wrapped in the clingy green dress she'd brought with her. It was mostly Lycra, came to mid-thigh, and had spaghetti straps. She'd designed it herself just a few months ago, so it was close enough to current fashion no one could say a word. The emerald green material accentuated her pale skin and brought out her eyes. She'd sewn satin ruching into the sides to help emphasize the curve of her hips but minimize her tummy, and made the top snug, since her rack was one of her best features.

Ty whistled behind her. "Are you sure *that's* not the dress you were wearing the night we met?"

He wore his gray blazer—Calvin Klein, though not this year's line. Still, it looked good on him, this time with a crisp white dress shirt beneath. Both brought out the rich copper in his skin tone and provided eye-catching contrast. His black slacks weren't designer, but they were slim and fit him like they were tailored, so it didn't matter much. He had a nice ass, and the pants, combined with the cut of the blazer, showed it off in the most exquisite way.

"You don't look so bad yourself." She pushed one of her diamond earrings in and admired him in the mirror. "Those broads are going to be crawling all over you again."

He walked up behind her. "I'll have to get better at dodging them. But please don't tell me to go play with them again." He placed his hands lightly on her hips. "Do you mind? You look too good not to touch."

She smiled. "I don't mind." Despite the difficulties ahead of her, she was determined to get through this miserable social engagement with her chin up. "I won't tell you to play with them again. I'm sorry I put you in that situation earlier."

"It's all right, I said I forgive you. I'm sorry I lost my temper."

"You had every right."

He caressed his hands up and down her sides. The sensation was terribly distracting as she tried to work her other earring in. *How far was he willing to go?* And would it cost extra?

She finished putting her earrings in and turned. "So, I know you're not a prostitute." She smoothed her hand down the front of his shirt, pretending to check for undone buttons.

He arched an eyebrow. His hair rested on his shoulders, thick and shiny. She wanted to drag her fingers through it, grab a handful, and yank him toward her for a kiss. The taste of his mouth still lingered in her memory, though she supposed he really didn't like tasting like scotch.

"No, I mean, I'm an escort technically, I guess. My mom calls me a gigolo." He smirked. His full lips were so tempting, and damn, had they felt good against hers.

She dropped her hand from his chest. "I know it says in our contract sexual services are not provided nor expected. It's against the law, obviously."

"Yeah, they have to put that technicality in there."

She stepped around him and walked to the bed, patting her hair. She'd piled it on top her head, but let a few curls spill down. "Do you ever have sex with the women you date, despite that?" She rifled through her clothes on the bed, not really searching for anything, but she didn't look at him while she asked this.

"I have, a … couple times." He cleared his throat.

"I mean, it happens. It has nothing to do with the service I provide. I mean, two adults who happen to be attracted to each other and have consenting sex is perfectly legal. It's not a big deal."

She glanced at him. "Do women ever offer to pay you to have sex with them?"

He held up a hand. "I don't want any more money."

"I'm not offering it." She grabbed up a pair of dark green heels from the floor. "I'm just asking a question. I'm curious."

He hesitated. "Yeah, sure, I've been offered. But I don't take it, because I don't think it's right. Like you said, I'm not a prostitute."

She walked back to the mirror. "What about the women you had sex with willingly?" She dropped the shoes next to the vanity and started rooting through her makeup bag for her perfume. "Did you ever see them again?" She looked at him in the mirror.

"One, yeah. I saw her a couple times after that. Off the clock, so to speak."

"Interesting."

"Shouldn't we be getting downstairs?" He pulled his phone out of his blazer pocket and looked at it.

"We should." She spritzed her perfume on.

They made the short walk to a bar next door, a modern place with an upscale, tropical motif. Most of it was open to the air and everything was white and wicker. However, there were a few interior rooms and the party was being held in one of these, on the second floor overlooking the beach. The room was all exposed wood with cushy leather furniture for lounging on, and there was an attached veranda with chairs and tables.

"The drinks are part of the package," she murmured to Ty as they walked in, and nodded toward a bar at the back of the room. "Knock yourself out." She held his arm and walked with a swing in her hips. She was more emotionally and psychologically prepared this time. At least she hoped so.

"I think I'll take it easy," he murmured in return. "I don't want to let my guard down too much or forget anything."

Everyone around them looked like money and class, wearing cocktail dresses and casual suits, high heels and gleaming loafers. Grace tried not to focus on labels, or the diamonds around Roxanne's neck, or the gold on Amelia's wrists.

"Oh hey, cute dress, Gracie," Roxanne cooed as she and Amelia slid up to them and blocked their path. "Is that Prada?"

Grace was tempted to say yes, but Roxanne was probably teasing her. She steeled herself. "No, it's actually a dress I designed myself."

Amelia held a glass of champagne. She sipped from it and looked Grace over as well. "Well, it suits your figure, that's for sure."

Ty spoke up. "I think she looks gorgeous. She's really good at what she does, I'm so proud of her."

Both women flashed simpering smiles. Their eyes glittered, predatory. Did they really find him attractive, or were they just flirting with him to aggravate her? Or test him? She would die if they ever found out he was bought and paid for. She'd never be able to show her face around them again.

"Want some champagne?" Amelia held her glass up with a giggle. She was mostly asking Ty.

Before they could reply, Carl strolled over. "Tybalt, my man." He grinned his wide, white, sharky grin. "Come on over and have a drink with us. We're thinking about getting a poker game started."

Amelia and Roxanne rolled their eyes and wandered toward the veranda, talking lowly and giggling. Were they talking about her? About Ty? Grace tried to corral her paranoia.

Ty smiled at her. "You mind if I hang out with the guys? I'll let you mingle."

She gripped his arm tighter. "Are you sure? You don't have to run off."

He patted her hand on his arm. "It's fine."

She didn't want to let him go, but if they hung all over each other it wouldn't look right. People who were dating didn't hang all over each constantly, right? Besides, she wanted him to fit in, and he was trying.

She reluctantly let him go and walked to the bar. After ordering a stiff drink, she strolled around and said hello. They were a large group, ten to twelve couples who buzzed around the same social circle due to jobs, club memberships, and organizations. It had been a while since she'd been able to participate in any fund-raisers or parties—or pay memberships—but she tried to act as if she'd been around the whole time.

"It's good to see you again, Grace." Patsy was a tall, dark-haired woman, a bit older than the others and slightly more tolerable to be around. She was the wife of a CEO, and she looked the part. Fashionable, put together, dripping in gold. Even her perfume smelled expensive.

"It's good to see you, too, Patsy." Grace kissed her cheek as they delicately embraced. They didn't want to mess up each other's hair or clothes.

"I haven't seen you around the club lately." She was speaking of the country club where Patsy and her husband were members, and Brent used to take Grace. "We've missed you." The place had a nice spa as well. Grace badly needed a facial and a foot rub, but she couldn't afford it right now.

"I've been working so much." Grace kept her tone casual. "Business is booming at the boutiques. I do miss you, though. And our brunches."

Patsy surreptitiously looked her over, but Grace didn't miss the scrutiny. "You're looking good. Have you been dieting?"

"A little, yes." She was about to take a sip of her drink but reconsidered.

"I wish I had your curves." Patsy sighed. "I work out all the time, but I can't seem to get any padding in the right places." She flexed her bare arm, showing a decent, but ladylike, bicep. "I need hips like yours."

Grace wasn't sure if that was a compliment, so she just smiled.

"Is that your boyfriend?" Patsy looked over to where Ty stood with the guys. He had a glass in hand now and was laughing. He actually looked like he might be having a good time. "I saw you come in with him. Sorry I wasn't at the get-together this afternoon, I got in late."

"Yes, that's Tybalt." Grace fidgeted. "He's a business owner, like me."

Patsy smirked. "He's young and sexy. A bit of a hood rat, rough around the edges. I see what you're doing. Brent would lose his mind. Have you talked to him? Have you told him you're dating again?"

Grace's heart climbed into her throat. Hood rat? Rough around the edges? Sure, he wasn't as well dressed as the other men, and certainly not as clean-cut, but she wouldn't call him a *hood rat*. Was that what everyone was thinking?

"Um, no, I haven't spoken to him." Grace tried to maintain an unruffled demeanor. "I haven't talked to Brent in a long time, and good riddance." She waved her hand with a sharp laugh. "What a bastard, don't you agree?"

"Maybe, but I always thought he was clever and funny." Patsy winked and took a sip of her champagne. "Of course, if he'd been *more* clever, he wouldn't be where he is right now."

Grace stiffened, her hands tight around her glass. None of them understood or cared what she'd been through. She didn't want them to, really. She didn't need their judgement.

"Yes." Grace took a quick sip. "And no, I don't think Brent would approve of him, that's the point." She lightened her tone. "He's a toy, something to pass the time with. We're not serious, but my, does he heat up the bedroom." She fanned herself. "Sometimes you just need a bit of fun. Something to take the edge off, you know?"

Patsy grinned. "Oh, I know it." She whispered, "My Pilates instructor."

Grace laughed uproariously with her. Ty glanced in their direction.

"I'll find someone more suited for me, in time." Grace twirled a curl around her finger. "Until then, I'll be his Sugar Mama."

Patsy winked. "You go, girl."

Grace finished her circuit around the room. More people noted that she hadn't been around lately and claimed they missed her. She was preoccupied fretting about how people were viewing Ty as rough and unseemly. Were they gossiping about her, laughing at how she'd brought some poor, bedraggled "hood rat" to their wealthy, lush retreat?

She finally found a stool and sat at a vantage point where she could watch him. He joined a poker game at one of the tables. The men were smoking cigars and drinking scotch, though Ty had a beer and wasn't smoking. He was unarguably the most striking man at the table, no matter what anyone thought of him. Shame and guilt boiled inside of her.

He worked hard, just like her. She could see it in him. On top of that, he had to do this job to supplement himself. He seemed genuine and kind beneath the suave act, and he rested easy in his skin. He was the sort of man any sane woman would kill for. And her mind kept going back to the way he kissed her earlier. The way he took command and pushed her against the wall and drove the obsessive thoughts out of her head with the touch of his lips. The way he made her knees weak. She thought of his hands on her hips in the room, the way he looked at her in mirror, the desire in his eyes and the way he spoke to her—none of it seemed like an act. If it was, he was a damn good actor.

He was exactly the opposite of her slimy, self-serving, fake ex-husband. And that's precisely why they thought he wasn't one of them. But if they thought that, they would soon think the same of her, and she'd be openly mocked and ridiculed, thrown out of their circle. She'd have to go back to the dreary, dead-end life she used to know before Brent, down among the dregs. Panic overwhelmed the guilt inside her and collected around her like a black fog.

She stood up and strolled to the table, where she placed a hand on Ty's shoulder. "Are you winning, darling?"

The men around the table chortled. They didn't have chips but were playing with actual money. Ty smiled up at her.

"No, but now that you're here, Lady Luck, maybe things will turn around." He took her hand and kissed it.

Carl leered at her through a haze of cigar smoke. "You're a knockout in that dress, Gracie. Why don't you teach my wife how to eat so she isn't just a skeleton with some silicone attached to her?"

That was the second time someone had called her fat without calling her fat. She resented it. She worked out. She had muscle. Her body shape was just on the fuller side.

Ty squeezed her hand. "You put all the other women in this room to shame."

Most of the men around the table smirked and nodded at this, though the more congenial ones gave him a dirty look. A few of them actually liked their wives, or at least tolerated them.

"Would you like another beer, darling?" She nodded at his bottle. "Or are you going to have scotch with the boys instead?" She said this almost as an encouragement, hoping he would take the hint. He was a good man, but the better he fit in, the easier the next few days would be.

He smiled up at her again. "Another beer would be great, thanks."

She squeezed his shoulder, a bit tight. "Now, don't lose all your spending money. I'm not giving you more if you throw it away on these silly bastards."

The men laughed. Ty looked up at her with an arched eyebrow, his expression startled. Better to play this angle. They would understand then, at least, why she chose to bring a common man with her.

She walked to the bar and felt eyes on her back. Not just the men at the table, but Ty. She ordered him another beer, brought it back, and kissed the top of his head. He didn't say anything or even look at her, just stared at his cards.

She went out on the veranda to get some air. The evening was warm and smelled like the ocean. She'd always been fond of the scent of salt and brine. She'd grown up near Coney Island and it reminded her of walking on the beach on Saturdays with her mother, collecting shells for craft projects.

Blissfully, no one wanted to chat with her and she was left alone for a while. About fifteen minutes passed, and then Ty came out. He had his jacket off, sleeves rolled up, beer bottle dangling from his hand. She caught her breath at the sight of him but looked away.

He walked over and leaned on the railing next to her and held out a folded wad of money. "I'm pretty good at poker, by the way."

"I see." She eyed the money.

"And I figure since I'm a kept boy, I better give it to you, ma'am." Sarcasm tinged his words.

"Technically, you are a kept boy." She plucked the money from his hand. "It's yours, though. I'll put it in my purse and give it to you in the room."

He took a swig of his beer and turned toward her. "Yes, after all, you don't want anyone to know I'm my own man."

She glanced around. "What are you talking about?"

"If you want to pretend you're my benefactor, you should have said that to begin with. You asked me to pretend I was your boyfriend and we have this great relationship, but now I'm supposed to be your lap dog?" His eyes flashed. "If you want to act like you pay me to fuck you, you could just flat out tell them you bought me. That would be easier than all this playacting."

"I panicked." She stepped closer, keeping her voice down. "Patsy said you looked 'rough' and I had to come up with something."

He jerked his head back. "Rough? What the hell does that mean?"

"You know ... not like them." Her heart was

pounding. "They're stuck up their own asses, if you haven't noticed. They think anyone without money should be serving them, not hanging out with them."

"Are you calling me poor?"

"I barely know you." She reached out and gripped his wrist. "I didn't say that. I think you're probably very industrious, and I—"

They were interrupted by Carl and several of his cronies. She let go of Ty's wrist and stepped back.

"So, golf tomorrow?" Carl chewed on the stub of his cigar. "Are you going to join us on the green, Tybalt? We always have room for one more."

Grace tried to intervene, but Ty spoke first. "I'm afraid I'm not very good at golf." He was congenial, but frosty. "I would just make a fool of myself. I'm sure you're all very good."

"In that case," Carl smirked, "we could always use a caddy."

Ty stepped away from the railing. "Enjoy your game, gentlemen. Grace, I'm going to head back to the room, I think."

"We have plans tomorrow," Grace quickly interjected. "We're going sightseeing. He can't spend all his time with you old codgers." She swatted playfully at Carl's arm.

Ty was already walking away. He left his beer bottle on a table.

"He better treat you right." Carl winked at her. "If he doesn't, give me a call. I know Brent wouldn't mind if I took care of you. Better than any old Brooklyn boy could."

Grace stared desperately after Ty. She was really messing this up.

Chapter Eight

"Looks like you're not having much fun in paradise."

Ty glanced up from his phone to look at the bartender. He'd gone back to the bar where they'd had their initial meet-up that day. He didn't know where any other bars were located on the resort and he didn't want to stray too far from where they were staying, truth be told, despite his current aggravation.

"Yeah, it's not quite what I expected." Ty looked down at his phone again.

He'd been contemplating calling home and having his sister wire him money so he could buy a plane ticket. But an international call—or even a text—would put a hefty fee on his next phone bill. He didn't even have his service turned on at the moment, for fear of incurring enormous roaming charges. He planned to call his sister tomorrow for a few minutes to check in. Maybe he needed to use that call now.

But what if he changed his mind?

He picked up the bottle of beer in front of him and took a drink. A simple Budweiser, though it still cost a lot more than back home.

"I saw you in here earlier, didn't I?" The bartender was an older man with thinning hair and heavy lines on his face. Despite that, he was spectacularly tan and looked hardy. Island living must be good for the body. "You were with that big group of people."

Ty nodded and set his bottle down. "Yeah."

"I noticed you because you didn't seem to fit in." The man was busy polishing glasses with a thick white towel. "I see people like the rest of your group all the time in this place. The jet-set class. No offense, buddy, but you don't seem the type."

"So I've been told." He idly turned his bottle on the bar top.

"You walked out with that pretty brunette woman." He plunked a glass down and smiled. "The tall curvy one. If you don't mind me saying, she's quite the looker."

"Yeah, she sure is." Ty gazed dully at his bottle as he turned it.

"She your girlfriend?"

Ty looked up at him. No need to lie here, right? This guy wasn't part of the game.

"No." Ty took a swig. "She's just … someone I met."

"Ah, well, she looked like she was into you. That counts for something, right?"

Was she into him? Or was that just more of her mind games? He'd thought for a few minutes that *he* was into her. When he kissed her earlier. When they were getting dressed in the room. Maybe that was all hormones, though. Being "into" someone wasn't the same as plain old wanting to fuck them.

"I guess." Ty looked at his phone again, still debating.

He didn't know the process for giving a client a refund, how it worked, how he'd go about it—he'd never had to do such a thing before. Would the agency ban him from working with them again if he walked out on a date? He still needed to keep this up for a while, to get the money for Becky. Wasn't his daughter's future worth the sacrifice of his pride?

"I'm not used to seeing people stressed out at my bar." The bartender picked up another glass and held it up to the light. "Most people who come in here are having a good time."

"Like you said, I don't really fit in, and it's hard

to have a good time when you feel like the most awkward man in the room."

He'd never been on a date like this before. Not even the ones where he stayed overnight or went somewhere. Most of his clients were shy and nervous and he had to take the lead. Even the ones that weren't, they were more into the aspects of the date, and him, than trying to keep up some charade. Sure, he played a role, but he'd never had to play a role quite like this before. He'd never had a woman make him jump through such complicated, flaming hoops.

"Maybe that means you're trying to be something you're not." The bartender started polishing the glass. "Maybe you just need to be yourself."

Ty rubbed his forehead. "I wish I could, friend, I wish I could."

"Everybody has to pretend to be something they're not from time to time. That's how it is." The bartender shrugged. "Being yourself isn't about the part you play, it's about being true to yourself while you play it."

Ty furrowed his brow.

The bartender leaned toward him. "Play the game, but remember who you are, deep down inside. Remember your purpose." He winked and pointed at him. "Everyone has a purpose. It's easy to get lost, but you'll always have your true north to help you find your way again."

Ty frowned and gazed at the wall of liquor bottles behind the bar. He knew his purpose, of course, and always had: provide for his family, secure the future for his daughter. No matter what sort of man of the world he pretended to be for his dates, he always kept that in mind. It wasn't easy, and sometimes it tore at his heart and soul, but he kept his eyes on the prize.

Realization struck him. Maybe he was judging Grace too harshly for doing the exact same thing.

What was *her* true north? What was her purpose? She was playing this game, playing this person she obviously wasn't, but she must have her reasons for it. He couldn't imagine why anyone would put up with these people, but maybe she *had* to, the way he *had* to sell himself. Maybe she couldn't walk away, like he couldn't walk away until he got what he needed.

"Do they teach you this wisdom in bartending school?" Ty smirked and picked up his bottle. He tilted it toward the man in thanks. "Is that where you learned to dispense such good advice?"

The bartender snorted. "Nah, I just been around the block a few times. I didn't always live in an island paradise, you know. I've seen the world."

"I bet you have."

Ty finished his beer, still debating between calling his sister and giving Grace one more shot at not treating him like a trained monkey. He could talk to her and try to figure out her motivations. He could tell her in no uncertain terms that he wouldn't put up with any further degradation. He could put his foot down, and if she violated his dignity one more time, he would end this and go home.

He plunked his empty bottle on the bar. The bartender wandered back over from serving another guest.

"Want another?"

Ty shook his head. "Nah, I only had enough for one." He wished he hadn't handed his money over to Grace in a fit of anger. Getting it back from her would also be degrading. He tossed his last dollar on the bar for a tip. "Thanks for the advice."

"He'll have another," a voice said behind him.

"It's on me."

Ty turned on his stool. For a moment, he thought the female voice belonged to Grace and his stomach clenched, in an unexpected way. It wasn't anger or dread. It was more like expectation, and when he saw it wasn't her, it immediately sank.

"And a dry, very dirty gin martini for me." Amelia slid onto the stool beside him with a coy smirk. "Thank you."

The bartender raised his eyebrows but walked away to get the drinks. Ty was cringing inside, so much it felt like all his muscles had locked up.

He could refuse, but he had to be polite. If not for Grace's sake, then for himself, because he wasn't a rude person. *Be yourself.*

"The answer is yes." Amelia plopped her silver clutch on the bar. She wore a tight white dress and very high heels. He might have found her more attractive if he didn't want to run away from her.

"Yes?" Ty frowned.

She swiveled toward him, her blue eyes glittering, her shiny lips curled in a smile. "Yes, I am stalking you. Since you're wondering."

Ty turned back to the bar, maintaining a poker face. "I wasn't, actually." What if Grace caught them together? Had Grace sent her?

"I saw you leave the party." She crossed her legs, nearly brushing his hip. "You looked like you were upset. Did you and Gracie have a tiff?"

He continued to face forward, peeling the label off his empty bottle. "No—yes. I don't know. But it's fine. We're fine." He flashed her a tight smile.

"I watched you playing poker. You were very good at it, and very confident. It's been a while since those jerks got their asses handed to them."

Ty sat back and rubbed his palms on his thighs. "Yeah, well. I've been playing since I was a teenager, so..." Was that something people from Park Slope did? He didn't even care anymore.

"It's so boring." She leaned closer to him. "I had to get away, so I came to find you. I was hoping you hadn't gone back to your room."

He flashed her another terse smile. "Thank you for the drink. I am going back to my room after I finish it, though." Would it be entirely uncouth to chug it?

"Oh, you don't have to rush off." She rubbed his upper arm. "Grace is still hanging out with the boys. They just love her, you know. Why don't you let me keep you entertained?"

The bartender returned with their drinks. Amelia slipped a credit card out of her clutch and put it on the bar. "Keep it open."

"I'm only having one," Ty said firmly. He picked up his bottle and held it up to her. "Thank you, again."

She picked up her glass delicately, by the stem. "I meant what I said earlier."

He took a quick drink. "What was that?"

"That you can keep me company while Carl is on the golf course." She plucked a strand of golden hair from her shoulder and wound it around her finger. "We have a very nice suite. I think you'd like it."

Be yourself.

He took another deep drink and grimaced at the burn. "Carl is your husband."

She took a tiny sip of her martini. "Mm hmm?"

"So you're married."

She giggled and set her glass on the bar. "Yes, I am. Very astute."

"Don't you think your husband would be a little upset if I came to your room?"

She rolled her eyes. "Please. Carl has had so many mistresses I've lost count. He could hardly condemn me for having a little fun of my own. You see he's already trying to put the make on Grace."

"Yes, I see that." Ty clenched his hand around his bottle. "And if you don't mind me saying, that doesn't sound like a very happy marriage."

Perhaps it wasn't his place to say such things, clearly it wasn't any of his business. But she was practically crawling into his lap right now and he needed to approach this from a different angle.

She seemed unoffended, and in fact laughed. "Oh, darling. It's not a marriage so much as a business arrangement. You see, my father owns the chain of banks that Carl works for. It was a strategic match. Carl has Daddy's trust, and Daddy gets to keep his little girl close." She continued winding her hair around her finger. Grace did that a lot, but he'd noticed it was only when she was nervous or distressed. "Our money makes a good, tidy life for us. It's sort of like a merging of empires, you see. People married for money and power in the old days, and they still do."

Ty thought that sounded hollow and extremely sad. Did Grace's ex-husband have money like that? Was their marriage a business arrangement, too? That might explain why she was trying so hard to be part of this world.

"Well, it must work for you." Ty kept his hand clenched around his bottle. "I think I'd rather marry for love, though."

She picked up her drink again and huffed. "Maybe we did love each other, once, in the beginning, but that's long since passed." She sipped. "A divorce would be too much work at this point. Let him have his fun, and I'll have mine." She nudged him with her knee.

Ty took a bracing breath, and another drink. He plunked the bottle down and turned to face her. He could play this role and be himself as well. He picked up his phone and slipped it into the pocket of his jacket, his mind finally made up.

"You're a beautiful woman, Amelia." He looked her in the eye. "And you seem like you have it together. You have style and class."

Her smile broadened. "Thank you, Ty—can I call you Ty, like Grace does?"

"Sure. Whatever." He shook his head. "But business arrangement or not, your husband shouldn't treat you the way he does."

She stared at him.

"He shouldn't talk to you the way he does, or flirt with other women in front of you. You shouldn't treat your wife like that. Hell, you wouldn't treat a friend like that, and you sure as hell wouldn't treat a business partner like that either."

Her smile sagged into a frown. She slipped her finger out of her hair.

"I'm sorry." He held up his hands. "I realize I don't know you or your husband. It's probably none of my business. But I think you should be told you don't deserve to be treated that way. No one does."

She looked down at the bar.

"You're gorgeous." He leaned toward her. "I'm sure you're smart and fun. I think you should tell your husband to knock his shit off. I've only been around him for a few hours and I already want to punch him in the face."

He'd probably gone too far. This would all be over, but he had to stay true to himself.

"I'm flattered you find me attractive," he went on. "But I'm sorry, I'm not going to do the same thing to

Grace." He picked up his beer and chugged the rest of it. He had to force himself not to belch after doing so. He put the bottle down, slid off the stool, and wobbled a little at the immediate alcohol head rush. "Thank you for the beer, and I'm sorry if I've offended you."

She looked at him, her eyes wide and bright. Her face was softer now, as if a mask had fallen away.

"I'm not offended." Her voice was low. "I want to punch him in the face sometimes, too. All the time, really."

"I wish you the best." He turned and walked away. He waited until he got to the door to let out the trapped air from knocking back the beer so fast, and winced. Damn, he hadn't chugged booze since high school. He was getting old.

He left the bar and went back to where their room was, preparing himself. He would talk to Grace and get this all sorted out. He would tell her exactly where his line was and that the consequence of her crossing it again was that he would leave. He would play the role she wanted, but he wanted to know exactly what that was from here on out.

The hallways were empty and quiet. His thoughts flashed back to Grace asking if he ever slept with his dates. Then they settled on the curve-hugging green dress she wore. Maybe the best way to work this out was through the physical...

"Ty, wait." A voice startled him. He stopped and turned.

Amelia was stepping off the elevator he'd just passed. She was holding her clutch, and still had that vulnerable, stunned look on her face. He felt sorry for her, but he wasn't going to let her use that to her advantage either.

"You *are* stalking me," he half-joked. "I'm going

back to the room."

"I know." She hurried up to him and gazed into his eyes. "I just wanted to say thank you."

"It's not really any of my business, but I meant what I said."

"No, it's okay." She placed a hand on his chest. "It's just, no one has ever said something like that to me before. No one has ever been so kind."

He glanced down at her hand, then back up. "That's a shame."

"It's just..." She stepped closer, so they were nearly pressed together. "It's such a miserable, lonely marriage. I don't mess around nearly as much as Carl does, though I suppose I have every right to."

He took her hand gently and pulled it off his chest. "I also meant what I said about not doing the same thing to Grace. I think you have a lot of issues to work out with your husband."

She gazed up at him, her lips turned into a pout. Her perfume filled his nose, light and floral. He didn't want it all over his jacket for Grace to smell.

"Have a good night, Amelia." He squeezed her hand and dropped it.

"Ty." She quickly snaked her hands under his jacket and slipped her arms around him, so fast he didn't have time to pull away. "Jesus Christ, you're so fucking hot. And the fact you're so damn sweet makes it even hotter."

"Um." He placed his hands on her shoulders but didn't push. If he accidentally knocked her down or something, this was going to be a disaster. "Please don't."

She tightened her grip. Her face was close to his, but he kept his head turned away so she wouldn't be able to kiss him.

"I won't tell Grace." She moved a hand down and squeezed his ass. "You just told me I was gorgeous. You think I'm hot, too."

He applied force to her shoulders, trying to be careful at the same time. "I'm not going to cheat on Grace. Amelia, stop."

She had to be drunk, or else he'd sparked some raging, irrational emotion in her by being nice. That was sad in itself, but he didn't care at the moment. He just wanted her to let go and get her hands off him.

"You don't understand how badly I need this." She was trying to catch his lips. "Please, Ty."

The elevator doors opened again, much to Ty's relief, but that relief quickly turned to horror as Grace stepped out. She stopped short and stared at them, her mouth open.

"Get off me!" Ty finally pushed her away. She stumbled, but thankfully didn't fall. She scowled at him, then looked over her shoulder, noticing Grace.

"Oh, Gracie." She giggled and wobbled on her heels. Drunk then, probably. Maybe she'd feel bad about this tomorrow. "I was just playing with your boy."

Ty tugged at his jacket to straighten it. Grace flashed him a burning look. He shook his head.

"Why don't you go back to the party, Amelia?" Grace's tone was icy. "I think Carl is looking for you."

Amelia laughed and waved her clutch. "Oh, I'm sure he is." She sauntered toward the elevator. She looked over her shoulder and gave Ty a wink. "Thank you, Ty." Ty dragged his fingers through his hair, his jaw tight.

Amelia got on the elevator, giving them a little wave with her fingers. Grace glared at her until the doors slid shut, then she turned that glare on Ty.

"What the hell are you doing?" she demanded.

Ty flung his arms in the air. Apparently, he'd be making that phone call after all. "Oh, you know, just being myself." He let out a sharp laugh, then gritted his teeth.

She narrowed her eyes. "What?"

He sighed and turned. He headed down the hallway toward their room, dragging his fingers through his hair again, yanking it in frustration.

"Fuck," he muttered.

Chapter Nine

Grace marched after Ty but was careful not to trip on her heels. She followed him through the door, into the room. She'd spent the last forty-five minutes alone with the sharks, not wanting to lose face, only to finally escape and immediately discover Ty in Amelia's arms.

And though she shouldn't care, the sight of it sent her heart crashing through the floor.

"What were you doing with her?" She slammed the door behind her. "Were you going to fuck her?"

Ty turned sharply. His eyes were blazing, his hair scattered around his face. "Did it look like I was trying to fuck her? She was molesting me. I couldn't get her off!"

If Grace was being rational, she knew he was telling the truth. When she caught them together, Ty looked like a cornered animal trying to escape. And she knew how Amelia was, through and through, that conniving bitch.

"Where have you been?" she asked.

"At that bar we were at today. She hunted me down like a goddamn predator."

"You can't just storm off like you did. I paid you a lot of money to spend this weekend with me and pretend to be my boyfriend."

He loomed closer, glaring into her eyes. "I *am* pretending to be your boyfriend. You keep changing what you want from me and I can't keep up. But I'll tell you one thing." He pointed in her face. "I won't be treated like dirt any longer. You can't pay me enough for it. If you keep it up, I'm refunding your money and going home."

She stared back at him. "I didn't mean to treat you like dirt." She had though, and it gave her an uneasy feeling in her stomach and an icky feeling on her conscience. "I'm sorry. I didn't mean to act like that, I panicked."

"What the hell is going on here?" He took his finger out of her face. "I don't get it, why are these people your friends? Why do you want to be around them? Unless you're more like them than I'm aware of, but I don't think you are. For one, you have a job and a talent that you're proud of. The rest of these women just have someone else's money and attitudes."

"It's complicated." She paused. "They're friends of my husband—my ex-husband. I can't extricate myself from this social circle without a lot of embarrassment. Well, more embarrassment than I've already endured anyway."

He squinted. "That doesn't make sense. If they're your ex's friends, why don't you just walk away?"

She gripped his arm. "I don't want to explain it right now." *Or ever, maybe.* "But I am sorry. I shouldn't have treated you that way down there. I don't think you're trash, or rough, or anything they think. You seem like a hard-working and honest man. And you've got a lovely personality." She did feel horrible for treating him the way she had. He didn't deserve it.

His face softened a bit. "I just need you to tell me what you want me to do, and quit changing the rules."

"I will, I promise. I just—I want you to keep doing what you've been doing. Just be my man. Just … be there for me."

She gazed at him. The deep brown of his eyes was so rich, so bottomless. Behind that handsome face was the soul of a good man, and it had been a long time since she'd met one of those.

"This is crazy," he said. "I mean it, if you do this again, I'll leave. Three strikes and you're out."

She nodded. "I understand." She spoke softly, "I

don't want this trip to be misery for you."

"It shouldn't be misery for you either." He took her hand from his arm and held it. "We're in the tropics right now, at a resort. This should be nothing but fun."

"Having fun" with this crowd was out of the question. But maybe she could have some fun with Ty.

She licked her lips. "I mostly paid for you to come along so I could have some nice conversation, not to mention something pleasant to look at." She dropped her gaze down his body. That suit fit him well, in season or not. He was a wet dream.

"And that's an expectation I can live up to." He drew closer. "You're a glamourous woman, no matter what they tell you. You're interesting and fun to talk to, and trust me, you're pleasant to look at as well."

She found it hard to pull in a breath, he was so close, and she wasn't sure how far she wanted to go— how far she was *allowed* to go. "You don't have to go back to the party with me. I shouldn't make you hang around them any longer."

He took her by the arm. "Why don't you stay here? You don't have to go back either."

Her stomach tightened. "You really weren't trying to sleep with Amelia?"

He gave her a stern look.

"I know, I'm sorry." She sighed. "I know how she is. I believe you."

"She's nothing compared to you. Even if I was free to choose, I'd choose you."

Her stomach fluttered now.

"You're not a prostitute," she reminded him. "Or a prisoner, like you're making it sound. If I stay here in the room, what do you want to happen?"

"You're paying me to be your boyfriend. Don't boyfriends and girlfriends have sex?" His eyes were intense, dark, shining. "But that's your call." He pulled her closer, until she was pressed against him. "Don't go back down there, either way. Stay here."

"I'm not going back," she whispered. Maybe this was wrong, maybe she'd regret it, but she didn't care. Those plush lips were irresistible, and she was tired of denying herself.

He chose *her*.

His mouth tasted like beer this time, and he smelled divine, the rich spice of his cologne filling her senses. She did then what she'd been wanting to do since the moment she met him in that airport, and raked her fingers indulgently through the long, thick strands of his hair. He backed her up and pushed her up against the wall, his solid, hard body pressed tight against hers. It must be a kink of his, pushing women up against walls. She didn't mind.

She kicked her heels off, so she dropped an inch or two shorter than him. They broke the kiss and she tried to catch her breath.

"It's been a while," she admitted.

"Then I'll make sure I do this right." His voice curled around her and made her shiver.

He swept her off her feet and she squeaked in surprise, and then laughed. She knew she was tall and bulky, despite all her attempts to appear petite, and she wasn't used to being picked up by men. He carried her to the bed and deposited her there, not gently, but with purpose. She scrambled back to get some space and started removing her jewelry. It was all too expensive to have it fall off and get broken in the bed. She tossed everything on the nightstand and switched on the lamp.

He stood at the foot of the bed, head tilted, his gaze questioning.

"I want to look at you." She sat back on her

hands. "You're gorgeous. I picked well."

He smirked and started peeling his jacket off. "I want to look at you, too. I'm a lucky man to land a job like this."

She got to her knees, in the center of the bed, and slipped her dress off her shoulders. He undid the buttons of his shirt and she watched raptly. How many other clients got to enjoy this show? Something deep inside told her not many, and she felt even more special.

"You could easily sleep with all your dates, I'm sure." She peeled the top of her dress down to reveal her bra. It was green lace and silk and matched her underwear.

"Maybe. But would you believe me if I said it's been a while for me, too?"

"Yes." Another shiver passed through her. He didn't sleep with all of them, but he *wanted* to sleep with her, and that was not just flattering, it was downright hot. "I believe you."

He undid his pants and pushed them down. He wore black boxer briefs that hugged the lean lines of his hips. His body was sinewy and toned, his stomach not overly defined, but still tight and flat. Dark hair started on his chest and shot in a thin line down the slope of his stomach, and disappeared into his boxers.

She wiggled her dress over her hips, then tumbled back on the bed and worked it down her legs. "Come here." She crooked a finger. For the first time in ages, she didn't feel horribly self-conscious about her body. Probably because of the way his eyes widened in appreciation when he saw her in just her bra and panties.

He crawled on the bed and slid up next to her. She pressed her body against his, against all that firm, smooth musculature and silky, hot skin.

"Why are you here, with these people?" He lifted

a hand and brushed her hair back, his touch as light as the breeze through the balcony doors.

She pressed a finger to his lips. "I don't want to talk about that right now."

His eyes shone in the lamplight, his skin even duskier in the muted yellow glow.

"I'm sorry," he murmured. "But maybe you can explain what the hell is going on in the morning, huh? I want to know."

She caressed a hand down his chest. "Maybe." She slipped it lower, onto his stomach. "Does it even matter? You barely know me."

"It matters." He caressed her side and down onto her hip.

"Stop talking about it right now. We have more important things to focus on." She didn't want to think about those people right now.

"You're right." He kissed her throat. "You're fucking gorgeous."

She raked her fingers through his hair again and clutched it. "So are you."

He slid down and buried his face in her cleavage with a soft, indulgent moan. She chuckled. Men loved her breasts. He then slipped his hand beneath the elastic of her panties. "I'm not doing this because you're paying me," he reassured her. "I want to do this. I want you to know that."

A hot rush of arousal flooded through her and she lifted her hips to his touch. He stroked her clit slowly with two fingertips, and she gasped. She fought the urge to grind against his hand, but only for a moment, before she gave in.

"What do you want?" he whispered against her ear. "Tell me your desires. I'm here to fulfill them."

She loved sex, but she hadn't had it in so long she

was starting to think she never would again. Too many complications in her life, too many issues for her to just pick up a man, and she certainly couldn't get involved in a relationship right now. What did she *desire*?

"I want you." She raked her nails across his shoulder. "Right here, right now."

He eased a finger inside her. It felt good, and she squeezed her inner muscles around it. It made her hungry for something thicker and longer, the thing that jutted hard and insistent against her hip right now. He was an adequate boy, just as she'd told Amelia and Roxanne.

He gazed down at her. "Yeah? You want me?"

"Yes." She touched his face. "I need you." She pressed against his hand, making him push his finger in deeper. "More than you can imagine."

"I don't need to imagine, I can feel." He pushed deeper and higher yet, and she gasped. "You're so wet."

She was burning up, needy, frighteningly vulnerable, but she didn't fight what she felt. He slipped his finger out and then yanked the cups of her bra down, so her breasts popped out.

"That's expensive and designer," she chastised him. She sat up, wrenched her arms around behind her, and popped the clasp on the back. "Please be careful."

He chuckled. "Sorry, I just needed to see those beautiful tits in the flesh."

"Are you happy now?" She tossed her bra away.

"Thrilled."

She laid back down and Ty sucked one of her hard nipples into his mouth with a lusty growl. Tingles rushed across her skin as it stiffened even tighter. Despite his professed love for her boobs, he quickly abandoned them and went downward.

"I thought you were interested in my tits?" Her

115

stomach quivered at the touch of his lips.

"They're glorious." He placed a kiss over her navel. "I want to taste you, though."

He pulled her panties down her legs, tossed them the way of her bra, and settled between her spread thighs. She quivered in anticipation.

"Are you as sweet as you look?" He gazed up at her, a gorgeous sight between her legs.

She laughed and bent her knees, opening herself wider. "I'm not sweet at all, darling."

"I'll be the judge of that."

She moaned in both relief and pleasure as he licked up her soaked slit. He knew exactly how to use that tongue. She ached with need and loved the sensation of yearning and desperation as it surged and expanded. It would eventually consume her with its demand to be filled. She'd forgotten how nice it was to experience this. It was good to feel *anything* again.

She drew her legs up and held them back, opening her needy pussy to him. He worked her clit with his tongue and fingered her nice and deep, this time with two fingers, then three. The wet, sloppy sounds coming from her were gloriously obscene. She released one knee and gripped his hair, clutching it just tight enough to keep him there and guide him in his task.

"Ty…" His name rolled off her tongue. Her body pulsed with pleasure.

She dropped her legs, planted her feet on the bed, and pushed up against his face. He made a muffled sound, though not of protest. Quite the opposite. Her thighs twitched, her inner walls clenching on the verge of spasm.

"Oh, fuck!"

She came hard, and suddenly, so fast it took her breath away. She shook and spasmed all over the bed, the waves of pleasure rolling through her. He clutched her hips and held on, licking her through it. Finally, she plunked them back down on the bed, trembling and panting. Her inner walls were still twitching.

He stopped and lifted his head.

"Want me to keep going?" His lips and chin glistened. He was breathing nearly as hard as her.

She did, and she didn't. She could easily come in that mouth again, but she wanted more.

"I want you inside me." She untangled her hand from his hair. "I want you to fuck me."

He gave her pussy one last, swift lick before departing, and sat up on his knees. His cock pushed out the front of his underwear, so the elastic pulled away from his stomach and showed off the thick dark hair below his navel.

"That looks nice." She sat up. "Let's see." She grabbed the elastic and yanked it down.

He popped out fully hard, thick and heavy and long. She nearly drooled.

"Like it?" He grinned. "By the way, you *are* very sweet."

She gripped the shaft—it was silky and hot in her palm—and stroked, making the plump slick head slide across her palm. He groaned, and it turned into a low growl at the end. She liked that sound.

"Am I?" She stoked faster. "My, you're excited to be here."

He gripped her shoulders, his eyelashes fluttering. "I'm excited to get in you. You're so soft and tight."

"Am I?"

"Oh, yeah." He cupped her jaw and stroked his thumb across her cheek. "Such a tight little pussy, and soaking wet for me. You need to be filled, I can feel it."

She loved dirty talk. It made her already molten

insides melt further. She stroked him fist over fist.

"Then you should come inside." She ran her tongue over her lips. "I'm a starving woman here." Foreplay be damned, she wanted him to fuck her hard and pound all this pent-up sexual frustration out of her.

"Get these off." She released his cock and tugged his underwear down his thighs. A thick dollop of fluid dripped from the tip onto her wrist. "We need a condom. Did you bring some? If not, I did." Wishful thinking on her part? At least it paid off.

"Yeah, I brought some." He pulled his underwear off.

She rubbed her hand across her mouth and licked the salty fluid from her palm, and then her wrist. She'd use her mouth on him later, when she wasn't so desperate.

He climbed off the bed, stark naked, and walked to his suitcase on a chair. She admired his round, firm bottom. Even if they never saw each other again after this trip, she would use this as fantasy fodder for the rest of her life.

He returned with a condom, tearing the package open. After working it onto his cock, he crawled back on the bed and settled between her legs. She boosted herself up on one elbow and reached down to spread her lips open for him, like the wanton jezebel she suddenly was. She wanted to watch him slide into her.

He gripped his cock and rubbed it against her, teasing. The anticipation peaked and her muscles tensed.

"Put it in," she begged. "Please."

"Anything you desire." He positioned himself against her opening and pushed in.

She moaned as she watched that thick column glide between her fingers and disappear inside her. A hot, hard pressure opened her up, so good, so intense. Their groins came flush together, his dark pubic hair tangled with the thin strip of hair on her mound. She fell back on the bed, arching luxuriously beneath him.

He gripped her thighs and draped them over his. "Goddamn, you feel so good, Grace."

"So do you." She squeezed her legs around him. "That's just what I needed." She whimpered before she could stop herself. "Fuck me."

He did, slow at first, with easy, smooth strokes that made her gasp each time he pushed fully in. They both shuddered with each labored breath. Urgent tension built low in her stomach, another orgasm already building.

"God, this is so good." He gasped. "You're perfect."

After a few more thrusts, she needed it harder. She tightened her legs around his waist, drawing him in and encouraging him to do it properly.

"Fuck, Grace." He swooped down and kissed her, his mouth hot and possessive. "You're amazing."

"So are you," she murmured in return. The sensation of him inside her, above her, all around her, was threatening to release her emotions from the cage she kept them locked away in, and it terrified her. "Please, more. Harder."

He snapped his hips and braced his hands on the bed, next to her shoulders. He pounded into her, just like she wanted, until she was wailing. Each time he drove in, a bolt of pleasure shot through her, pushing her toward satisfaction one inch at a time. She reached down to rub her clit, not caring anymore if she was making a spectacle of herself. She wanted to come again so badly it was all she could focus on.

"Grace," he panted. "Yes."

"Yes!" she shrieked in return.

Each thrust shook her entire body. His sweaty skin glided across hers. The ocean breeze rolled over them, cool and salty.

She rubbed harder, the pleasure so high and frantic she was trying to both push him away and pull him in at the same time. "I'm going to come." Her voice was whining and ragged and foreign to her ears.

"Yes, do it." He changed his strokes and made them shallower and quicker, little jabs that poked at that swelling tension and would soon make it pop. "Come for me again."

Another breath-holding moment and she reached the edge. She shrieked and stiffened, her head thrown back, hand clamped over her pussy and around his cock. The orgasm started deep inside her, rolling out into powerful shudders that gripped her from head to toe. She shook and moaned. Her inner walls spasmed, pulling him in deeper and milking him.

"Oh my God." Ty pumped into her through it. "Damn, that's so beautiful."

He quickened his pace, though she could barely stand the further stimulation. She opened her eyes and gazed up at his sweat-sheened face. His eyelids drooped, his mouth slack, hair swinging damp and tangled around his face.

"Your turn," she urged him, her head woozy. "Come inside me." She reached up and stroked his shoulders and straining biceps.

"Fuck." His voice was short and desperate. "Almost…"

A few more thrusts, and he plunged inside her and held there. A groan ripped out of him, from deep in his chest.

She rubbed her hands up and down his sides, enjoying his shudders. Her pussy twitched, and she could feel him throbbing in there, warm and thick, as he filled the condom. She was euphoric and feared she might either suddenly scream or burst into happy tears.

This was well worth the money.

"Damn." He panted, reaching down. He gripped the base of his cock and pulled out. The sweet ache he left behind made her groan.

He toppled over, onto his side next to her. "Wow." He dragged his fingers through his hair, chest working hard. "Thanks?"

She laughed and rolled toward him. "No, darling, thank you." She rubbed his chest.

They were quiet for a few minutes, catching their breath and cooling off.

His eyes were narrowed into slits, a lazy grin on his lips. "I hope this isn't the last time we'll do that on this trip?"

Her body buzzed with afterglow. She felt better than she had in weeks, months. She'd done something right, finally, bringing him here.

"Oh, no." She raked her nails across his sweaty skin. "Not even the last time tonight, hopefully."

This trip had gotten a thousand times better.

Chapter Ten

Waking up to the distant sound of waves and a tropical breeze across his skin was like heaven to Ty, but even better was waking up to a soft, supple, beautiful woman lying next to him. For a moment, he thought he might still be asleep and dreaming. This was far, far removed from waking up to the sound of his mother and sister arguing, or a little girl taking up most of his bed with her foot wedged in his ribs.

Not that those things didn't hold an important place in his life, but a vacation was just what he'd needed.

Grace was tucked in the crook of his arm, her hair in his face and the warm swell of her breasts pressed against his side. Though they were both sweaty, he didn't want to move. She soon stirred and rolled onto her back, rubbing her eyes. Ty shifted onto his side and gazed at her, smiling. Her breasts were above the sheet and he resisted the urge to reach out and squeeze a dusky pink nipple.

She cracked one eye open and peeked at him.

"Morning." He smiled wider.

Even with her makeup mostly gone and her hair a mess, she was gorgeous, maybe even more so. He rubbed her stomach. He wanted to pull her against him and kiss her fully awake but didn't. This was work, after all, and despite the fact they'd gotten *very* familiar last night, she was still in charge.

"Good morning." Her voice was rough with sleep. She sat up and fluffed her hair, then yawned and stretched.

He gazed at the pale curve of her back and his cock stirred. He willed it to behave. *Not right now.*

"Did you sleep good?" He rolled onto his back and stretched as well. "It's nice waking up in paradise."

The morning light shone in her eyes. "Mm, what time is it?" She rolled away to grab her phone. As she did, the sheet wound around her waist and he got a delectable view of her bare bottom. It didn't help his cock behave in the least.

"Do we have a breakfast date?" He focused on the balcony doors, looking out at the ocean to distract himself. "Do we have to meet up with your friends?"

"Thankfully, no." She flopped back next to him, staring at her phone screen. "They probably got much too drunk last night to be up this early. That's why rich people only do brunch." She smirked, and he thought she might actually be making a joke. Was she starting to loosen up?

He could go for a few more rounds of working that stuffiness out of her, if not.

Be-have.

"I'm sorry about last night," he said. "I shouldn't have stormed out of the party. It wasn't very professional of me. And I shouldn't have given you hell. It's not my place to question what goes on in your life, I barely know you."

She looked at him. With a sigh, she placed her phone on her chest. "Don't apologize. I'm the one who should be sorry, and I am. I didn't mean to treat you like that. You didn't deserve it. You had every right to get upset."

He edged closer and looked into her eyes. "I'm glad we ended the night on a positive note, though."

"A stupendous one." She gripped the sheet around his waist and balled it in her fist. "Better me than Amelia, hmm?" She kissed him.

"Way better." He grinned, but then frowned. "I

feel bad for her, though. Her husband treats her like shit."

"Carl is a piece of work."

"I feel like she wouldn't do those things if she was treated better, if she had some respect for herself. She should get away from him and try to find her self-esteem."

Grace stroked a fingertip over his lips. "You're such a good man." She looked away, ran a hand down her body, and groaned. "God, I'm so sore. I haven't had a workout like that in ages."

"Want me to kiss it better?"

She picked up her phone. "I need a shower first. I feel so dirty." She rolled away, taking the sheet with her—leaving him exposed—and crawled off the bed. "In the best way, mind you. Take it as a compliment."

"I am."

She dropped the sheet and he watched her walk, like a naked goddess, across the room. He gave up arguing with his cock and let it do as it would. Sprawled on his back, nothing to cover him, his appreciation was obvious. She looked over after grabbing up a toiletry bag and robe, and smirked.

"I'm going to have to tip you well."

"I don't mind providing some of my services for free."

While she showered he got out of bed, managed to get his cock to stand down, found his underwear, and put them on. He walked out on the balcony and gazed at the ocean—so vast it seemed endless, stretched out blue and crystalline to the horizon. A long strip of white sand lay below, dotted with morning sunbathers and umbrellas. He took a few more pictures with his phone.

He made some coffee with the in-room espresso machine. He'd been thinking about getting one of these—an industrial one, of course—for the store. The old coffee machines still worked, but the store as a whole definitely needed updating. Also, getting up to speed with the times would bring in more clientele. His father had always been content to stick with what worked.

Of course, the more updating, the less money that went into savings, and the future stretched out further and further, unchanging and bleak. At least for him. He listened to the water run in the bathroom as he sipped his coffee and tried to get his thoughts off that. He only had a short time here, and he wanted to enjoy himself.

When Grace emerged, she wore a pink silk robe, her hair a wet tangle on her shoulders, face clean. She looked like a different woman—a real, honest, simple woman.

"Want some coffee?" He nodded at the machine. "I'll make you some."

She rubbed her hair with a towel in her hands. "I'd love some. The water pressure here is amazing, by the way."

He got up and went to the espresso machine. "I'll get cleaned up too and we can go grab some breakfast. Unless you want to order room service?"

"I think I'd rather go out. It's so lovely here. It's been raining so much back home, it's good to see the sun."

"I know, right?" He started making her a cup. "I feel like I need to build an ark somedays." That reminded him about another thing that needed updating: the gutters and the drain in the back room. It clogged and flooded constantly.

Focus on the moment.

He brought her the coffee. She took the cup with a gentle smile and tossed her towel aside.

"You said you'd tell me what's going on this morning." He sat down with her on a sofa near the balcony doors. "Why you're here with these people, who clearly aren't your real friends."

She brought the cup to her lips, her long elegant fingers wrapped around it. "I said *maybe* I'd tell you."

He took a sip of his own coffee. Maybe it was better not to pry. Do his job, make her happy. That was literally all that was expected of him.

She lowered the cup and sighed. She seemed to deflate. "No, you deserve an explanation. I dragged you into this insanity, I should at least make things clear."

"You don't owe me anything, but I admit I'd like to know, if you want to tell me." They were so close their knees were touching. He slid an arm across the back of the sofa behind her.

She stared down into her cup for a moment, then looked up. Her brow was furrowed, her eyes glittering. "You realize by now I have an ex-husband."

He nodded.

"The divorce was finalized a little over a year ago. It was easy enough." She gazed out the doors. "He's in prison. It makes things a bit simpler."

Ty nodded again. "I guess it would."

"Brent was the head of the finance department at his company. He's quite wealthy, not just from his job, but family money. But it wasn't enough, apparently, to keep him from embezzling funds from the company's investors. They found out, and they weren't happy."

Ty winced. "Oh, man." He would pretend Carl hadn't already fondly told him about this.

She looked down at her cup. "My father left when I was a child, and I didn't grow up with money, like Brent did. A great lack of it, actually. My mother died shortly after I graduated high school and I was on my own."

This was … unexpected.

"I tried to attend design school, I wanted to open my own boutique, but—it was expensive. I worked several jobs at a time, as a cocktail waitress, a server, a bartender. Whatever bar or restaurant would let me shake my ass and tits for a few hours and collect tips." She winced. "I knew better than to call that flight attendant a stewardess, people have it so hard in the service industry. I was being rude."

Ty was silent, not sure how to react. This was *really* unexpected, after the airs she put on.

"Brent brought a colleague to dinner at an upscale restaurant I was working in at the time." She flexed her fingers around the cup. "He was so charming and incredibly handsome." She paused. "He was my knight in shining armor—savvy, rich, and he wanted me. He also wanted to pay for my school. The fact that a wealthy, successful man pursued me sucked me into a fairy tale, just like that." She snapped her fingers. "It blinded me. I thought I was the luckiest girl in the world. And he took advantage of that."

Things were starting to make sense. She wasn't like the others here, who obviously never knew anything about being poor, because she came from a much more humble background.

"I let him court me for almost six months, but I don't think that's what he was really doing. He was training me. He was turning me into the kind of girl who would fit into his world. He bought me everything, helped me get through school, and when he asked me to marry him, he also bought me my first boutique."

Ty got an uneasy feeling. This sounded like brainwashing.

She gazed out the doors again. "By the time we married, I was fully integrated into his lifestyle—I only had him, his penthouse, his money, and his friends. But I was so easy to persuade, because what was the alternative? Go back to being slapped on the ass for a few dollars while handing out martinis?"

Definitely brainwashing—or at least manipulation.

"It was all such a whirlwind. We'd just celebrated our third wedding anniversary when he got caught. When the accusations against him first started, he assured me they were false and it was just jealousy and people trying to defame him." She sighed. "It soon became clear that wasn't the case."

Ty gently touched her back. "That must have been terrible for you."

"I had four boutiques by that time, and I didn't know how to run them on my own." She let out a humorless laugh. "I certainly couldn't finance them on my own. I'm ashamed to admit they weren't exactly booming businesses, but his money allowed me to keep them open and spend time working on my designs."

He moved to rubbing her back.

"I only have one now." Her voice was soft and tiny. "There was this woman, this fabulous, powerful woman, who would come in at least once a week and she loved my designs. We went to lunch together sometimes. After Brent went to prison, she knew something was wrong, and I broke down and told her. It turned out she was looking for a place to sink some of her money, privately—she wouldn't say why, she must have been trying to hide it—and so she offered to become a limited partner in my business. She keeps me afloat, while her business investment remains private. But in some ways, that makes it even more terrifying. If I lose this last one, I take her money down with me."

"I'm sorry, it sounds like a mess." He kept rubbing.

"It's been quite a ride." She huffed out another sad laugh. "From waiting tables to the heights of society, then back down again. I've got whiplash. More than a bit."

"So that's how you know these people."

She nodded. "They're Brent's friends, not mine. But I was so dazzled when I met them. I couldn't believe they invited me into their circle." Her face sagged. "They don't condemn Brent for what he did. They think it's funny and that he'll be out of prison in no time. Carl already has business opportunities lined up for him." She took a sip of her coffee and her hand shook. Ty was silent, letting her go on.

"The trial was pretty cut and dried, but the investors he embezzled from didn't want to be publicly revealed, so they remained anonymous and were just represented by a team of lawyers. No one even knows the names of the people he robbed. I suppose that's his sweet little secret, the bastard. They still took him down, though."

Ty furrowed his brow. He recalled Carl telling him the people Brent had stolen from were "small fries" and that he should have gone higher up the food chain. If no one knew who they were, how did Carl know?

"He won't sit in there much longer," Grace said softly. "I'm sure his friends will get him out."

Ty patted her back. "They're terrible people and you don't need them."

"Leaving them behind is difficult, though. I don't have the money to hang out with them anymore and I don't fit in, but—they're all I have. Everyone from my old life before is gone, all the people I knew then, all my old friends. There's no one to fall back on. I'd be alone."

He frowned. "Your husband screwed up your mind and made you think this is all there is. You can make new friends."

Her eyes brimmed with tears. "I can't go back to being a cocktail waitress. I can't fall that far, all the way back to the bottom. I couldn't—I couldn't even fully pay for this trip until the last deposit from my store cleared, just this week. I held my breath all month hoping I'd make enough."

He cupped her cheek. "Money isn't what makes a person valuable. There's nothing wrong with hard work."

A tear slipped from her eye. She pulled away and wiped at it. "I had a taste of the good life. Have you ever had that? It's addictive."

"I haven't, but that doesn't mean I don't want it. Doesn't everybody?"

She sniffed.

"I've only known you for twenty-four hours." He took her hand. It was soft and warm, and trembled. "But I already see you have talent and ambition. It seems like you struggle, but there's nothing wrong with that. In fact, it makes you much better than someone born with a silver spoon in their mouth who treats people like shit just because they can."

She put her other hand over his and was silent, looking down.

"If they're judging you because of your shoes and handbag,"—he shook his head—"they were doing the same thing when your husband was around. Those aren't friends, they're vultures. They have to find something to pick apart so they can feel better about themselves."

She drew a deep breath. "I've spent so long feeling ashamed. Ever since Brent was arrested. I was just starting to get the hang of high society when it was ripped away."

Ty snorted. "If this is high society, I'll take being poor any day."

She looked at him, her eyes shining. "I'm so sorry. I sound like them, don't I? You work hard, I'm sure, and you struggle as well. And here I am, talking about how much I detest that."

"The fact you can be ashamed of talking like that, and they can't, says a lot about you."

She sighed again and played with his fingers. "I need to remember who I was before the money and glamor put a blindfold over my eyes. Truth be told ... I haven't been truly happy in years, even before Brent went to jail."

He nudged her with his shoulder, wanting to cheer her up. "I could make you happy, at least for a few days."

She gave him a watery smile. "Oh, you already have. I haven't gotten laid in ages. It was amazing."

"I'm glad I'm doing my job, then." He rubbed her hand. "You know, even without all this, any guy would be lucky to have you. You're beautiful and witty."

A hint of pink lit up her cheeks. "I can't imagine dating again, not right now. I have a hard time trusting men."

"I can see why. But you know, we're not all manipulative assholes."

She gazed at him a moment. "I need to find a man who takes pride in the family business, and can wear a suit and look sexy as hell on top of it."

He chuckled. "I don't know if that's me." He hesitated, wondering if he should bare his soul as well. "Honestly, I don't want to run the family business. I never did. I always saw myself doing something different."

"So why do you do it?"

He flashed a wry smile. "The artisan bakery pays the bills, you know."

She grimaced. "I'm sorry about that."

"It's fine. No, it's really just…" Again, he hesitated. Unburdening his woes on clients was a huge no-no, but she deserved some reciprocation after that emotional admission. "My grandfather opened the store when he was young. It passed to my father, but two years ago he died from a heart attack, and it landed in my lap."

She squeezed his hand this time. "I'm sorry."

He shrugged. "Greek men are prone to heart disease, and he didn't exactly take care of himself. But I thought I had more time. I thought I could go to school and make something of myself, and my father would be an old man and have to sell the store someday because I'd already be immersed in my own life and career. That's why they tell you not to drag your feet."

"So now you're running the store, and there's no time to go to school."

He nodded. "It takes a lot of time and money running a business. But you know that already, don't you?"

"Do I ever." She released his hand, then flopped back and sifted her fingers through her wet hair. The sun picked out the burgundy highlights in it.

"You enjoy what you do, though," he said. "I don't get much personal satisfaction from selling cigarettes and cheap beer and trying to keep the coolers from turning into hot boxes every other day."

"You could sell the store." She continued stroking her hair. "Have you considered it?"

"That's kinda complicated." He looked down at his hands and rubbed them together. "I own the entire building and we live in the apartment above it."

"We?" She paused in detangling her hair.

This was why he didn't talk about his personal life on dates. However, he'd gotten in too deep to stop now.

"Yes. Me, my mother, my sister, and … my daughter."

Grace sat forward, her mouth popping open. "You have a daughter?" She sounded pleasantly surprised.

"Yes, she's four." He smiled. "And quite precocious."

"Are you married?" She cocked her head. "I can't imagine a wife being all right with this job."

"No, I'm not."

"A girlfriend, then? A very understanding one?"

Discomfort prickled beneath his skin. "No." He shook his head. "It's kind of hard to be a man whore and have a relationship."

She smiled, coy and yet sweet. "I know *I* would never allow you to do such a thing. I'd keep you all to myself."

He grinned. "If I was with a woman like you, I wouldn't want to do this job."

She twirled a strand of wet hair around her finger, and it reminded him of Amelia so much he wanted her to stop. "I always thought I'd have children. Brent and I talked about it a few times. I'm very glad now that we never moved ahead with it."

"You'll find the right man to have kids with, I'm sure"

She dropped the strand of hair. "So her mother isn't in the picture anymore?"

"I shouldn't talk about my personal life with you." He tried to keep his tone neutral. "It's unprofessional. I'm supposed to be showing you a good time."

"Because I paid for your services, we can't be human beings?" She touched his wrist. "I don't mind. I wouldn't be asking if I just wanted you to shut up and look pretty."

She *had* wanted that, at first, but the fact she'd changed her stance on it in a single day was kind of … nice.

He was silent a moment, then spoke reluctantly. "Her mother, Cassandra, was my high school sweetheart. We knew each other for a long time. We were on-again-off-again, but we kind of screwed up, and that's how Becky happened."

"Becky." Grace smiled. "Short for Rebecca? That's a cute name."

"Her mother died shortly after she had her."

The mirth faded from Grace's eyes and expression. "Oh, no. I'm so sorry."

"She had preeclampsia. Had a stroke during the birth. Never woke up." His throat tightened as he spoke. His chest felt as though someone were squeezing it. "She never met Becky."

Grace clutched his hand. "That's terrible. I'm sorry."

"We weren't in love." He blinked a few times. "But we were going to try, for the baby, you know? For our daughter." He tried to pull in a breath. Every time he thought of this, it just seemed to hurt more instead of less. Time hadn't healed that gaping wound yet.

"I'm sorry." Grace squeezed his hand tighter. "You're a good man for wanting to support the two of them even though you weren't in a relationship."

"My dad died a couple years later." He let out his breath. "It's been a really rough road."

"And here I am, complaining about my silly problems." She looked at him with profound sympathy. "At least no one died in my world."

"Hey, your problems aren't silly." He put his

hand over hers. "There's all kinds of tragedy in the world. One person's suffering isn't lessened by another's."

"Life is so very unfair, isn't it?" She rested her head on his shoulder. "We're at its unforgiving mercy."

"Yes, we sure are." He pressed his cheek against the top of her head, into her damp hair. "I started doing this job last year, much to my mother and sister's disapproval. I'm doing it for the money, but not for personal gain, or to put it into the store."

She lifted her head and looked at him, her eyes limpid and gleaming in the sunlight, her chin on his shoulder.

"I'm doing it so Becky never has to run the store. So she can go to school and have that life I wanted." He rubbed her knee beneath the robe. "I'm going to put her through private school, and then college. Most of the money I make from my dates goes to that. She's going to be a doctor, or a lawyer, or anything but a goddamn grocery store owner."

She smiled. "You're a good man."

"I know I can't do this forever, but while I'm still young and have my looks, I'll milk it as much as I can."

"Selling your body for your daughter's future." Her tone was light. "Very noble."

"You sound like my mom." He slipped his hand up higher and pinched her thigh, then looked around, out at the ocean and the sprawling resort, then back at the gorgeous woman leaning against him. "But God, I don't know how anyone can work under these conditions."

She laughed and gripped his hair, and pulled him down to her mouth. He liked the way she grabbed his hair. Her mouth tasted like mint. He sucked at her tongue until she let out a soft, contented sigh. His cock was perking up again.

"Now we know each other's secrets." She stroked her fingertips against the nape of his neck. "I'm a destitute cocktail waitress with a felon ex-husband, pretending to still belong to the upper echelon I was never really a part of."

"And I'm a ghetto grocery store owner with a tragic backstory and bills up to his eyeballs, slinging his cock around just to get by." He gave her a sly grin. "How about I get a shower and we go have the sort of wild, uncouth fun that lowlifes like us are meant to engage in?"

She gripped the front of his robe and slung one leg over his, long and sleek. "That sounds wonderful. I want my money's worth."

No more behaving.

Chapter Eleven

As suspected, the real fun was off the resort. Grace looked up things to do locally and found an abundance of tourist attractions, restaurants and bars, shopping, and activities they could engage in that didn't involve having their noses in the air. When Roxanne texted to join them for brunch, she didn't respond.

Ty wore a white t-shirt and boardshorts, and he looked like a bronzed god under the tropical sun. He had his hair in a haphazard ponytail, showing off the smooth muscled column of his neck and tempting her to bite it. She wore her bikini and a big floppy sun hat. His gaze often strayed to the valley between her tits, where she was slathered with sunscreen and glistened with sweat. She didn't mind at all. His gaze was nothing like Carl's.

They ate a marvelous breakfast on an airy patio overlooking the ocean, went on a sightseeing tour, drank rum from coconuts, and bought too many overpriced chintzy trinkets. They held hands and laughed and Ty pressed her into alcoves and shady secret spots to ravish her mouth. The sun was hot, the breeze humid, and the tension between them scorching.

She'd left the resort this morning feeling vulnerable and tender after her confession, but by afternoon she felt like she'd started a whole new life, and her spirits were higher than they'd been in years.

"I love the ocean." Grace leaned on a stone wall, her arms folded on top of it. They stood on a bluff overlooking the beach, and the view was breathtaking.

Ty played with the string of her bikini top across her back. "Better than a swimming pool. We should go jump in it."

"Would you believe I've never been in the ocean before?" She looked out across the glittering blue expanse. "I've been to the beach many times, but never actually got in. Brent took us to Cancun for our honeymoon."

"You went to Cancun for your honeymoon and didn't even get in the water?"

She shrugged. "It was a resort of course, and there were pools, like here. I was trying to be part of his world, do what everyone else did. I didn't want to look like some classless tourist or mess my hair up. I was so worried about looking perfect."

Ty shook his head. "That sounds so weird. People go to the ocean all the time to have fun, doesn't matter how rich or poor they are. What's so classless about it?"

"I don't know." She looked at her fingernails, gleaming and perfectly manicured. "I was so afraid to do anything wrong, anything out of place. I wanted to fit in so badly. I felt like I was being scrutinized constantly, even by him."

She had never dared to confess such things before. This was almost as good as therapy—which she probably needed as well.

He slipped his hand down her back, then wrapped his arm around her waist. "You're back in this world now. C'mon." He tugged at her. She hesitated.

"Come on." His plush lips curled into a smile. "Let's go jump in the ocean like the peasants we are. Maybe it'll wash the filth off us."

She laughed. He took her hand and they walked down a sandy slope to the beach.

People were lying everywhere on towels and blankets. Kids ran around. Everyone was laughing, drinking, playing. Music came from beneath big, rippling umbrellas. Easy, happy, fun times, the kind she hadn't had in ages. She'd learned how to fit into high society, now she had to learn to fit back in the real world. Was she ready for that?

Ty peeled his t-shirt off, standing near the water's edge. She admired his body. He wasn't a gym rat, but he was lean and nicely built. She wanted to lick the sweat from his chest.

"Come on." He kicked his sandals off and dropped his shirt next to them. "You can take off your top, too, if you want." He grinned.

She didn't want that kind of attention on her. Really, she didn't want anyone but Ty looking at her right now. She untied the sarong across her hips, kicked her sandals off, and walked down to the water to join him.

He whistled. "Goddamn, you're beautiful."

"Yes, with all this meat on my bones. They just couldn't quit bringing that up last night." She had to speak over the roar of the waves coming in. Standing in front of the water, it seemed even more vast and fathomless, its power and majesty magnified. She could easily be dragged out and never seen again.

"They're just jealous." He gave her bottom a playful, gentle swat. "You're gorgeous and their wives are as severe and sharp as their personalities. Don't let them get you down. Come on." He gripped her hand and pulled her toward the water.

She followed him down the soft slope to the point where the froth flashed across the sand and then quickly withdrew. The water was much cooler than the air, but not startlingly cold like she expected. It lapped at her toes and curled around her ankles. The creamy, smooth sand rippled beneath the surface and mesmerized her. How far out could they go and still be safe?

"I've never been in the ocean either," Ty said as they swished out until the water filtered around their knees. He still held her hand. "But that's just because

I've never been to it."

"Well, here you are."

He smiled. "Thank you, for choosing me. For lots of reasons."

She let go of his hand and bent to splash in the water. "Thank you for actually showing me what a good time feels like again."

"That's what you're paying me for, isn't it?" He waded out further, ahead of her.

"Yes, but you're going above and beyond, trust me."

They played in the ocean, splashing each other and jumping at the waves as they rolled in. Eventually, she got down in it, let it wash over her entire body, and paddled around. The water flowed and ebbed, a primal force, and it felt both dangerous and thrilling at the same time. They seemed so far from the beach, and all she could hear was the rush of water and wind.

"This is amazing." She draped her arms over Ty's shoulders, and they bobbed together in the chest-deep water. "I don't know why I've spent so much time in swimming pools."

He wrapped his arms around her waist. Droplets glistened on his skin like diamonds. His hair was wet and nearly out of the ponytail now. She reached behind his head, slipped the tie out, and stroked her fingers through those thick black locks.

"I like it better loose." She continued dragging her fingers through it. "You're a handsome man."

"You wanted me to be all fashionable and proper yesterday," he teased, and pulled her tighter against him. "I had to act like some spoiled kept boy, remember?"

She smoothed her hand over the top of his head, slicking the front of his hair back. "There's no need for that anymore. I don't want you to be uncomfortable for the rest of our time here."

"I can still be whatever you need me to be, that's my job." He played with the tie of her bikini top. "Just keep me in the loop, okay?"

"You're a person, not an object." She stroked his cheek. The rough, dark stubble on his jaw tantalized her fingertips. "I'm sorry I treated you that way."

"No more apologizing. We both said we're sorry and we both forgave each other."

She realized suddenly he had undone her top. She gasped as the tie fell away across her back and the cups loosened, setting her free.

"Ty!" She swatted his shoulder.

He laughed. "No one can see us out here. We're too far from shore."

She glanced toward the beach. No one was close to them in the water.

"My services are still yours." He slipped a hand under one of the cups. "I am at your command." He tweaked her nipple, which was already hard from the cool water.

"Is that so?" She locked her legs around his waist. "I don't want you to get the wrong idea."

He tilted his head. She wished she could see his eyes, but they were hidden behind the sunglasses he wore. "Was I getting the wrong idea last night?" he asked. He rolled her nipple between his fingers, making tingles rush across her skin.

"I don't want you to think I'm using you as a prostitute. Because you're not, and I know that."

He pushed her up a little, so her boobs were right in front of his face. He pulled her top up and gave the nipple he'd been toying with a firm suck. She gasped and looked toward the beach again and wrapped an arm around his head.

"We're going to cause a scandal," she murmured.

He moved to the other side and gave the other nipple the same attention. She bit her lip and squirmed against him, their bodies sliding together beneath the water.

He drew back and looked up at her. "I thought you wanted to cause a scandal."

She wiggled her top back down. They had bobbed out farther, and the waves undulated around them. "I don't mean by getting arrested. Let's not take it that far."

He smirked and slipped his hands onto her ass and squeezed. "You never lived this wild and free, back before the rich folk caught you in their net?"

She tilted her head back, so the sun streamed down on her face. Had she? The men she'd been with before Brent seemed like boys compared to her ex's swagger and status. She'd had some fun back then, but it all seemed long ago, another lifetime. Was this *really* that wild and scandalous? Or was this just what normal people did?

She looked back down at him. "I need to take my reentry a little slower." She flipped his sunglasses up so she could look into his eyes. So lovely and dark. If only this moment were real. If only they were actually a couple, happy and carefree in love, floating in the middle of the ocean without the weight of the world to pull them down. But he was only a dalliance she'd bought, a distraction. Something superficial, like the rest of her life, devoid of true meaning.

The thought made her stomach knot up and her spirits sag. Why couldn't she just live in the moment?

"That's fine." He caressed his hands up her back. "I'm sorry if I'm pushing you."

She wasn't sure why she was balking. She could handle a lot of things right now, if only she let herself.

Even if this was all pretend, it was perfectly fine to have some fun, wasn't it?

"I'm the one who's sorry." She pulled his sunglasses fully off. "I'm much more of a prude than I imagined myself to be."

He squeezed her and smiled. "Just because you don't want to get dirty in public doesn't make you a prude. I shouldn't be getting all handsy. It's just..." He flicked his gaze down to her chest, which still bobbed in front of his face. "You're hard to resist."

He met her eyes again, and she found herself lost in those depths, so vibrant and honest. He wasn't just saying what she wanted to hear. He meant it. Or at least he was very good at pretending he did.

"I don't mind you being handsy." She put his glasses back on him. "Do up my top, you perv." She wiggled off him and turned around. He tugged the strings behind her.

"We should go get drunk," he murmured next to her ear. He snaked his hands around and cupped both breasts beneath the water.

She gave an exaggerated gasp. "In the middle of the day!"

"At some cheap, seedy bar."

She hummed as he kneaded her breasts. "Even worse. You mean, you don't want to go to one of the overpriced swanky places on the resort? You want to drink *cheap* beer and *bottom shelf* liquor? How droll."

He squeezed both nipples, pulling a little squeak out of her. His cock was pressed tight—and hard— against her bottom. "Oh dear, what will your friends think?"

She snorted. "They wouldn't set foot off the resort, don't worry, they'll never know. They're too afraid a local might look at them, or worse, try to speak to them. Let's go have some real fun."

He smoothed his hands down her sides with a soft groan. "Okay, I'll behave myself. No more touching until you say."

She smiled. "You can touch me all you like. Don't worry, we can still get naughty—in private. This place seems to bring out the beast in me."

He growled playfully and snapped her re-tied top string. "No, I think you're just a beast."

After they emerged from the water and grabbed up their discarded clothes, they took a walk up the beach and found the perfect place: a little bar with sandy floors and thatched walls, tables that wobbled, and a darkly tanned, heavily mustached bartender who mostly spoke in grunts. The place wasn't too crowded and the booze selection was minimal but cheap.

"This reminds me of one of the first bars I ever worked in." Grace sipped her rotgut vodka and soda. "It was a dump and it seemed like every night my ass got grabbed at least twenty times before happy hour was even over. But I made great tips and the owner was a nice older man."

Ty had a bottle of beer. He leaned on the bar and grinned at her, his hair slicked back and clinging to his neck. "I think I've been to that place. It sounds like the places I usually go, anyway."

She eyed an old pinball machine in the corner, half the lights on it out, but it still looked functional. "You play?"

He huffed. "You're looking at the Bensonhurst 1998 World Pinball champion."

She arched an eyebrow. "Really?"

He chuckled. "No, but I did play a lot with my sister when our dad would hang out at the bar. Come on." He jerked his head toward the machine.

She went with him, hand-in-hand. She was still damp from the ocean, and her hair smelled like saltwater. When was the last time she'd let herself become so disheveled? It felt amazing. It felt *real*.

Ty wasn't joking about being good at pinball, despite his exaggeration. She stood next to the machine and watched him rack up points, the blinking lights and bells going off as he scored again and again. She sipped her drink and couldn't stop smiling. The bar was playing some wild tropical steel drum music over the speakers and she shook her ass to it.

Finally, Ty lost his ball and beckoned her over in front of him. "Your turn."

She walked around to the front of the machine. "I don't think I'm going to beat that." She set her drink on the little table next to them. "You were lighting this thing up like the Fourth of July."

He sidled up behind her, so he was pressed against her back. "Don't worry," he murmured. "I'll help you out." He slipped his hands over hers on the paddle buttons.

She grinned over her shoulder. "Oh yes, Mister. I've never played one of these fancy machines before. Can you help me?"

He kissed her shoulder. "You just stand here looking pretty. I'll do all the work."

She giggled hysterically as they played. He worked the paddles with his hands over hers and racked up points once again. His body pressed warm and slick against her back was all she could focus on, so she was glad he was actually the one playing the game.

"You *must* be a master," she said. "You can even play with your cock grinding into my ass. I'm impressed."

He jerked his hips against hers. "I don't know

145

what you're talking about."

The ball finally slipped down the shoot and the machine rang out a disappointed tune. Ty stepped back but placed his hand on her stomach and drew her back with him.

"Had to fall from grace eventually," he lamented.

She picked up her drink. "Is that a pun?" She turned around but stayed close. Not just to preserve his dignity, but because he was like a magnet, and she was inexorably drawn to him.

He picked up his beer. "Or maybe I'm falling *for* Grace..."

He took a swig of his beer, maintaining eye contact. She didn't care who was watching them. Let them watch and be jealous. She was in another world right now. She was just about to kiss him, right there in public, when a familiar voice interrupted.

"Well, look who it is. There you are!"

She looked around, her heart leaping into her throat. Then, she quickly plastered a fake smile on, an automatic reaction.

"Carl." She stepped away from Ty. "What on earth are *you* doing here?"

She'd been tragically wrong in assuming none of them would step foot off the resort. Carl was dressed in pressed white shorts and a pink golfing shirt, tanned and coifed and looking a thousand times richer than any of the locals in the room.

"We missed you at brunch, Dollface." He stood near the bar. No way would he come to a place like this to drink. They didn't sell aged scotch, after all.

"Ah, yes, well. We slept in." She looked at Ty. "Then we thought we'd do some touristy things. You know, sample the local flavor."

Ty's expression was neutral, but irritation shone

in his eyes. Grace urged him to follow her to the bar. Carl leered at her, looking her up and down as she approached.

"I'm here to buy cigars." Carl held up a wad of money. "The Cuban kind." He winked. "There's much less chance of them being stale than when I have them imported. I can examine the merchandise first."

Of course, he would only be slumming it if he wanted something.

The bartender brought a wooden box over, set it in front of Carl, and opened it. Inside were rows of fat brown cigars.

"The girls were asking about you at brunch." He plucked one out and waved it under his nose. "I was hoping you'd show up, too, since you left the party so early last night." He raked his gaze down her body, slow and obvious, as he twirled the cigar between his fingers. "You brighten up a room, Gracie."

She kept her smile on, though her insides recoiled. Even when she'd been married to Brent, Carl didn't restrain his opinions of her. He had being a creep down to an art.

Ty stepped up beside her and slipped an arm around her waist. "Could you stop that?" His tone turned dark.

She stiffened.

Carl put the cigar down and picked up another one. He smiled easily at Ty. "Stop what?"

"Looking at her like a piece of meat and talking to her like that. Especially in front of me."

Grace held her breath. She should nip this in the bud, play it off as lighthearted as she could, but she inexplicably found herself struggling against getting involved. She *wanted* to see what happened, and it horrified her.

Carl chuckled. "He's a scrappy one, Grace. Brent would have a laugh. You're trying to get back at him after all, aren't you?"

She opened her mouth, but Ty cut her off.

"You mean her felon ex-husband? Gee, why would she want to 'get back' at him after everything he did to her?"

The bartender raised an eyebrow at Ty. If they got thrown out of some island dive bar, she wasn't sure she'd ever live it down with the others.

Carl seemed to find the entire exchange amusing. "I know your sort, Tybalt. Is it really Tybalt, or did you make that up? I'm curious when they started letting dagos run businesses in Park Slope."

Anger flared up in Grace, and she couldn't keep silent. She lurched forward. "Carl, that's out of line!" She flung her hand out to stop Ty from jumping forward.

"You can do better than this, Gracie. If you really want to get back at Brent, that's fine. He'll be out of that hole soon enough." He smirked. "He'd rather I take care of you, in the meantime."

Ty pushed around her. "I'll punch your fucking capped teeth out of your head if you say one more word, you piece of shit."

Grace gripped Ty's arm. "Don't." A surge of emotions flooded through her—outrage, shame, guilt. "Just leave it."

Ty stared Carl down. Carl remained nonchalant, toying with the cigars, smug and superior.

"Your sort always resorts to violence," Carl said. "You can't refute what you are. Stay out of things you don't understand, hood rat."

Grace pulled Ty back so he wouldn't throw the punch he'd balled his fist up for. "Let's go." She glared at Carl. "You're so rude. I don't care if Brent is out soon." Defiance swelled in her, stoked by rage. "I never want to see that lying, worthless piece of shit again as long as I live. I hope he gets shanked in there."

Carl laughed. "My, you have gone to seed, haven't you?"

She dragged Ty away forcefully, because she was certain he *would* punch Carl if she didn't get him the hell out of there. "Come with me." She lowered her voice, putting command in it. "Do *not* hit him, I'm warning you."

Ty seethed. His arm trembled beneath her hand. She turned and walked him toward the door at the rear of the bar.

"Hope to see you at dinner tonight!" Carl called after them.

They stepped out into the sun. She finally let go of him but positioned herself so he couldn't run back inside.

"I'm going to knock him the fuck out." Ty jammed his sunglasses on. "He shouldn't talk to you that way. To either of us!"

She gripped his shoulder. "Please don't start a fight here." She realized she was trembling, too.

"What kind of bullshit is this?" Somehow, furious, he was even more attractive. "The way these men treat you like a sex doll, the way they think what your husband did was funny?" He gestured to the door. It was only a screen door, and she was sure Carl could hear him. "These are the biggest assholes I've ever met in my life, and I've met a lot of assholes. How can any human being have their head so far up their ass and still breathe?"

She pulled him down the beach. "I know, I agree. But I didn't bring you here to fight them."

"It's not right, Grace!"

She hurried ahead, but he didn't follow her. She turned and looked back at him. Her vision swam as tears pricked her eyes. Her breath caught, and it was hard to pull it in, hard to think straight.

"You can send me home if you want," Ty growled. "I'll give you your money back. But I am not going to put up with anyone talking to you, or me, or anyone else like that."

"Yes, they're terrible people!" Her voice cracked. She clenched her fists. "But I don't know how to get myself out of this life right now. It's all I've known for years. I've been completely immersed in this world, terrible as it is. I don't have other friends. I don't have anything, Ty!"

He walked up to her and gripped the sides of her face. "Never see them again, it's that easy. It really is. You're better than this. You can find new friends."

Her eyes brimmed with tears. "No one has ever stood up for me like that before." She could barely speak, her throat was so tight. "No one has ever defended me like that." Her heart felt like it would pound out her chest. "But I can't just walk away, it's *not* that easy."

"Grace."

She pulled out of his grip, wiped her eyes, and started down the beach again. "We're going back to the resort."

"Grace!"

"Now!" she snapped back, though she instantly regretted it. "I'm not paying you to fight my battles. Just shut up and come on." She kept walking, and the tears fell.

Another wonderful day completely dashed and ruined. She ought to be used to it by now, but she wasn't.

Chapter Twelve

"I can't believe you want to do this. You'll bring disgrace on this family. Don't you think we've suffered enough the past couple years?"

Ty sat at the kitchen table, face in his hands, rubbing his forehead. If he had to listen to much more browbeating tonight, he might just pack a bag and find a friend's couch to crash on. He couldn't make his mother see the upside of this, or the ways it would help. All she could see was—

"My son wants to be a whore." She wasn't actually doing anything in the kitchen, just puttering around and slamming things on counters. *"He wants to sell his body, as if we've sunk that low."*

Ty lifted his head and gnashed his teeth. He didn't want to yell at his mother, and it would only make things worse if he did, but it was difficult to keep his patience.

"I'm not going to be a whore, Ma." His voice came out louder than he meant it to. *"I'm not selling my body. I'm just going on dates!"*

She glared at him, her eyes glittering with a mixture of anguish and outrage. When he was little, that look put the fear of God in him. It wasn't so far off now.

"There are more respectable ways to make money." She leaned on the counter, as if this was all too much for her and she might collapse. Those dramatics wore on him, too. *"You don't need to be a gigolo. What would your father say about this?"*

That argument would come up a million more times over the next year. It was her go-to when she started getting upset about it all over again.

"Ma." He stood up from the table. *"They'll give*

me three hundred dollars to take a lonely woman out to dinner. Five hundred if I take her dancing or something after. How is that a bad thing?" He approached her, forcing his voice to a low and reasonable volume. "I'm not going to sleep with them. I'm just getting paid to help someone have a good time."

She sniffed and turned away. "We don't need money that badly. Who knows what could happen to you. Do you think men are the only ones capable of acting crazy? A woman could kill you and stuff you in her trunk!"

Ty rubbed his forehead again. He shouldn't have told her, but she would find out. There was no way he could play off going out several nights a week—if he was lucky—as just hanging out with the guys. Especially if he went out dressed up and came back with cash.

"Ma, every dollar we make from the store either pays our bills or goes right back into it." He tried not to get emotional, since she was emotional enough for both of them. "I can't save anything. Luci wants to go to school and I want Becky to have some kind of future that isn't this. How the hell am I supposed to make that happen if I can't get extra income from somewhere?"

She turned sharply. That fierce sparkle in her eye grew more intense.

"What's wrong with this? This is a good future for your daughter. She has a home, a family, a business that can support her someday! Are you trying to spit on everything your father and grandfather built up for you?"

Ty couldn't tell her how he really felt, how every day these walls seemed to be getting closer and closer and all he wanted to do was run. Run and never look back. But he couldn't do that.

"Wouldn't you rather Becky had a better

chance?" He was walking the line, and he knew it, so he tried to be careful. "What if she could become a doctor, or a scientist or something?"

His mother pressed her lips together, still glaring.

"And Luci wants to go to community college. There's too much income in the store for her to get the grants she needs. Don't you want her to be able to do something, too? What if she could work in an office, or start her own business?"

His mother sighed and shook her head. "There are more honest ways to make money."

"Then show me one, Ma!" He flung his hands up. He couldn't hold back the frustration and anger any longer. "Show me where the hell I can make five hundred dollars a pop several times a week that isn't illegal or won't drag me away from running the store. Someone has to take care of us!"

"Don't swear." The glitter in her eyes turned to the bright sparkle of tears. "There has to be something other than this. It isn't the answer."

"It's just dates." He dropped his arms. "It's perfectly legal, and it makes a lot of money. Yeah, it's not going to be the answer forever, but I'm young and good-looking right now, why not try it? I'll only have to do it in the evenings, I can still run the store during the day. It's perfect."

He'd found out about the agency through a friend of a friend, a guy who was going on dates and turning a nice income. Ty wrestled with the idea for a while, on one hand thinking it was insane, on the other thinking it was genius. He hadn't dated anyone since Cassie died, and before that their difficult, tangled relationship made it hard to see anyone else. He missed female company, so it was a win-win. He'd gone for the screening and application process before he told his family. He didn't *want to start drama if the agency didn't even accept him.*

But they had, and now here was the drama.

"I'll be careful," he assured his mother. "I won't let some crazy spinster chop me up with an ax. And I'll only do it for a while, until I've got some nice savings built up for Becky's college fund. C'mon, Ma. Don't be like this. You know there's no other way to get this kind of money without selling drugs or gang-banging."

She shook her head again. "What am I going to tell the ladies in my bridge club?"

Ty rolled his eyes. "You don't tell them, Ma. It's not like I'll be flaunting it or it's our only source of income. Just don't mention it. I'll keep it discreet."

She tottered past him and across the kitchen. "I just hope your father isn't looking down on this. My son, the gigolo. Well, you do what you think is best for this family, Ty, and I won't interfere." That was her sanctimonious voice, and it was worse than her typical crowing.

"Ma!"

She drifted out of the room, crossing herself with a sniffle.

Ty heaved a sigh and dragged his hands through his hair. She would come around. Maybe.

He gathered up his folder from the table—he'd wanted her to look at the contract and all the legal paperwork so she could see it was aboveboard. She wouldn't so much as glance at it, of course. He was about to head out of the kitchen when he noticed his sister leaning next to the doorframe out in the hallway. She had her arms crossed and one eyebrow cocked. She was good at picking up where their mother left off.

"I'm sure you have something to say, too." He tucked the folder under his arm. "Get it over with, I have to go do inventory."

She shrugged. "How would you feel if I decided to go down to the corner and turn tricks to pull in extra money? Just wondering."

"I'd fucking kill you. It's not the same thing and you know it. I won't be turning tricks. I'll be going on dates, that's it. Wine tastings and chick flicks and shit like that."

She titled her head. "What if I decided to become an escort? You know, just go on dates. Be arm candy for lonely guys."

"It's different."

"Why, cause you're a guy and I'm a girl?"

"Yes!" He glanced down the hallway. Becky was taking a nap. He lowered his voice. "You wanna go to school, don't you?"

"I don't need you to pay for my college with your dick. I can get a part-time job."

"Yeah, well, Becky can't." He slipped the folder from under his arm and brandished it at her. "You can sit around here and carry on the family legacy if you want, but you're gonna grow old here, Luci. If you're lucky, you'll marry one of these bums from the block. You'll move into some dump down the street, but not so far away you won't have to come in every day and run the register. But you'll never escape. This will be your life, until the day you die. I'm not letting that happen to my daughter. I can still change things for her. You can change things for you, too."

She stared at him, and she had the same disdainful anger in her eyes their mother had. But there was something else there, too—a quiet, sad understanding they both shared. If they didn't try, this was going to be their prison for eternity.

She turned and walked away without another word. A minute later, she came back, her purse slung over her shoulder. It was a purple canvas bag with stars printed all over it. She loved anything star-patterned.

"I'm going to get groceries for Ma." Her voice was stilted. "You want to come with me?"

"No, I got work to do. There's always something, you know?"

"Yeah, I know."

She turned and left the apartment, and he stood in the silence, wondering if this was such a great idea after all. It seemed like the only choice right now, no matter how awkward. If he didn't start digging, this hole was just going to fill in with more and more dirt.

Until he couldn't breathe.

* * * *

Ty stood in front of a rack of colorful wraps, beach towels, and flip-flops. He held up the thin piece of pink material, a scattering of silver stars splashed across it. It was something to wear over a swimsuit, but Luci could probably use it as an accessory with a number of outfits—as a scarf, or a belt, or a wrap over a skirt. She could just throw it over a lampshade, if she wanted to. Regardless, he thought she'd love it. The stars were iridescent and shone rainbow in the light.

He'd been in the gift shop for a while, seeking gifts to take home to his family. He didn't know where else to go, or what to do with himself. He didn't want to be in the room with Grace right now. Despite the wonderful day they'd had—up to a certain point, of course—he didn't even want to be on this damn island anymore.

Was three thousand dollars' worth it? He hadn't even known Grace forty-eight hours and it was a wild ride—sometimes fun, but also more demeaning than he cared to put up with. Sure, the sex was great, but that was all hormonal. He hadn't had sex in a while and she was a hot woman, *of course* the sex was great. The toll on his pride, not so much.

She wouldn't quit yanking him back and forth, and frankly, he was getting sore.

He tossed the scarf-wrap thing in his basket and continued browsing, trying to find the perfect thing for his mother. Something that wouldn't remind her he had been away for the weekend being a man whore—literally, this time—but of course he wouldn't be telling her that part.

As he looked over the racks and shelves, he tried to reason with his anger. He thought of how they'd bared their souls that morning. He felt sorry for Grace and he saw the position she was trapped in. Money and class were shiny golden rings for people at the bottom. After all, wasn't that why he was addicted to making money and acting like some sort of suave man of the world? And even though it was an act, he couldn't deny that he enjoyed pretending to be on a level he couldn't even hope to attain in real life. He felt bad for her, he really did. And he understood.

But maybe his tenderhearted reaction was just an aftereffect of having his head buried between her legs. He should probably jump ship now before she whipped him around again. Could he handle one more day of this?

He picked up a glass with "Barbados" written on it and a cheesy beach scene drawn around the bottom. His mother didn't need more dishes. He put it down and picked up a gaudy playing card case with sequins in the shape of a palm tree on it. Something to take her cards to bridge club in, maybe?

"It's all cheap crap. But I suppose you're into that, aren't you?"

Ty looked up. Dismay filled his stomach as Amelia flounced toward him through the racks. She wore a short white dress, hat in one hand and sunglasses atop her head. Her shiny lips were pinched, her gaze severe. He put the case down and braced himself. Judging by her words, she wasn't here to hit on him—which he was at least grateful for.

She stopped a few feet away, on the other side of a short set of shelves. Her nose was literally in the air.

"Did you threaten my husband?" She spoke imperiously. "You thug piece of trash."

Ah, so she'd already heard. He resisted the urge to roll his eyes. "Did I threaten him? Is that what he told you?"

"You tried to punch him."

Ty looked around. There were a few other people in the store, and glances were tossed their way.

"I never threw a punch at him." Ty kept his voice down. "I suppose he didn't bother to tell you what led up to me wanting to punch him, though?"

She stalked around the shelves. He held his ground but set his basket down. He would come back and get the stuff, if need be. He wasn't going to cause a scene in public.

"I don't know who you think you are." She looked him up and down, hands on her hips. "It's obvious you don't belong here. I should have expected Grace to drag something like you on this trip. She can't find a decent man to save her life."

Ty snorted. "Oh, you mean a decent man like her husband who's in prison?"

"You're more of a lowlife than he ever was. Trashy, classless, violent little gutter rat." She closed in, though she wasn't the least bit intimidating. Even in heels, she was barely as tall as him.

He smirked cruelly. "Hasn't stopped you from trying to get in my pants, has it?"

She shoved him in the shoulder, hard enough he stumbled back a bit. He was startled, then anger swept through him.

He glared at her. "Don't put your hands on me."

"How dare you say the things you said to my husband." She curled her upper lip. "He's a thousand times the man you are, and he could buy and sell you over, little boy. You dare think you could raise a fist to him?"

Ty laughed. He couldn't resist provoking her further. "I seem to remember you saying you'd like to punch him, too, hypocrite."

She shoved him again. He gritted his teeth. The clerk was staring at them from the counter.

"Don't. Touch me." He eased toward her. "I didn't threaten your husband. He called me names and treated Grace like trash. I'm not going to put up with that, not from him, or from you."

Her eyes glinted. "I think you need to leave, you and Grace both. You're not welcome in our party anymore."

He rolled his eyes. "You're not queen of this island. We can be here if we want. Why don't you just stay the hell away from us for the rest of the weekend?"

She pointed a finger in his face, her bright red nail gleaming. "If you dare to come near us again, we're calling the police."

"Go ahead." He barked out a laugh. "What are you gonna tell them, that I told your husband to go fuck himself because he called me a dago?" He shook his head in disgust. "You have some real problems, lady. I actually felt sorry for you last night. I didn't think you deserved that piece of shit, but maybe you're more suited for him than I guessed. You need to work out whatever issues you have, but I can't help you with that. Get out of my face, and I won't tell him you were climbing me last night. Imagine what he'd think if he knew you were getting yourself all dirty."

She shot out a hand and gripped his shoulder, balling his shirt in her fist. Her nails dug sharply into his flesh. "Don't you threaten me, fucker." Her eyes were wild. So this was the crazy woman who was going to attack him, like his mother feared.

Her nails hurt, which made him react without thought. Still, he attempted to restrain himself as he gripped her wrist and twisted her hand off his shoulder. He flung her arm away. "Stop it!"

She stumbled back, much more than was warranted. She flailed at the shelf and gripped it, and let out a high, terrified, and much exaggerated shriek. "Leave me alone! Help, this man is attacking me!"

The clerk hurried out from behind the desk. Ty groaned. No way. *No fucking way.*

"Security!" Amelia screamed. "I need security, this man is trying to hurt me!" She continued to swoon and cower. "Please, someone help me!"

The clerk rushed over, frowning at Ty, and gripped Amelia's arm. Ty thought about bolting out of there, but that would look bad. Better he stand his ground, and maybe someone would believe him.

Right. They'd totally take his word over a rich, beautiful, hysterical woman's. He was certainly going home now, probably in police custody. Wouldn't his mother and sister be pleased to see him?

A security guard hustled into the store. Everyone was staring. Amelia sobbed dramatically in the clerk's arms.

He sighed. "Jesus Christ."

Chapter Thirteen

Grace sat on the bed in her robe, still damp from her second shower of the day. Washing the brine off her was the only thing she could do, and she'd hoped the shower would also give her head and emotions some clarity. It hadn't.

She brushed her wet hair, gazing out the balcony doors. The sky was blue, the ocean sparkling beneath the lowering golden sun, and nothing of the scene reflected the gray, raging storm inside of her. How could she be in this beautiful place and feel this way? How could she have the sort of brilliant, whirlwind day she'd had and be left sitting here, an aching, conflicted, self-hating lump?

Ty left the room almost as soon as they returned, claiming he was going to look for gifts to take home to his family. His voice was gruff and he wouldn't meet her eyes. She wanted to stop him, apologize, try to make him understand why she'd reacted the way she had to Carl's taunts. But she couldn't get any words out and he left, slamming the door behind him. If not for the fact his things were still in the room, she'd fear he might not come back at all.

She stood up and tossed her brush on the bed. He couldn't expect everything to change in one day, could he? Just because she told him her woes didn't mean she was prepared to tackle them. Though they'd had a marvelous day, the sort of day she used to have back when she was a different, carefree person, she wasn't any less stuck in this life than she was this morning. He couldn't expect her to give them the finger and ride off into some—what, new and uncertain life? Into nothing. Into loneliness and isolation.

A knock sounded at the door, startling her out of her reverie.

Her heart leapt into her throat. Who could be visiting her? Had Ty forgotten his keycard? No, she'd watched him jam it angrily into his pocket before he left. Maybe he'd lost it?

She walked to the door, heart hammering in her ears, and touched the doorknob. The knock came again, hard and insistent. She cracked the door open and peeked out. Her stomach sank, and then turned queasy.

"Gracie." Carl eyed her. "Is this a bad time?"

She eased the door open and pulled her mask on. "I just got out of the shower, I'm not decent." She stroked her fingers through her wet hair. "You know I don't like being seen without my face on."

He smirked. "You're a hot broad no matter what, don't worry. Is your chivalrous boyfriend here?"

She stood stiff, clinging to the door. If Ty came back right now, they would get into it, and he might really punch Carl this time. She didn't need that.

"No." She tried to keep her tone casual. "I don't think you two should be around each other, truth be told."

"I couldn't agree more." He stepped forward. "I'd like to talk to you." It was obvious he was inviting himself in, and like the weak creature she was, she stepped back and opened the door wider as he pushed in.

"I'm not sure this is an appropriate time." She clung to the door still as he slid past her, and then closed it. She wanted to leave it wide open, in case she needed to run, but he would either see that as an insult or force it closed himself. As soon as it clicked shut, the pounding in her ears intensified. She was trapped, alone with him.

He turned to her, his predatory gazing homing in on her. His presence filled the room, malicious and threatening.

"Grace, I think you should send that uppity little

boy home before he ruins your vacation."

She pulled her robe tighter across her chest and folded her arms. "And how is he going to ruin my vacation?"

Carl eased toward her, and she tensed. "He doesn't fit in here, and we both know it. He knows it. I don't know what gutter you fished him out of, but you don't have to do this."

She gazed at him. When he reached out and stroked her cheek, she flinched involuntarily.

"You're a lovely, smart woman." He lowered his voice, trailing his fingers along her jaw. "You can do better than that. I think you've made your point."

She drew away from him. Fuck propriety. "What point is that?" She walked across the room to the vanity and scanned the items on it for one she could use as a weapon. Spray perfume in his eyes? Hit him with her curling iron?

"That you're getting even with Brent." His tone was casual, almost mocking. "That you can still get some young, meaningless piece of ass. It's all right to slum it now and then, Grace, if you're just looking for a bit of fun. But really, what made you think it was a good idea to bring him? You know it's in poor taste."

She turned, staying close to the vanity. "I'm not slumming it, Carl. He's my boyfriend. And he's not from the gutter. You're also laboring under the delusion that I care at all what Brent thinks."

Truly, beyond the first few months, she hadn't longed for that man at all. Seeing through his scams and lies had turned him into a dark figure in her mind. All she wanted from him now was what belonged to her.

Carl strolled over. She backed against the vanity, bumping it with her hip.

"I think you should send him home," he

reiterated, and stopped in front of her. "If you want, leave with him, but he's not welcome here anymore, not after the way he barked at me like a puppy."

She bristled. Did she dare snap back at him? Did she even have the guts to stand up to him the way he needed to be stood up to? The way Ty had?

"I paid my own money to come here." Her voice lacked the power she wanted to instill in it. "Anyone is allowed to be here. You can't throw me out. You don't own the place."

She felt light-headed. This could be the end, truly, if she sassed him too much. She would find herself alone whether she wanted it or not.

He tucked his hands into the pockets of his shorts and heaved a heavy sigh. "Grace, you're making a fool of yourself, do you realize that? Everyone's talking about you right now. You're not acting right."

Her cheeks flashed hot. Her worst fear was them mocking her, talking about her behind her back. But why did she care? Why did she want these vultures to like her?

She tilted her chin up. "You said some very rude things to him earlier. He may not be your sort of man, but you had no right to speak to him like that. He's still a person."

Carl shook his head. The look of disdain and disappointment on his face only fueled her fear. "Is he really that good in bed?" He smirked. "Has he got you wrapped around his dick, is that what it is?"

"Carl, you should leave." She jerked her robe across her front again and turned away. "You know the way you're talking is uncouth."

He gripped her arm and she stifled a yelp. He turned her back to him, so he was directly in her face. Her mind flew to the vanity again, wildly trying to figure out how she could fend him off. Would anyone hear her if she screamed?

"I'm going to give you some choices here, Gracie." He spoke lowly. "I want you to think about them, really consider them before you answer."

She tried to pull away. He held her tighter, so much it hurt.

"You can both leave, or you can stay and he leaves." He stared into her eyes. The superiority gleaming in those hard, cold depths made her blood turn to ice. His power pressing down on her made her unable to move, unable to fight back. "If you stay, you have a chance to redeem yourself. We can get past this and all will be forgiven. Just a silly little incident that we'll sweep under the rug."

She swallowed hard and hated herself for finding that tempting.

"But if you make this difficult." He pulled her forward, so she was almost touching him. "I'll make things difficult for you, too."

The threat was so obvious it finally made her react. She yanked out of his grip and stumbled back. "Stop touching me." Her voice shook. "Get out of my room." She pointed at the door, and her hand was trembling, too.

He seemed unfazed. He smiled easily. "Send him home and come to dinner tonight. Join us, say you're sorry, and this will all be forgotten."

She snatched up her curling iron. "Get out of my room." She pointed it at him. The world was crashing down around her, but she wasn't going to let him do something awful to her on top of it. She would leave with her dignity intact.

He laughed, his face scrunching up in an ugly grimace. "Or you can both stay here and make this difficult, like you obviously want to."

"Get out." She spoke firmly, though everything inside her was crumbling.

"As I said, I'll make things difficult in return. I'll make some arrangements with Brent."

She stared at him. He didn't seem to be bluffing, but what the hell did that mean?

"Arrangements?" She narrowed her eyes.

"Yes, Gracie. You know I have some very good lawyers in my pocket. Men who can pull even the tightest of strings. All I have to do is throw some money their way. You know I have plenty of that."

"If you could get Brent out of prison, you would have done it by now." And what, exactly, would Brent do? Did Carl think he would come after Ty? She didn't believe Brent would bother himself with such things—but maybe she was wrong.

"I'm not talking about getting him out of prison. I'm talking about helping him deal with the government, and his money they have tied up. I'm talking about making sure you never see a dime of it."

Her heart seemed to still, then. She couldn't even hear it in her ears anymore.

"I can make sure you go back to the dirt he pulled you out of." Carl shrugged. "I know you don't have the money left to fight it."

She lowered the curling iron. Tears pricked her eyes, but she blinked them back.

"I deserve half that money." She could barely push the words out. "It came from my boutiques."

Carl shrugged again. "He bought those boutiques for you. Why shouldn't he get the money from them?"

She dropped the curling iron to her side. "Because I made that money! He didn't help me." Her vision blurred. "I worked hard for it."

"I couldn't care less. But I do care about being talked to like I come from the same landfill as your 'boyfriend.' So I'll gladly make sure you never see that money. It wouldn't be hard for me to get Brent to agree. He's a shrewd man, and you were just a passing fancy. When he gets out he'll have a lot of other things on his mind."

She turned away as tears spilled down her cheeks. She had no doubt he was telling the truth. He had the power and the money to close that door for her forever. Life wouldn't just become lonely, she would be destitute as well—she'd lose it all and be back to waiting tables.

"So." His tone was firm. "Send your white knight home and come to dinner tonight. Tell everyone you're sorry for acting like such a lowlife, and we'll laugh it off and go on with our lives. You made a mistake, Gracie, but it doesn't have to get worse. You'll figure out how to act right one of these days. It just takes practice."

She wiped her eyes and turned back to him. "You're so cruel, Carl." She shuddered. "How can you treat me like this?"

His lips curled into a taunting smile. "Because I can, Gracie. You're only making this hard on yourself. I can make your life much easier, you know. I can keep you from slipping any further."

She knew what he meant by that, and it was more than just keeping his lawyers in a cage. She would rather fling herself off the roof.

A pounding came at the door then, making her jump. She looked at it. Who the hell was it now? Could this get worse?

"Maybe that's your boyfriend." Carl smirked and walked to the door, like this was his room. "I can help him pack, if he needs some assistance."

She hurried after him. Carl yanked the door open,

and she stopped short, staring wide-eyed into the hallway. Her mouth dropped open. It *could* get worse, and had.

Ty was there, but he wasn't alone. Flanking him were two broad, burly men in security uniforms, and they were holding each of his arms. Ty looked angry, and he flicked his gaze between her and Carl, and furrowed his brow. This couldn't look good, but on the other hand, his situation looked much worse.

Amelia breezed around the security guards. She clutched her hands to her chest, sniffling, her eyes bright and brimming. "Carl! Thank goodness you're here." She flung herself against him, as if she actually valued his protection.

"What's going on here?" Carl slipped his arms around her and glowered at Ty.

Grace tried to get her brain to work. "Yes, what the hell is going on?"

"You know this man?" one of the guards asked her.

She stared at Ty, gripped with fear. "Yes…"

"He tried to assault me!" Amelia shrieked. "Oh my God, he's like a damn animal. Who pushes a woman around like that?"

Grace boggled at Ty. Amelia's hysterics were obviously put on, but my God, what had happened? What had he gotten himself into?

The guard spoke again. "This woman is saying he tried to assault her in the gift shop downstairs."

"I did not," Ty spoke sharply. "She kept shoving me and I just pushed her hand off me. I didn't try to knock her over."

Amelia clung to Carl. "I confronted him about trying to punch you. It was silly of me, but I couldn't stay silent and not defend your honor." She gazed at him with huge watery doe eyes. "I know it was stupid, he's a savage, but I was out of my mind with rage."

"You attacked my wife?" Carl snarled at Ty.

"No!" Ty snapped back. "She attacked *me*."

"I want charges pressed," Amelia demanded. "I won't stand for this. He's ruined our entire vacation."

Grace was in a panic. She didn't believe Amelia, not for a second, but this was a bad situation. Like Carl, Amelia had the money, the status, and the upper hand to make things work in her favor. They were both in trouble.

"Shame on you." Amelia gnashed her teeth at Grace. "Bringing this scumbag here. How could you do this to your friends? You're a piece of trash, just like him."

Grace's stomach turned. She didn't know how to talk her way out of this. What would happen to Ty if they arrested him here? Could she get him home? Did she have the money to do so?

"I didn't attack her, Grace." Ty looked pleadingly at her. "She was pushing me, I swear. She's making all of this up."

"I am not!" Amelia wailed. "My God, you're a monster. Please have him arrested, this is unbelievable."

The other security guard, who looked quite put-upon, sighed and looked around at all of them. "The gift shop is pulling their security footage right now. We'll go down in a few minutes, check it out, and call the police in. We'll get this sorted out."

Grace was trembling all over. She thought she might crumple. Everything was going gray.

Amelia drew away from Carl, suddenly calm, and cleared her throat. "Wait, is that really necessary? Isn't that a task, looking at the footage? I don't want to cause them all that work."

The disgruntled guard looked at her. "They got cameras all over this place, they probably got a clear shot of everything that happened. It'll make things easier. You won't even have to give a statement, they'll just take him in." He tugged at Ty. "We'll keep him downstairs in our office until then."

"Wait." Amelia held a hand out and touched her hair with the other. She did that when she was nervous. "Maybe—maybe I'm misremembering things, I was so distraught. Now that I think of it."

Grace narrowed her eyes. Ty did as well.

"Darling." Carl touched her back. "Let them take care of him. He belongs in a cell."

"It's just, maybe it didn't happen exactly the way I think it did." She clasped her hands. "It's just a misunderstanding, I think. I'm not going to press charges."

The security guard became even more irritated. "Lady, you want us to call the cops or what?"

Grace glared at Amelia, anger slowly replacing terror. She was lying, and she knew the security footage would show that. She might even get charged with assault herself, if what Ty was saying was true.

"No, I don't think so." Amelia gave a nervous laugh. "It was just an accident, I'm sorry. Let him go, please. He didn't push me, I was mistaken."

The two guards looked at each other. Now they both seemed angry. They let go of Ty's arms. "You sure?" the first one asked.

Carl was frowning at Amelia. She continued to titter and touch her hair. "I think I had too many mimosas at brunch. I just misunderstood things. I'm very sorry, gentlemen, for wasting your time."

Ty shook his arms out, glaring at Amelia. "Maybe I'd like them to take a look at the security footage anyway. Maybe *I'd* like to speak to the police."

Carl's expression of confusion turned stony cold. Amelia's eyes widened. While it would be satisfying to see Amelia dragged away in handcuffs, the repercussions would be immense. Grace could just imagine the hell the two of them would rain down on her and Ty in the aftermath.

Grace grabbed Ty's hand. "Darling, come on. Let's just forget about this, it's not a big deal." She flashed Carl and Amelia a false smile. "It's just a little misunderstanding."

"The hell it is," Ty said.

Grace dragged him into the room, still smiling, and waved at the guards. "Thank you so much. I'm sorry about the trouble."

Ty was fuming, but he didn't resist. She would put him on a plane after this. Maybe she'd join him. He would probably never see or speak to her again, but she had much more important things to sort out right now.

The guards grumbled, shook their heads, and started down the hallway. Amelia, instead of being grateful, just looked smug.

Ty stepped forward and pointed at Amelia. "Listen here, you lying bi—"

Grace turned and clamped a hand over his mouth. "I think you should go," she told the other two. "We need to talk. Alone."

Amelia huffed. "Trash. You're lucky." She flounced down the hallway.

Ty wrenched out of Grace's grip. He had nothing to say though, thankfully. He stormed off toward the bathroom.

Grace grabbed the door and started pushing it shut. "You should go comfort your wife, Carl. She's obviously distraught."

Carl didn't move. He gazed in at her as she closed the door. "See you at dinner tonight, Gracie," he spoke ominously.

She shut the door and fell against it, her forehead pressed to it, hands shaking on the knob.

Why couldn't she wake up from this nightmare?

Chapter Fourteen

"You don't have to leave. I'm not asking you to leave."

Ty jammed his clothes into the suitcase. He couldn't look at Grace, in part because he was angry and he didn't want to take that anger out on her, but also because she sounded so desperate and sad. If he looked her in the eye, he might give in. He'd experienced way too much insanity for the brief time they'd been together. It was time for him to go.

"I don't think it's a good idea that I stay." He looked around for the rest of his stuff. There were his pants from last night, on the floor next to the bed. Reminding him, taunting him. "This is all too much." He strode over and snatched them up.

"She knew she was lying!" Grace grabbed his arm as he tried to walk back to his suitcase. "That's why she wouldn't press charges. They would have seen on the security camera that she was the one who attacked you."

He stopped and dared to look at her. As expected, his stomach clenched up, but he fought the wave of pity that threatened to break over him. Her eyes were wide and shining, her lashes wet, tracks of tears down her cheeks. She clung hard to his arm, her grip like that of a frightened child. Her wet hair hung limp around her face and all he wanted to do was kiss her.

Instead, he pulled away.

"I believe you, Ty." Her voice wavered. "I know you didn't hit her. She and Carl are angry because you dared to stand up to them. That's something I could never do and I admire you so much for it."

He grimaced and yanked at one of his pant legs, as they were inside out. He tried to do the same to the other one, but they were all tangled up. Frustrated, he just jammed them into his suitcase.

"Ty, you're a better human being than anyone else here, even me. You deserve to hear that. And I'm so sorry—" Her voice cracked, and then it dissolved into a watery whine of sobs. "I'm so, so sorry."

He heaved a sigh and turned. She was crying into her hands. His instinct was to grab her, pull her into his arms, and comfort her. But again he resisted. If he kept letting himself get sucked into this, the madness would continue. If he stayed here one more day, who knew what the hell might happen to him. He'd almost been arrested.

She turned and walked to the vanity, grabbed up a handful of tissues from the box there, and mopped at her face. He turned back to his suitcase.

"You have every right to want to leave." Her voice was thick and miserable. "I don't blame you one bit, and I won't try to stop you. I won't even ask for a refund. I want you to keep the money and provide for your daughter. God knows after what you've gone through this weekend, you deserve twice the amount."

He heaved another sigh and turned, hands on his hips. She sat down at the vanity and continued wiping her eyes and nose.

He was going to regret this. "Grace, I think we should both leave. I think that's the best solution here."

"I can't leave."

"Yes, you can. It's easy. Walk out the door with me. Get on the plane with me. I know you said everything can't change overnight, but it can *start* to change."

She looked up at him, and her eyes glinted. They were filled with not just anguish but bitterness and anger.

"I can't leave. Carl just threatened me."

He stared at her. "What?"

She looked at herself in the mirror and touched her hair, fruitlessly. "He told me if I don't come to dinner tonight and apologize for my behavior, I'm going to regret it."

"*Your* behavior?" Ty marched over. "You're not the one who needs to apologize."

He stopped next to her and she looked up at him, still so vulnerable and pitiful that all he wanted to do was scoop her up. What kind of bizarre universe was this? He felt like he'd been sucked into some trashy reality show about the world's most horrible rich people.

"Let him stomp his feet, Grace." He put a hand on her shoulder. "Let him blow smoke. He can't do anything to you."

"Yes, he can." She looked down, her voice going watery again. "He said if I don't do as he asks, he's going to mobilize his lawyers to help Brent, to help him make sure that I never get a dime of my own money."

Ty boggled. He tightened his grip on her shoulder. "What do you mean?"

She looked up at him again, tears streaming anew down her face. "He said he'll make sure I don't win the court case. I know he has the power to do that, he's not bluffing. He'll get Brent to agree to it and … I'll never pay off my debts. My boutique will close. I'll be back to waiting tables. He'll ruin my entire life." She dissolved into sobs.

Ty wasn't sure if he wanted to go make good on getting sent to jail, or throw up, or run as fast as he could away from this crazy mess. Were there really people in the world this spiteful and cruel? Had he stumbled into their lair and nearly gotten trapped in their web?

"We barely know each other, I understand that." She spoke through her tears. "But please don't leave. I need you for moral support. You've been kinder to me than anyone has in a long time."

She flung her arms around his waist and pressed her face to his stomach. He teetered and put his hands on her shoulders. Her face was wet and hot through his shirt, and she shuddered with ongoing sobs.

"I won't let them know you're here," she spoke muffled against him. "I'll pretend I sent you away, but please, Ty, I need you." She gripped the top of his shorts and looked up at him. Her face was red and wet, her eyes swollen. "You're the only thing keeping me from leaping off the balcony right now."

Goddammit.

How much worse could this get, realistically? And was it even about him right now? If he walked away and left her to the sharks, he would never be able to forgive himself. He couldn't just go back to his life and never spare another thought for how she might be doing. Or what had been done *to* her.

"All right." He sighed and wrapped his arms around her shoulders and pulled her back against him. "I'm here. I'm not going anywhere."

****

"At least leave with me tonight, after dinner?"

Ty knew beyond any doubt if they stayed there the rest of the weekend, though it was only one more day, her "friends" would continue to make her life a living hell, especially Carl. Also, the longer they stayed, the more risk there was of someone finding out he hadn't actually left.

"I would have to make an excuse," Grace said. "If I leave early, they'll see it as me running away from them, with my tail tucked."

They were sprawled on a lounge, in front of the open balcony doors, stark naked, the warm breeze off the ocean caressing their sweaty flesh. Ty couldn't explain how comforting her had led to this, but he didn't try to stop it. An insatiable desire welled up in him, demanding to be fed even in this craziest of moments. The same desire flared in her, and her tears turned to ecstasy, if only for a short time.

"So what?" He propped himself up on his elbow and looked down at her. "As long as you grovel to Carl tonight, he won't pull that trigger, right? What does it matter after that?"

She shook her head and looked out through the doors. "I don't trust him."

She was a vision, lying there in the afternoon sun. Her hair spilled in wild dark tangles, now dry, across the back of the lounge, her creamy skin on display for him, smelling of sweat and soap. She was soft and gentle now, like a real person, instead of the sexy fantasy she'd been last night. Somehow, that made her even hotter.

"Listen to me." He cupped her cheek and turned her head so she was looking at him. "You don't need them after this trip. You don't need to stay friends with them. He can't hold his threat over your head forever."

The anguish in her eyes didn't abate. Her forehead crinkled. "You don't know him at all, then." She paused, and the crease in her forehead deepened. "He'll hold it over me every day until I actually win the court case. Only then will I be able to leave them behind."

He stroked her cheek. "Maybe you can get some lawyers to fight back. I mean, if the money is yours, you deserve it. He can threaten you, but he can't change the law."

He couldn't imagine what it would be like if some rich woman married him, fully immersed him in her world, brainwashed him to leave the rest of his life behind, and then suddenly vanished, leaving him to flounder with her horrible friends slashing at him from all sides. He'd probably feel helpless, too, with no idea how to change his fate.

"I can't afford more lawyers," she said. "Carl knows he has me under his thumb. If I don't do his bidding, I will be sunk."

He settled back down beside her and sifted his fingers through her hair. "There's no shame in being broke and struggling, if it comes to that. Trust me, I know what it's like, and I think if you reach back in your memory, you'll know it, too. You kind of get used to it. And you know, you can start over, and you don't have to start over at the bottom, waiting tables."

Her brow furrowed again, this time in question.

"You can make your boutique thrive on its own." He slipped his hand down onto the long, smooth column of her throat. "It's not easy. I juggle the bills every day, but I make it work. I can give you some pointers. Maybe you can downsize or take from something less important to make something more important work. Or get a loan. Something. You can keep your shop going. Then, downsize other parts of your life. There's ways to do this without subjecting yourself to Carl in the desperate hope you'll get the money."

She didn't say anything, though she swallowed hard so he felt it beneath his hand.

"I've lived in the shit for a long time." He caressed over and onto her shoulder. "You sink or swim. Sometimes you have to swim real hard to keep your chin above it. You have to sacrifice and scrape. It sucks, but you adjust. You prioritize what's important and cut off things that aren't. It's painful at first, but it builds character, or so I'm told."

She snorted. "Character. Isn't that what we tell ourselves?" She put her hand over his. "When I was a cocktail waitress, I lived in a tiny apartment and took the bus to work. Things were very real back then. Gritty and plain. But..." She frowned. "I had friends, I went out, and I drank too much, laughed too much, slept around. It was a wild time."

"Then your husband swooped in and carried you off to the land of enchantment. But now it's turned into a land of horrors."

She rolled toward him and draped a leg over his. "I already had to close the rest of my boutiques. I have to find a new place to live soon because Brent only paid up the lease on our penthouse to the end of last year. I can barely keep the lights on right now."

"You don't deserve what you're going through, and you don't deserve to have those idiots tear you apart. It's not right." He sighed. "They're not friends. They're self-serving monsters who think everyone else is below them. Screw them."

"If I leave tonight, I'll lose face." Her eyes welled with tears. "Even more than I have. They're going to mock me relentlessly, but who knows ... maybe if I try to salvage our friendship, Carl will help me financially, at least until the lawsuit comes through. It's worth a shot."

Ty frowned. How could she believe that? Why would she subject herself to it? He could only imagine the expectations Carl would put on such a favor.

"If he was going to help you, he would have done it by now." Ty gripped her cheek. "He wouldn't be laughing about your ex either. And I can just imagine what he'd expect in return for floating you a personal loan."

She drew away and wiped her eyes. "I'm stuck, Ty. As much as I want to, I can't just run away and tell them to go fuck themselves. They're the only lifeline I still have."

"You're better than this." He pulled her back. "I see it in you." He kissed her, gentle but firm, feeling possessive, feeling like maybe if he just kissed her hard enough she would get the point. He'd only known this woman two days, but he couldn't watch her beat herself up like this and let them humiliate her. He couldn't do that to anyone.

She broke the kiss. "As I said earlier, you've been kinder to me than anyone has been in a long time. I can't thank you enough for defending me. But this is still a very complicated situation, and I have to figure a way out that doesn't involve them cutting me off at the knees."

"Leave with me tonight." He gazed down at her, their faces inches apart. "Tell them something came up back home. Something with your business. You have to go."

She shook her head. "I can't let Carl think I'm hiding, or humiliated. I'll give him his damn apology and laugh it off, so he doesn't send his dogs after me. That's all I can do right now."

He sighed, sagging against her.

"You won't have to see them again, I promise." She gripped his hair. "I'll tell them you left. You can go enjoy the island while I deal with them."

He huffed. "I don't think I can have much fun after this."

"I know. Neither can I. But it's only one more day." She pulled him down for another kiss.

He pressed against her, caressing down her side. Despite his irritation and outrage, he responded once more to her touch, her scent. They were soon wrapped in each other's arms again, desperate and passionate. He paused long enough to grab another condom from the box on the floor.

She was wet and open for him, her moans lusty and eager as he filled her. He'd already taken her in every way imaginable: on top, beneath her, from behind, over the arm of the lounge. He pushed her legs back now, hooking them over his shoulders, and drove into her as deep and hard as he could, chasing another orgasm and dragging her along with him.

"Ty!" She raked her nails up his back, already sore from her previous passion. He didn't mind. He wanted her to mark him up. He wanted to go home with the memory of her all over his body.

She was so tight and hot inside he could barely stand it. His groin and thighs were soaked with her, the lounge was soaked with her, and her musk was all he could smell. He was in heaven. His orgasm was weak and rather dry, considering he'd already come once, but nonetheless satisfying. After, he buried his fingers inside her until she was shrieking and twisting, coming all over his hand. Her soft sweaty thighs locked around his arm and her juices slicked him to the wrist. He could spend the rest of the weekend like this.

After, they lay panting, tangled together.

"I need yet another shower," she said. "God, I haven't had this much sex since—I don't think I've *ever* had this much sex." She laughed weakly.

He rubbed her stomach. "Same here. Despite everything, this is the best date I've ever been on."

She lifted her head. "I've started to forget I bought you. It's certainly one expense I don't feel remorse over."

He grinned. "I'm actually a man whore now. My mother is justified in calling me a gigolo."

"I don't want to think about you going back to that life." She dropped her head back. "I'll be terribly jealous, thinking about you doing this with other girls."

He caressed the glistening curve of her hip. "I don't do this with all the girls." He, too, wondered how he could go back to dating random women for money after this. Jesus, it had only been two days. He couldn't think like that. It was incredibly silly and premature. *Dial it back. She's little more than a client.* But was that the truth?

They took showers separately, because Ty knew if they got in together it would lead to more fucking, and frankly, he didn't think he had another go in him right now. He let her shower first, then took his. The scent of her shampoo and bodywash hung on the humid air, and despite his exhaustion, it filled his head with dirty thoughts as he cleaned the sweat and sex from his skin.

She dressed for dinner, though he still wished he could convince her not to go.

"You look stunning." He checked her out. "Did you make that dress, too?"

She wore a maroon dress, cinched at the side. It came to her knees and traced every exquisite curve of her body like it had been painted on. Her cleavage was on display, but it didn't look trashy. Instead, she was both elegant and sexy as hell.

"I did." She smiled at him in the mirror as she did her makeup. "I'm glad you like it."

He walked over to her and smoothed his hands across her hips from behind. "Don't let them make you feel bad about yourself, you're gorgeous. Your curves are sinful."

She smirked, her lips bright red now. "I'm glad you like those, too."

He watched her apply mascara, mesmerized by her every move. Either she'd picked it up in high society, or she naturally possessed it, but there was an elegance about her that enraptured him.

"I'm going to call home." He kissed her shoulder, which was exposed by the dress. "Check in on things. You don't mind, do you?"

She arched an eyebrow. "It'll cost a fortune, won't it? Even *I* don't have an international plan."

"Yeah, but I've been bracing myself for it. I have to make sure everything is cool. I promised I'd give them a call."

She worked an earring in. "Back when I was a cocktail waitress, I couldn't even afford a real cell phone. I always had one of those prepaid ones." She sighed. "I might have to go back to that. It would be cheaper."

"Don't be ashamed. Think of it as being frugal. Maybe I should do that, too, now that I think of it."

She smiled. "You should go out tonight and have some fun, while I'm kissing ass. One of us ought to get the most out of this."

He swatted her bottom. "Oh, I'm getting a lot out of it, trust me." He winked.

He went out on the balcony for privacy. He was doubtful about the rest of the evening—he probably shouldn't leave the room, so he wouldn't run into any of them. He was sure by now Carl had told all his buddies what happened, and they might be waiting around some corner to pummel him with golf clubs.

That was silly, though. Rich men didn't beat people up, they just tossed ineffective insults at you about public assistance and taking the train.

He sat down, turned his phone on, and winced as he made the call, already attempting to calculate the cost in his head. It rang twice, and his sister picked up.

"Ty?" She sounded out of breath and anxious.

Worry sparked in his chest. Had the place burnt down after all?

"It's me, Luci. What's wrong?"

"It's Becky."

He felt like his heart literally stopped. "What? Is she okay? What happened?"

"She started not feeling well shortly after you left, then she started running a fever this morning. It's pretty high, and I'm worried. I haven't been able to get it down, even with children's Tylenol. I might have to take her to the emergency room. Ma says we can call Uncle Vic to take us. I don't think she needs an ambulance, that's an expense we can't afford right now anyway."

Panic swallowed him. He clutched the phone to his ear and looked around wildly as though he could locate a teleporter to transport him home immediately. "Yes, take her right now. Don't worry about the money."

"She's been asking for you."

Guilt gripped him along with the fear. He'd been so far away from home, lost in paradise with a beautiful woman, having sex, fighting douchebags like he was some kind of hero, while his daughter was sick and longing for him. It was enough to make him feel sick, too.

"I'm coming home right now." He tried to think, raking a hand through his hair. "I have to find a way to get a flight, but I'm coming. I don't know if they can just change my ticket or not."

"All right, I'll take her. Don't panic. You'll have to call me as soon as you get back in the States. That should be a while though, shouldn't it?"

He stood up and paced in a frantic circle. Various solutions raced through his mind.

"Wire me some money." He gripped his hair. "Have Ma go down to the Western Union on the corner and wire it from the store account. Just send a thousand dollars, I have no idea how much a last-minute ticket will be."

"That's a lot of money, Ty."

"I'll figure it out!" He struggled to keep his voice down so Grace wouldn't hear. "Don't worry about it right now. Get Becky to the hospital. I'll text you my flight details, and I'll call you as soon as I get back to the US." He had no idea how long and difficult this trip might be, but he'd make it.

"Okay, we're going right now."

Ty hung up and rushed back in the room. His heart raced and he could barely string his thoughts together.

"I have to go, Grace, I'm sorry." He hurried to his suitcase.

Grace sat on the bed, putting her heels on. "What?"

He ran around the room, grabbing up his belongings. "It's my daughter, she's sick, she's running a really high fever and they can't get it down. My sister is taking her to the emergency room."

Grace stood up. "Oh, no."

He stopped and looked at her. "I'm not making this up just so I can leave, I promise. Trust me, I wouldn't tell a lie about my daughter."

She frowned. "I don't think that at all, Ty."

"I'm really sorry, I know you need me right now." He looked around frantically. "Where the fuck is my phone?"

"It's in your hand."

He looked down at it and shook his head. "My mother is going to wire me some money so I can get a plane ticket. I can't stay here while she's in the hospital, especially since I can't just call and find out what's going on without racking up enormous charges. My sister told me not to panic, but you know that's the easiest way to make someone panic." He let out a high, insane laugh.

Grace watched somberly as he jammed everything in his suitcase. "I hope she's all right."

When he finished packing, he turned to her. "I'm so sorry." He took her hands. "Please consider leaving tonight, too, please. Don't stay here with these people. Don't let them threaten you."

"I have to do what I have to do." She squeezed his hands. "I had a wonderful time with you. You made me feel better about myself than I've felt in ages. That's well worth the price I paid for your companionship."

He gave her a light kiss so he didn't smear her lipstick. "When you get back to New York, call me. We'll have to get together—maybe go on a date or something?" He managed a smile. "I hope this isn't the last we'll see of each other."

She smiled, too, though it was sad and forced. She looked scared. "I really hope not as well."

He let go of her hands and grabbed his suitcase. "I hope they can get me on a flight tonight." He took a deep breath, trying to calm down. "I feel so guilty, having all this fun while my daughter is at home suffering." He focused on her. "Not that I regret spending time with you, not at all."

"Try not to worry too much, she has your mother and sister there, right?" She stroked his arm. "I'm sure she'll be all right. They'll get her fever down. Little kids get sick like that sometimes. I'm sure it's nothing serious."

He remembered something else then and groaned. "I'm sorry about the ticket you bought me to get home. You're taking a loss. When you get back to New York, I'll compensate you. I'm really sorry how this all went down."

"Stop apologizing." She hurried over to the vanity and pulled something out of her bag. "Get home to your daughter, and don't worry about the money right now." She handed him a paper with a confirmation number on it. "Take it and see if you can get it changed. It'll probably cost less if you do it that way."

"Thank you." He took the paper. "I promise I'll pay you back, though." He was haunted by the feeling he would probably forget something, but he had to go. "If I leave anything, will you bring it back with you?"

She stepped in and kissed him again. The scent of her perfume wafted over him, momentarily distracting him from his distress. "Of course, get home safely. When I get back home I'll call you to see how she's doing." She smiled faintly. "And so we can make arrangements to get together again."

He sensed a deep, abrupt sense of finality here, despite their words, and it made his heart ache. "I'll talk to you soon, Grace." He drew back. "Thank you for everything. I really enjoyed my time with you."

"I enjoyed it as well, more than you can imagine." Despair shone in her eyes, the sort of resigned disappointment that expanded in his own chest. "Go. Hurry."

"Thank you." He rushed to the door, then stopped and looked back at her. "Don't ask Carl for money. The interest he'll charge will be more than you can pay. You'll find a way. Don't give up."

She flashed him a tight smile. "You're very good to say that, thank you."

He left, though it hurt. He was torn apart by the guilt of leaving Grace and the guilt of not being at home. His daughter was more important than anything else though, more important than a fling or a vacation or playing superhero. He just prayed everything worked out and he could get home fast.

Chapter Fifteen

Grace stood outside the doors of the restaurant, struggling to breathe. She stared inside at the tables draped in white tablecloths, filled with well-dressed people, the sparkle of crystal and glint of silver everywhere. The room was filled with the noise of quiet chatter, laughter, and the clink of glasses. She felt like she was standing on a cold and dingy street, like some homeless child, staring through a window into a wealthy, bright, unattainable world.

Her "friends" were in a private dining room, as they usually rented when they came to places like this. No need to rub elbows with the unwashed vacationing, touristy masses. All she had to do was step inside and walk to it. They would invite her in with their usual forked tongues and sly, condescending smiles. She merely had to hold her head up and refuse to flinch.

No big deal.

Ty's advice echoed in her head. She should turn around. Go back to the room, pack, change her flight, and never speak to them again. She didn't need them. She didn't need to be part of their vindictive little circle any longer. But she did need the money from the lawsuit, and Carl would make sure she never saw it if she ran.

She stepped into the restaurant and tried to keep her posture straight and her chin up. She wished more than anything Ty was next to her, but Ty was gone and she would probably never see him again, despite their promises to get together.

A mere six hours ago, she'd been soaring at heights she hadn't reached in longer than she could recall. She'd felt something like her old self, that girl she liked and respected. Ty's advice brought clarity to her mind. His hands brought joy to her body. Though she'd only known him a short time, he was like Prince Charming come to save her, to wake her up with a kiss. She felt alive again.

Now, she'd crashed back to earth where everything was tangled and painful and bleak. Her prince was gone. She knew how these things worked. Maybe a few texts, maybe a phone call, but he'd forget about her eventually, go back to dating women for money, and she would be left with herself. Fate held her here, and it was fate she had to follow whether she liked it or not. She blinked tears from her eyes as she walked across the room. It was all right. She'd be all right. *You'll figure this out.*

She reached the entrance of the private dining room, a set of double doors, one closed, the other open so servers could go in and out. A host in a suit and bow tie stood next to a podium. He gave her a pleasant but bemused smile.

"Can I help you, Miss?"

She took a deep breath. "Yes, I'm with this party. Grace Bennington."

He checked the list on the podium, nodded, and his smile turned genuine. He gestured her toward the door. "Welcome. Your friends are inside already."

Access to their world, at least for now.

She steeled herself, put on her best fake smile, and strolled casually into the room. Into the lion's den. The snake pit. Hell.

The room was big and airy, with open windows looking out on the ocean. A chandelier hung from the ceiling. Two long tables filled the space, and they seemed to be divided along gender lines—the women were at one, the men at the other. As always, the men were boisterous and loud, having their pre-dinner cocktails. Carl sat with his back to the doors and didn't notice her immediately. The women, with their martinis and wine, were the first to greet her.

"Fashionably late as always," Roxanne chided, though there was little humor in it. "You do like to make an entrance, don't you?" She swept her with a cold, disdainful gaze. Amelia would have told her by now what happened.

Grace chuckled and acted casual. "Well, it takes a lot to put this together, hmm?" She smoothed a hand over her hip. Her curves were gorgeous, after all. Ty had told her so.

"And of course you had to put your dog down." Amelia glared piercingly over her martini glass. "I do hope he won't be bothering us again?"

Her chest ached. She felt like she couldn't breathe, let alone speak. Somehow, she managed to get words out. "He won't be." Grace gave her a terse smile. "He's gone home, and I'm very sorry for what happened today. It was a terrible misunderstanding."

The women up and down the table were peering at her. A few whispered to each other. She wanted to crawl under the tablecloth.

"I see." Amelia sat back. "I must say, even though maroon is out of fashion, you really pull it off, Grace. It looks good on you. I usually avoid it because it makes me look like an open wound."

Titters raced up and down the table. Before Grace could speak, a hand slipped onto her lower back.

"Gracie, so good to see you here." Carl flashed her a toothy, predatory smile. "And alone, no less. I think you look far more stunning on your own. Nothing to detract from your natural beauty."

Amelia snorted and drank her martini.

Grace kept her smile on. "Yes, well, Tybalt has gone home. And I'm very sorry about the sordid incident this afternoon. He understands how inappropriate it was."

Carl rubbed her back. "All is forgiven, Gracie. Sit down and have a drink. We can chat some more after dinner." He winked.

She felt like she was walking through a nightmare as she made her way to an empty seat at the end of the table. All eyes were on her, but she met no one's gaze.

Patsy sat next to her, the one who had called Ty a "hood rat" the night before. She leaned toward Grace, obviously already sloshed on red wine. "Don't listen to those catty broads," she murmured. "Amelia told us what happened, with her usual dramatics. Poor little victim." She swirled the wine around in her glass. "If he hit her, believe me, she deserved it."

Grace pressed her lips together. Did she dare defend him? "He didn't hit her." She spoke quietly. "It was just a misunderstanding. He's not like that."

Patsy winked. "A few more glasses, maybe I'll sock her myself."

Grace would honestly pay good money to see that.

Dinner was the horrible affair she expected it to be. She was so tense and distracted she had no appetite, and even her martini tasted terrible and caustic. She was painfully self-conscious, and every word anyone said to her sounded like the taunt of schoolyard bullies. She nonetheless had to put on a brave face in the onslaught. She thought continuously about Ty, wondering if he'd gotten on a plane, if he was on his way home right now, if everything would be all right with his daughter. Wondering when he would call her.

He won't call you, fool. Despite everything that had happened between them, he was just a boy she purchased for the weekend, a superficial distraction. She gave him money and he did his duty of making her feel good. Though he'd made promises on the way out, there was nothing in the world holding him to them. She could not let her emotions get involved. Best to keep those locked away in the vault she'd buried them in when Brent was arrested.

During the second course, Carl sidled over to their table and pulled up a chair next to hers. She'd thought she couldn't get any stiffer, but she was wrong.

"So your man went home, Gracie?" He slid his arm onto the back of her chair. "That's a shame. I was hoping he and I could continue our conversation from earlier today." His voice was cool and relaxed, but an ominous threat peeked through his tone.

She forced yet another smile, so hard she thought it would crack her face. "I don't suppose he's up to that sort of conversation."

"Isn't he?" Carl arched an eyebrow. "It seemed like he was when he started it. You two looked like you were having such fun, too. I didn't mean to ruin it."

She gripped her fork tight. If she said the wrong thing or made a wrong move, he would surely make her life hell. It didn't matter what happened to her right now, as long as the future turned out in her favor. She had to focus on securing the long-term. That would make the present bearable.

"You didn't ruin anything, your presence is always welcome, Carl." She went back to eating, mechanically. "Don't worry about him, he's gone."

He leaned back and dragged a hand slowly across her shoulder. She shuddered internally.

"We should have drinks after dinner," he said. "I think you and I have a lot of catching up to do." He stood, smirked, and wandered off back to the men's table.

Grace felt a scream rising in her throat and

stuffed it down. She wanted to scrub his touch from her skin.

Patsy smirked. "Carl has been hounding you for ages, hasn't he? That sly dog. No wonder Amelia is being such a bitch."

The woman next to Patsy shot Grace a coy look. "If you leave Tybalt, Grace, I'll take that sexy boy off your hands. Or at least distract him for you. I don't mind a roll in the dirt now and then." She and Patsy tittered and clinked their glasses together.

Grace took a drink to squelch the scream again. She was starting to panic as tears welled in her eyes. She managed to blink them away, though.

Before dessert, she excused herself to the ladies' room. Amelia regarded her with a sour glare as she passed by. Thankfully, no one else was in there, and she marched directly to a stall and locked herself in. Then, she burst into the tears she'd been holding back since she came down to dinner, but probably even since before Ty left.

After a few minutes of quiet sobbing, she pulled herself together, took a few deep breaths, and dabbed at her eyes with a wad of toilet paper. She needed to find her resolve. Looking weak in front of these people or letting them know how much they were getting to her, would only make them eat her faster.

She took out her phone and checked it in the false hope of a text or missed call from Ty. Her messages were empty. She thought about calling him, but if he wasn't back in the US yet, or was up in the air, his phone would be off. She could text him anyway, but to what purpose? He would get in touch with her if he really wanted to and when he had the opportunity.

She also didn't want him worrying about her when he had his daughter to worry about. Crying about her problems to him was selfish. His daughter, after all, was much more important than some client with loads of drama that he'd had to put up with for the past two days.

Instead of dwelling, she looked through the pictures she'd taken today: the two of them drinking from a coconut together, making stupid faces with their sunglasses on, standing in front of the ocean. A genuine smile touched her lips for the first time in hours. She tried to remember the things he'd said to her—that she was strong and resilient, and better than them. Life wasn't that bad at the bottom and she could recover no matter how far she fell. But it was difficult to believe all that, because there were years of thinking otherwise and years of the "good life" she had to deprogram herself from first.

She emerged from the stall, fished her makeup out of her purse, and went about fixing her face in the mirror. Her eyes were red and puffy and her mascara smudged. As she was finishing up, Amelia and Roxanne walked in. She quickly snapped to attention and put a smile back on. She stole another quick glance in the mirror to make sure she didn't look like she'd been crying.

"We thought you got lost in here," Roxanne said. "Did the shrimp cocktail not agree with you?"

Grace chuckled and snapped her purse shut. "I'm fine, thank you for your concern."

Roxanne shrugged. "Just wondering." She leaned against the wall next the stalls. Was this an ambush?

Amelia sauntered over to the sinks where Grace stood. Grace played with her hair in the mirror and tried not to crawl out of her skin.

"Is Tybalt actually your boyfriend?" Her voice was cold and accusing. "Or is he just some guy you picked up and took on this trip so you wouldn't be alone?"

Grace looked at her, terror rising. "I've talked about him before. We've been seeing each other casually for a few months. I know I've mentioned him."

"You never told us his name." Amelia narrowed her eyes. "Did you pay him to come on this trip? Because you got a shit deal."

Grace tried to act affronted, when truly, deep down, she knew the game was up. "How dare you." She swung her purse over her shoulder. "I don't have to pay men to hang out with me." She looked Amelia over. "And by the way, maroon might be out of season, but white certainly doesn't look good on a woman your age. It brings out your imperfections."

Amelia's mouth dropped open.

Grace marched to the door with her head held high and her hands shaking. She couldn't take this anymore. She couldn't take *them*. Her façade would soon crumble, but when it did, she was determined to take everyone kicking and screaming down with her.

"Amelia told me he tried to get in a fight with Carl," Roxanne taunted. "What a lowlife. You could have at least paid someone with class to pretend to be your boyfriend."

Grace looked over her shoulder as she opened the door. "There's a difference between class and status, you dried-up whores. Just because you've got one doesn't mean you have the other."

Amelia's mouth was still hanging open.

Grace looked her over sourly. "You're one to talk about men. Every single person here knows your husband thinks of you as nothing more than a meal ticket with tits, and he even had to upgrade those."

She flounced out of the room, a surge of empowerment moving her feet. What the hell was she doing? Where the hell was this coming from? She was nearly giddy with panic. Ty would be so proud of her.

Back in the dining room, she considered her spot at the women's table, then grabbed up the remains of her drink and walked over to the men's side of the room. Might as well crash and burn in spectacular fashion.

"Is this a boys-only club?" She stood behind Carl's chair and placed a hand on the back of it.

He looked up at her and smirked. "Not if you're asking to join."

She could see the writing on the wall, and this was her last chance to get out with any kind of prize.

She sat down in an empty chair next to Carl. Most people were up and about, mingling. These women didn't eat dessert after all, and the men just wanted to work on getting drunk.

Carl leaned back and watched her as she crossed her legs, angling them toward him. Much as she didn't want to sleep with this vile monster, if he would give her some money she'd endure it. She hoped Ty hadn't felt the same way about her.

"I see you've come to your senses." Carl raked his gaze down her body and focused it on her legs. "Your boy toy is just that, isn't he? Not really a relationship there." He looked back up at her face. "You're too hot for him and you know it."

She tried to think of nothing but her objective. "It's complicated, but you shouldn't have teased him today, Carl." She swatted his knee playfully. "He's not as sophisticated as you. Very few men are. Cut him some slack."

"There's no room for slack in this world, darling. You should be on my arm. You should be with a man who can treat you in the way you've become accustomed. I know Brent left you high and dry. You need someone to take care of you."

Just then, Amelia marched back in the room, Roxanne close behind her. She stopped and glared at Grace and Carl, her hands clenched at her sides.

Grace's stomach was in knots. "Oh, really? And what would your wife have to say about that?" She wiggled her fingers at Amelia in greeting.

"She has her own fun, make no mistake about that. Why can't I have mine?" He waved a hand. "We're married for the strategic comfort it provides, what with her father being my biggest supporter. She can't stop me from doing what I want." He leaned toward Grace. "And I have a big house. You're welcome to stay anytime. She wouldn't even know you're there."

Amelia didn't approach them but stormed back to her seat. She actually looked upset, not just affronted.

Grace's smile faltered. "Yes, I know you're a man of means." She switched the flow of the conversation. "And as you said, Brent left me destitute when he went to prison. I was blindsided, honestly."

"Like I said,"—he picked up his scotch—"I'll get him out of there sooner rather than later." He reached out and put a hand on her knee. "He might want to fight me for you, though. That could cause some friction. I know you're divorced but he'd have every right to be jealous."

She glanced at his hand. She wanted to fling it off her. Punch him in the face. None of them understood or cared how much chaos Brent's sudden disappearance created in her life. She was the one who had to suffer while the bank and the law stripped away his assets, while she had to close her stores and sell things at pawn shops. And all the while, Brent's indifference—and even outright refusal to communicate with her from prison— only made it harder. The last time she visited him was to serve the divorce papers.

"I don't really think we're compatible anymore." She bobbed her foot, moving Carl's hand, hoping he would take it off her. "We had a good run, but sometimes I wonder if we were ever really in love."

Carl shrugged and slid his hand off her. "Well, you know he has a thing for pulling girls up from the gutter. It's like his hobby." He sipped his scotch. "You're the first one he actually convinced to marry him, though. He said he wanted to try to start looking respectable and get a few kids out of the deal. The wholesome American dream, you know."

She stared at him. She felt as though everything inside her stilled—her heart, her lungs, and her blood.

"His ... hobby?"

"Oh, yeah." Carl chuckled. "He loved to slum around and find a girl from the bottom he could easily impress with his money, be her Prince Charming and all that. He was actually engaged to this girl who worked in a massage parlor a couple years before you came along. She ran off with some Mexican, though. He didn't tell you about it?"

All the sneaking suspicions she'd had during their marriage were suddenly confirmed. The excessive heaping of gifts on her was a smokescreen. Removing her from her "lowly" life and friends and isolating her was intentional.

She blinked a few times. "No, he didn't tell me that."

"It doesn't matter." Carl put his hand on her knee again. "You need someone more thoughtful in your life. Probably the best thing for you that fate intervened. I told him he needs to focus, find a woman on his level, and marry for money. *That's* the American dream."

She'd been brainwashed by Brent because Brent was very good, and very practiced at brainwashing. It was horrifyingly clear now.

"We ought to go have that drink." Carl grinned. "It's stuffy in here." He looked around the room, perhaps searching for his sulky wife. "I don't think anyone will miss us."

"Of course." She was like a robot right now.

She would not sleep with him after all, she vowed. She would kiss his ass and even his feet, if need be, but she would not climb into bed with him.

As they left the room together, she noted Amelia and Roxanne watching them with murderous glares. Amelia's eyes were shining. Had Grace's words in the bathroom hit their mark? Suddenly, those two catty women were the lesser of two evils and she would rather stay and fight them. Her insides were cold, her brain numb. How the hell would she get off this island without being torn apart?

They left the restaurant and went out onto the boardwalk. A person could walk from one end of the resort to the other on it, never touching the sand itself. God forbid. She thought of being in the ocean with Ty, bobbing through the waves with him. It seemed like a million years ago now.

The evening was warm and breezy, the sun starting to sink into the water, painting everything above and below with a palette of pastel color. Gorgeous, romantic even. As Carl took her arm her chest ached so hard she thought she might keel over. She wanted Ty. He was miles away by now and probably out of her life forever. She had to get over it.

"Let's take a stroll first." Carl's tone was suggestive. "I've been dying to get you alone."

Chapter Sixteen

"Are you sure there's nothing earlier I can get on?"

The ticket agent was probably getting tired of Ty's question, but she kept a polite smile plastered on her face. She'd checked her computer enough times he knew they'd looked hard and deep enough. She couldn't create a miracle for him.

"Yes, sir. If you want to rebook the ticket you have, the earliest I can put you on is the 6:00 AM flight. That would route you through Ft. Lauderdale and then get you to JFK by 1:00 PM tomorrow."

That felt like ages from now. He pictured Becky lying in some hospital bed, hooked up to monitors and full of needles, crying for him all the way until tomorrow afternoon.

"There are, of course, two flights to Miami tonight." The agent's voice remained a baseline pleasant but firm. "But they're both full, so you'd be on standby, and we couldn't honor your current ticket for that."

"And that would cost..." He couldn't think right now, let alone retain information. He rubbed his forehead.

"Three hundred more than what you're currently looking at now to change your original ticket."

He winced and pinched the bridge of his nose. Changing his ticket was already going to cost more than he could afford, and the sound of money draining out of the store account filled his ears. They didn't *really* need to fix that leak in the ceiling right now, did they? They'd been making do this long, with buckets. The coolers could probably hold out another six months without a new motor as well, if he could get his buddy to do a little cheap maintenance work on the system.

"I need to make a call." He stepped away from the desk. "Thank you, I'll be back."

The agent nodded.

Ty walked over to the area where people stood with their bags waiting to check in. He pulled out his phone and heard the whooshing sound of disappearing money once more as he turned his service on and made the international call to his sister.

"Ty."

"How is she?" He strolled away from the crowd, trying to keep his voice down. "Did you go to the hospital?"

"Yes, they just took her back. They're going to work on getting her fever down first." She didn't sound as worried as the first time he'd spoken to her, which was a good thing. "She said one of her friends at school is sick, so that's probably where she picked it up. Are you on your way home?"

He looked at the paper in his hand, the one Grace had given him with his ticket information. "Not yet. I have a ticket my client gave me, but they said the only way they can change it is if I take a 6:00 AM flight tomorrow morning. I can get a new ticket tonight, but I'll be on standby, and it costs a lot more."

"How much are we talking?"

When he told her the prices, she made a shocked, squealy sound. He sympathized.

"You said she gave you a ticket." Luci sounded a bit more stressed out now. "So shouldn't it be free? I mean, you already have it."

"No, 'cause I have to change it to another flight. But that's the cheaper option."

"What time does that flight go out again?"

"6:00 AM."

"What about the actual time out, on the ticket she gave you. What time were you guys supposed to be leaving originally?"

He looked at the paper. "Noon, but that wouldn't get me home until tomorrow evening. There's a layover."

"Maybe you should just do that instead, Ty. We can't pull that much money from the account. It's ridiculous, especially if it's free if you just leave when you were supposed to."

"I can't stay here that long." He jammed the paper in his pants pocket. "I can't sit here tearing my hair out while Becky's in the hospital."

"Maybe you should have thought about that before you left."

Anger surged up in him, and he couldn't restrain himself. "She wasn't fucking sick when I left!" Several people glanced over, and he lowered his voice. "Are you seriously browbeating me right now? Seriously?"

Luci's voice grew strained. "You can't keep running off like this. We need you here. Look what can happen."

"Okay, I'll stop doing jobs when I come back." He gripped his hair. "And you can figure out your own fucking way to finish paying for school. Get used to banging on the cash register, because that's your future. That's all you get."

He was upset, so much he was trembling, and he regretted the words even as they came out of his mouth. It wouldn't help anything, clawing at each other from a distance. He wanted to be magically transported home right now and standing at his baby's bedside.

"Text me and tell me how much money you want Ma to wire." Her voice was cold. "See you when you get here."

"Luci, let me know how she's doing. I'll keep my

service on!"

The line went dead.

He sighed and dropped his phone from his ear and looked helplessly around. The place was full of tourists, happy and well-rested from their vacations, and the people streaming in looked excited to be here. He felt a million miles away from all of it. He might have found some comfort if he spied at least one person who looked as miserable and anxious as him.

After some tough deliberation, he decided to exchange his ticket for the sure, moderately cheaper flight at 6:00 AM. He'd be in agony spending the night here, especially if Becky worsened, but taking less money out meant his mother and sister might forgive him sometime this year. Also, despite his worry, he knew Becky was in good hands with her aunt and grandmother. Probably much better hands than his.

After swapping the ticket, he debated what to do next. He could sleep there in the airport and make himself extra miserable, or he could go back to the resort and sleep next to Grace. She would at least lend him an ear while he fretted. Poor girl. She *definitely* deserved a refund.

He plunked down on a bench to collect his thoughts. A man sat on the other end, an older guy, his hair in dark, tight shiny curls, his skin a deep brown. He had a thick black mustache. Ty noted the man was watching a couple who stood a short distance away. They had just come in and their bags sat around their feet. They were arguing loud enough Ty could make out most of what they were saying.

"I told you not to harass him," the woman chastised the man. She was a middle-aged white woman, dressed in such a deliberate, flawless way it reminded Ty of the people he'd just left behind. Not a hair was out of place despite her current flustered state, her jewelry flashing, nails manicured and bright red. "We've only lived here a year, it's not like you know the roads better than a man who drives them every day."

The man was equally well put together, prim and polished from head to toe, and he was a storm cloud of anger. "I'm not going to let some lowlife cab driver who can barely speak English swindle me, Marion. He was deliberately taking us the long way to soak us. You have to watch out for that down here. They're all trying to pull a scam."

The man on the other end of the bench looked at Ty and rolled his eyes. Ty subtly shook his head. On his own cab ride here, the very nice, mannerly, and well-spoken cab driver explained that an area of the main road was under construction and they'd have to wait in a line of traffic if they went that way. The detour was much faster.

"You still should have tipped him." Marion huffed. "After the hard time you gave him. You know we have to come back here. Who knows if he could show up at our house. You don't want him to get some posse of thugs to jump you, do you? You have to watch out for that down here, too."

The man next to Ty gave a gruff laugh. Ty smirked back at him in sympathy and comradery. *Exactly* like the assholes he'd left behind. They were everywhere.

The couple gathered up their bags and made their way to the ticket counter, still bickering about useless cabbies and the possibility of getting rolled.

"It's always the same, isn't it?" The man had a vaguely Indian accent. "Especially here, where it's full of these rich tourists. They're always visiting or moving here, and they expect everyone to bow down and kiss their feet, like it's their own personal island."

Ty dragged his fingers through his hair and started pulling it back. "Yeah, I know the type." He slipped the hair tie off his wrist and secured his hair with it.

"And they're sure everyone is out to get them." The man grunted. "These uppity folk, they think every non-Caucasian with a blue-collar job is a criminal. We're all in a gang or something. Obviously, if you look the wrong way at us we'll come over with our friends and beat your skull in and fuck your wife."

Ty chuckled. He thought of the way Amelia had acted, the whole "attacking her in the gift shop" incident. It was the same back home sometimes, depending on what neighborhood he ended up in. The bigger and more opulent the houses were, the more anxious the side-eyes became.

"They're sheltered." Ty looked down at his bag between his feet. "Every time they go out in the real world they treat it like they're visiting the zoo."

"Of course. And the cages barely hold us, you know. We're savages."

Ty slipped his phone out of his pocket and stared at it. He should go back to the resort, he knew that. Grace would probably be glad to have him there, and he wouldn't mind a soft bed over a hard airport bench. But did he have the right to keep putting her through this? He didn't want her to have to deal with his personal life any more than she already had.

He also pictured her, surrounded by those sharks, all alone in the water. Trying to navigate those deep, confusing, choppy depths. His heart ached for her. It made his stomach twist. But he couldn't run in and play hero either. Just because he made her pussy happy didn't mean she wanted him to be her knight in shining armor. He barely knew her. He had to keep reminding himself of that.

"Where you headed?" the man asked.

Ty looked over at him. "Nowhere, tonight." He sighed. "Brooklyn, New York, in the morning. That's the earliest I can get a flight that doesn't cost an arm and a leg."

"That home for you?"

Ty nodded. "My daughter, she's sick. I mean, not like bad sick. She's got a fever that won't break and my sister has her at the hospital right now, but…" He looked back down at his phone. "I'm worried. I can't get to her as fast as I want to. It's driving me crazy. She's in good hands but I want to be there, too."

"I know how it is. I got two of my own, five and eight." He fished his phone out of his jacket. "One of them gets a sniffle and I'm up all night."

Ty gazed at the flight board above the ticket counter. So many flights, none of them he could get on. "I think she'll be all right, I'm just chasing my tail, you know? Being so far away. I shouldn't be hanging out here in paradise while she's suffering."

The man leaned over and showed Ty his phone. On the screen was a picture of him, smiling, holding two dark-haired, grinning little girls on his knees.

Ty smiled. "They're so pretty." He brought up his own pictures on his phone. "So yeah, cutting my trip short."

"You here on vacation?"

"Just a weekend thing." He pulled up a picture of Becky, holding her Hello Kitty doll, and showed it to him. "I was supposed to fly back tomorrow anyway."

The man smiled fondly at Ty's phone. "They're so precious, aren't they? They take up your whole heart, and then you realize what your heart was for all along."

Ty smiled gently and gazed at the picture. "Yeah,

I know what you mean. Even when nothing else in my life makes sense, there's her."

"I hope she'll be all right. I know she will, man. God has this. Just leave it up to Him."

Ty didn't know if he trusted much in God, but it was something his mother would say, too, so he just nodded. He turned off his phone screen and went back to contemplating.

"You here with friends?"

Ty shook his head. "A woman."

"Did she leave already?"

"No, she's back at the resort we were staying at." He pictured her again, at their mercy, and guilt gnawed at him. It was already eating him up from not being with Becky, but apparently he had a little more guts left to chew on. "I had to try to get back home, though. She understands."

"Your girlfriend?"

"No." Ty turned the phone over in his hands. "I don't know her that well." He didn't want to explain the situation to this guy, and he certainly didn't want to tell him what he did for money. "She's just—a friend."

"Yeah, I've heard that one before."

Ty chuckled.

"She pretty?"

Ty smirked. "Yes, gorgeous." He pictured her long legs and ample breasts. The way everything she wore fit her just right. He had to see her again when they got home, no matter what else happened. Even if it was forbidden. That just made it sweeter.

"You like her?"

Ty nodded. "Yeah, she's an interesting woman. I had a lot of fun with her."

"So why you sitting here?" The man lifted his hands and shrugged. "You said you can't get out until morning. Why don't you go back to her?"

Ty wondered the same thing. Maybe he felt like if he stayed here, a miracle might occur, and he'd get on the next flight out. Or maybe he was punishing himself for being here in the first place. He needed to do penance.

Ty sighed. "This woman—she's got a lot of problems right now, a lot of things going on in her life." He kept turning the phone over in his hands. "I don't know that I'm the right person to fix them for her." He frowned. "It's complicated."

The man snorted and sat forward. "Problems? Down here? What ever happened to going on vacation to get away from your problems?"

"Problems travel, too, you know. They don't care about your location." He stopped fiddling with his phone and placed it on his knee. "Everyone's got problems though, I know that."

"Tell me about it." The man ran his hand over his curls and patted them. "The thing about problems though, is they're better when you're not going through them alone. Trust me, if it wasn't for my wife I would have gone crazy a long time ago."

Ty looked at him and arched an eyebrow.

"You might not be able to help her, but maybe you can just be there, you know? And hey—you got problems right now, too. Do you wanna be alone, breaking your ass all night on one of these things?" He knocked on the armrest beside him. "Or do you wanna go back and both of you can be with someone while you go through your problems?"

It all sounded so simple, and yet...

"I don't want to impose on her." Ty spoke carefully. "She's got her own life, and well, I don't think I can really be a part of it. Maybe, eventually. But like I said, I don't know her that well. And I don't want to heap all my angst on top of hers right now either. She's got enough to worry about."

The man chortled. "Best way to get to know someone is going through a crisis together. That's what they say anyway."

Ty wasn't sure who "they" were, and he wasn't sure about that adage either. He'd heard the opposite, often, that people who bonded over a crisis were left with little else when it was over. He sometimes thought that was the case with Cassie, Becky's mother. Her own mother had just passed away when they met in high school, her father was hardly ever around, and she needed someone to talk to and comfort her. Even as the years went on, and they were on-again-off-again, she often clung to him in times of hardship, and he was always there to try to patch things up.

Maybe he was just used to saving women.

Cassie was from his neighborhood though. She had never been married into money, and she certainly didn't hang in the social circles that Grace did. He was way in over his head with her.

"Even if I want to help her, I don't know that I *can* help her." Ty contemplated his bag between his feet again. "I mean, some things are just beyond my scope."

The man leaned over, gripped his shoulder, and gave it a friendly shake. "Mister, you should stop doubting yourself. I bet you're smarter than you give yourself credit for." He slipped his hand off his shoulder. "Or, you know, they give us credit for." He gestured toward the counter.

The couple was still trying to obtain their boarding passes and were now arguing with the agent, who was a black woman. Maybe it was a coincidence, maybe they argued with everybody, but it seemed to underline the point and made Ty feel even more rage toward those stuck-up, racist assholes back at the resort. The same assholes he'd left Grace with.

He narrowed his eyes as an idea came to him. Maybe he *could* work with what he had. The only way he was ever going to win against them was to play the same games they did, after all.

Ty sat up straighter and smiled at the man. "I think I will go back to the resort. You know, it's not going to help my daughter just sitting here, stewing in my guilt. I might as well try helping my friend. That, I can actively do right now."

The man gave him a thumbs-up and hauled himself to his feet. "I hope your daughter gets better. Don't worry too much."

Ty reached out and offered the man his hand. He shook it. "Where are you heading?" Ty noted he didn't have any bags.

"Oh, I work here." He chortled and pulled out a hat. "Skycap. I haul bags around for these demanding types." He indicated the couple again. "I was just on break. Now it's back to the hamster wheel. Good luck with everything—your daughter, and your friend. I know it's all gonna work out for you." He pointed up. "God's in control."

As he shuffled off, Ty drew a heavy sigh. He wished he had such faith, or faith in anything really right now. Faith that his life would get better, the bills would get paid, his daughter would grow up healthy, and he wouldn't have to own a grocery store for the rest of his life. Grace was probably hoping for many of the same things. Maybe the skycap was right. Maybe they should hope for them together, it would at least make the wait more bearable.

He got up, grabbed his bag, and looked at his

phone. He could call Grace and tell her he was coming back, but she might be at dinner and wouldn't answer. He could just surprise her. If she didn't want him there, he would come back and bust his ass in a chair all night, waiting for the sun to rise and his ride home.

"Worth a shot," he murmured. If he ran into the others, he had an idea how to get them to step off, too. Cater to the rules of their game, no matter how absurd it was.

Soon, he was headed back into the lush green of the island, with the setting sun to his left over the ocean. Such a beautiful sight, stretching pink and orange across the water. The warm breeze flowed in the cab windows. He kept checking his phone for missed messages and calls, even though it never left his hand.

He texted his sister: **Please keep me updated with what's going on, often. I don't care if it costs money.**

He took a few deep breaths. He'd get back. His daughter would be okay. If not God, then someone had it. Someone was in control of the situation. He had to have faith in that or he'd lose his mind.

A text came back, quicker than he expected. **They're giving her fluids and getting her fever down. Chill, I'll call you. It's all right at the moment.**

He sagged in relief and gazed out at the sunset. He took a picture of it to show Becky. She loved the color pink, and there was so much of it in the sky and on the water right now, like a sign from her that everything would be okay. He put his hand over his heart and closed his eyes for a moment. Hopefully, she could feel him, too.

They drove back toward the resort, where those awful people waited, but Grace was there, too, and she was the exception. He was going to put his savior complex aside for the night and just be with her, just be there for her. And she would be there for him, too, at least keeping him distracted and keeping the existential loneliness at bay. If that was all they could do for each other, it would be enough. Though he didn't have much money left, he tipped the cabbie extra.

Chapter Seventeen

Grace stood at the boardwalk railing and gazed out at the ocean. The sun was nearly below the horizon now, the sky above it heavy with thick orange and pink clouds, the same colors reflected across the water. The breeze tugged at her hair. She wanted Ty to see this sunset and appreciate it with her. Instead, her flesh crawled as Carl slowly rubbed her lower back. He stood so close she could smell his cologne and it made her want to retch. If she actually did, maybe she *could* blame the shrimp cocktail.

"Carl, can I ask you for something? A favor, perhaps?" She pulled up her resolve and eased closer to him, despite the urge to run away as fast as she could. "You're a very wealthy man. And a generous one."

Carl slipped his arm around her waist and drew her closer yet so that she was pressed against his side. "One of the wealthiest and most generous men you'll ever meet, darling."

Both of those things were far from the truth—there were men much wealthier, and much, *much* more generous, but she wasn't going to argue.

"You know this has all been very difficult for me, financially. Waiting on this money to get freed up has been a nightmare." Her whole body was rigid, and she could barely breathe. "I know there's not a thing Brent can do, in there. I don't blame him at all." She blamed him for everything, especially after the truth bomb Carl had just dropped on her, but he was Carl's buddy. If she badmouthed him, unless it was to downplay his prowess to boost Carl's sexual esteem, this wasn't going to go well for her. Carl would take Brent's side in any matter. He'd shown that to be true already.

Carl hummed in sympathy. "Yes, I expect you haven't had an easy time of it." He rubbed her hip in wide circles. "I'm sorry I threatened you earlier. I panicked."

She looked up at him, arching an eyebrow.

"I didn't want you to run off on me." He chuckled lightly. "The thought of losing you made me lash out. Will you accept my apology? I was a jerk."

In no way was he actually sorry or serious. "Of course." She emitted a dramatic sigh, to try to sound pathetic. "Here I am, though. Struggling to get by. The only real income I have now is from the boutiques, and, well, it's not quite what I would like." Of course, she had never told any of these people she only had one left. "It's not enough to keep me in my lifestyle, the one I've grown to like so much." She nudged him with a playful elbow in the side.

He turned fully toward her, slipping his other arm around her waist as well. She was now pressed up tight against his body and she couldn't escape easily if she needed to.

"Darling Gracie, why has it taken you so long to come to me?" He reached up and stroked the errant strands of her hair back. "I expected you'd come crawling long before now. I prepared myself for it. You didn't have to hold back so long."

She swallowed. "I've been trying to preserve my pride, I guess." She lifted her chin and looked him in the eye. "I've been making do."

"You haven't made do nearly as well as you could have." He stroked his hand down her arm. "I could give you everything you want, you know. Brent wouldn't mind, he doesn't even have to know. All you have to do is ask."

In a grim flash of horror, she knew she had to

accept. If he gave her any money, she would be stuck in his web forever. Even if he didn't demand she have sex with him in return—which was slim—he would expect her gratitude forever, or at least until she got her money from the courts and could disappear. He would be involved in every aspect of her life in every way he possibly could.

This was a mistake. A desperate, stupid mistake. It wasn't the answer. There had to be some other way.

"Maybe I shouldn't ask so much of you." She tried subtly to shrug off his hand. "It's not right to ask you for help, not with Brent being your friend. I realize it puts you in an awkward position."

He smirked. "I'm never in an awkward position. And you need it, quite a lot. You're not managing at all, Gracie. Your life is in shambles."

She stared at him. "No, it isn't."

He leaned closer, almost in her face. She drew back a little.

"You only have one boutique left." He tightened his hold on her. "You closed the other three and sold off your assets. The other one is still open only because you have an investor. You've been pretending you're doing just fine, but you're not. You'll be out of the penthouse in just a few months. You can't keep up the bills on it."

She blinked a few times, her cheeks flashing hot. "How do you know all that?"

"Oh, I've done my research. Keeping tabs on things, you might say. I've been looking after you."

She didn't know how to respond. She was flabbergasted, and more than a little humiliated. Did the others know as well?

"Your bank account is dry, business is dry at your boutique, and you can barely pay to live, let alone come on this trip." He reached up to her hair again and played with a loose strand of it. "But it doesn't have to be that way. You don't have to struggle. That's what I'm here for."

She looked away, her face burning. "I think I should go back to my room. I don't want to continue this conversation. It's too embarrassing for me, Carl."

"Embarrassing, why? Because you might end up back at the bottom, where Brent found you? As I said, that doesn't have to happen. Unless that's where you want to be. But I think you've come to enjoy this luxury. You don't want to let it go."

She struggled against his grip. The worst part was that he was right. "Let go of me, Carl." She pushed at his arms.

"Or maybe gutter rats always make their way home." He dropped his arm from around her waist. His voice turned cold, the way it had been in the room when he was threatening her. "From the first time Brent brought you around, we all knew he was just doing his usual. No matter how much he tried to shine you up, it peeked through, that dirt on you. And now that you don't have him filling up your coffers, your shine is fading."

She stepped back. "You can't talk to me this way." Fury overtook humiliation. "How dare you."

In that moment, she knew there were no further options. She knew what Ty had been trying to tell her all along was true. She didn't need their judgment and ridicule. She didn't need to be around these horrible people, trying to be something she wasn't. She was better than this. She could *be* better than this.

Though tears blurred her vision, she wouldn't grovel. "I may be from the other side of the tracks, but that doesn't make me less of a person. In fact, I'm a better person than you, and all the rest of these vapid, self-absorbed morons." The words had been pent up inside her for a long time and now they came out in a rush, the way they had with Amelia in the bathroom. "I can't believe I've continued to associate myself with you." She let out a sharp, shaky laugh. "Or I even married that piece of shit behind bars in the first place. I hope he rots in there. I hope you end up joining him."

Carl just laughed.

He sneered. "Honey, the only reason I let you stay around and tolerated your lackluster presence is because of that ass and those tits." He looked her over. "And God knows in a few years those will be gone, too."

She couldn't stop herself. In a flash, she reached out and slapped him across the face. She drew back with a gasp, horrified at herself.

He laughed again.

"And that gutter punk you brought here with you, is that supposed to impress us, or make me jealous? What street corner did you pick him up on? Is it the one you usually work?"

Despite being mortified at herself, she flung out her hand to slap him again. He caught it easily. He grabbed her other arm as well, hard, so hard it hurt. She yelped. Panic shot through her.

"Don't you get uppity with me," he said in her face. "You want some money, huh? Is that what you were going to ask me for? Well, you're going to work for it. You'll have to earn it. You can earn it, can't you, baby? With that pretty mouth of yours and that fat ass?" He reached around and gripped it.

Tears slipped down her cheeks. She twisted against him. "Let me go, you bastard!"

He shook her. "Play nice now, honey. You'll get a treat if you do."

She shrieked again. He yanked her toward him and kissed her, rough and sloppy. He tasted like scotch and it made her recoil. She wrenched her head away and tried to scream, but he grabbed her chin, pinching her cheeks hard.

"Stop fighting, Gracie. You know this is the best you'll ever do."

She was terrified. Could she scream loud enough to summon help? Was anyone close enough to hear? Did she have the strength to throw him off?

As it turned out, she didn't need to try. A woman's voice called out.

"Let her go, motherfucker!"

Grace looked over Carl's shoulder, wide-eyed. Amelia was marching along the boardwalk toward them, her heels clicking hard on the wood. Her eyes blazed, her mouth pulled in a grimace. She stormed up to Carl as he let go of Grace. She grabbed him by the arm and whirled him around to face her.

"You fucking pig." She snarled. "I'm tired of this, the way you act, the way you treat me."

Carl growled and shook her hand off his arm. "What do you want? Are you drunk? Why don't you go back and finish getting sloshed?"

Amelia put a finger in his face. "You're not going to keep humiliating me like this." She looked at Grace, her gaze full of bitterness and disgust. "You keep parading your sick bullshit in front of me, crawling on top of any woman who gets near you."

Grace stood stunned, tears wet on her cheeks, not sure what to do. She wanted to run away, but Amelia might need help.

"Oh, please." Carl brushed his arm off where she'd grabbed him. "You screw lowlifes all the time. Every driver you hire, you fuck. Not to mention our chef, and the gardeners—should I go on? You'll throw your fake tits at any scumbag who smiles at you. Are you saying me fucking her somehow offends your delicate sensibilities?" He jerked a thumb at Grace.

Grace's rage rose up once more. She was tired of being talked about like this. Before she could open her mouth, though, Amelia spoke again.

"You're the lowlife." She spat right on his designer silk shirt. "That's why I stopped fucking you ages ago!"

Grace gaped at Amelia. Had she rattled something in her earlier by insulting her and pointing out the obvious?

Carl didn't laugh this time. His expression turned dark, his eyes glittering. "Listen, you cunt." He grabbed Amelia by the arm. "If it wasn't for me, you wouldn't be where you are today." He flung her around and slammed her against the railing of the boardwalk. She squeaked.

"Carl!" Grace lurched at him. "Stop!" She didn't like Amelia, but she wasn't going to watch her be manhandled.

"You wouldn't be where you are without my father!" Amelia shrieked back at him. "Scumbag. Loser!"

He lifted his hand as if to hit her, but Grace blocked it. He snarled and turned on her, and then grabbed her by the throat. Grace's eyes popped wide. She clutched his wrist with both hands.

"Who the hell do you think you are?" he demanded. "Don't either of you put your hands on me."

Even together, they probably didn't have a chance of taking him down. Still, Grace would try. She wasn't going home with a black eye. She reached back into her memory, of bar fights and brawls at the places she'd worked at. Even women had gotten involved sometimes and she had to jump in and break things up. Did she still have it in her?

It didn't matter, because someone else showed up

just then.

The figure flew at Carl seemingly from nowhere and slammed into him from behind. He instantly let go of Grace's throat, as well as Amelia.

Grace stumbled back and was gratefully shocked at who she saw. She thought for a moment she must be imagining things. "Ty!"

Ty was a seething mass of rage, his hair loose and scattered, dark eyes burning. He backed Carl down the boardwalk.

"You keep your fucking hands off her." His voice was deadly.

Carl laughed at Ty. "Or what, you punk? What are you going to do to me, boy?"

Ty answered his question by swinging and hitting Carl with such a vicious punch, the crack resounded on the air. Carl crashed to the boards with a surprised groan. Grace shrieked and clamped her hands over her mouth. Amelia rushed up beside her.

"What am I gonna do?" Ty marched around him, to Carl's head. "This." He pressed his foot over his windpipe. "Assholes like you have had their foot on my neck for years. How's it feel, you woman-beating rapist?"

Grace took her hands from her mouth and yelped. "Ty, don't!" She didn't want him going to jail, especially not with his daughter sick at home. Why was he even here? Why hadn't he left? Not that she was complaining.

Carl squirmed and clutched Ty's ankle, but Ty was apparently pressing down hard enough to keep him from fighting back effectively. Carl coughed and gagged.

"How's it feel?" Ty asked again. "Just like you've been doing to everyone else, including your own wife, huh?"

Grace hurried over. "Ty, stop." She looked wildly

up and down the boardwalk. If a cop or security guard came along, Ty would surely be arrested.

"You listen to me." Ty bent over Carl. "If you ever touch Grace again, or even contact her, or bother her in any way, you'll regret it." Carl stared up at him with bulging, frightened eyes. "And if you do anything to me, this is what'll happen." Ty's lips twisted into a vicious smile. "Some of my close acquaintances will pay you a visit. You know the sort of acquaintances I'm talking about, huh? Some Italian fellas, of the highest order. They'll make what's happening to you right now seem like a picnic. They'll show up at your house when you're least expecting them. Do you understand what I'm saying?"

Grace boggled. Was he talking about the mob?

Carl, still struggling, nodded against the boards. His face was bright red.

"You know people like me, us lowlifes, we have connections." Ty gave a harsh laugh. "Connections you don't want to mess with. Us ethnic guys, we strong-arm our way through life. You want that arm on your throat?"

Carl shook his head, his legs working fruitlessly.

Grace's heart was hammering. She was shaking. She wasn't sure if she was terrified or elated, or both.

"Don't ever bother her again," Ty reiterated. "And if you try to stop her from getting her money in court, it's going to be the last thing you ever do." He took his foot off Carl's neck.

Carl rolled away, coughing and gasping. Amelia hurried to her husband. She stood over him, breathing hard, staring at Ty. Her expression was somewhere between fury and confusion, hard to read.

"Don't mess with me." Ty pointed at her. "You call the cops about this, my friends will know. And even your rich Daddy can't do anything about it." If he was bluffing, it didn't show. He sounded dead serious.

Amelia looked down at her husband. He'd rolled onto his stomach and was groaning and muttering. He didn't get up. For the first time since Grace had met him, he was truly subdued.

Grace found her voice. "Good-bye, Amelia. I don't think I'll be coming for brunch anymore."

Amelia hauled off with a scream and kicked her husband in the ribs with the tip of her high heel. He hollered in pain and swore profusely. Grace was impressed and a little envious. She wanted to do it, too. Tears slipped down Amelia's face.

"You can do better than this, Amelia." Grace looked at Ty. "Trust me."

"Get off this island," Amelia said, lowly. "Go."

Ty grabbed up his bag, which he'd dumped on the boardwalk before attacking Carl apparently, then clutched Grace's hand and dragged her down the boardwalk, away from the couple and back toward the resort. She followed in a daze, barely able to comprehend what was going on.

"I thought you left," she managed to get out. "What are you doing here?"

"I can't get a flight out until morning." He walked with purpose, hair bouncing on his shoulders. "Come on, we're grabbing your stuff and getting out of here."

That sounded like a good idea. She'd stay in the airport all night, or sleep on the beach, on the side of the road, but she wasn't staying here to see the fallout.

"You really have connections in the mob?" She was still terrified Carl would call the police. "Is that what you were implying?"

He smirked back at her. "Of course I do, don't all us dirty Wops?"

Grace stared at him, then smiled. "The only people he would actually fear. I think Carl believes you."

"That's all that's important. He won't bother you again, Grace. I promise."

She wasn't sure he could make that promise, but for now she let herself believe it. She felt like the chains that had held her since Brent went to prison—since the day she met him, really—had finally loosened and she was working her way out of them. Soon, she would sprint in the open air and leave this life behind forever.

She started laughing as they hurried through the hallways toward the room. For the first time in years—so many long, joyless years—she knew who she was. She felt like herself again.

"You ready to get the hell off this island?" Ty asked. "And the hell away from them?"

She squeezed his hand, her heart and spirits soaring. "Yes. I'll go anywhere, as long as it's with you."

He pulled her into his arms and lavished a deep kiss on her, and she was free.

Chapter Eighteen

Ty jerked awake as someone shook him. For a moment, he didn't have a clue where he was, the time, or what was going on. However, it all quickly came back.

"Ty." His sister stood over him, a paper cup of coffee in hand. "Sorry, thought you might want something to drink."

He pushed himself into a sitting position with a wince. He'd been slumped over in the narrow, distinctly uncomfortable chair, and the arm had been digging into his side as he was dead asleep. He rubbed his ribs. "Is she okay?"

"Yeah, she's still asleep." Luci sat down in the chair next to him. "Her fever hasn't come back. We should be able to take her home in a couple hours."

Ty flopped back against the chair and rested his head on the wall behind him. His whole body ached, head to toe. It had been a long, tiring day—had it even been an entire day yet? He couldn't figure it out right now, he'd been on a plane for most of it.

He shifted his jacket off his chest, where he'd had it draped like a blanket, and took the cup of coffee. "I'm glad she's going to be okay. It scared the hell out of me." He took a sip and flinched. Hot, black coffee. Exactly what he needed right now, but his addled brain wasn't expecting the heat.

"It scared me, too." His sister eyed him. "Did you have fun in Barbados, at least?" She reached over and lifted his hand. "Apart from this?"

His knuckles were still red and swollen on his right hand. He'd only punched a guy once before, when some junkie was threatening his mother in the store. That guy was frail and brittle though, and Carl was quite solid. The power Ty put behind the punch amazed even him.

When he'd seen him with his hands on Grace like that, anger just overtook him and gave him momentum.

"Yeah, it was a blast." He flexed his fingers and grimaced. He didn't think he'd broken anything, but he'd suffer for a few days, and holding a pen wouldn't be fun.

"You should have a doctor look at that." Luci sat back in her chair. "Or at least get a nurse to give you an ice pack."

The white, sterile corridor was quiet, filled only with the beeps of monitors from the open doors of nearby rooms. Some staff milled about at the other end of the hallway.

"Nah." He took another, smaller sip of coffee. "Then I'd have to explain how it happened. I don't need the police coming around."

He hoped his threat to Carl, along with the show of force, would be enough of a deterrent. Ty did in fact know some shady types, but they sure as hell weren't in the mob and probably couldn't do much to a rich guy like that. He had to pray the guy in the airport was right— guys like Carl always assumed the worst of people on the lower rungs of society, that they were all dangerous thugs who crept in the shadows and could pose a threat at any time. He really, *really* hoped Carl thought that way. Otherwise, he was screwed and his big display was for nothing.

"So tell me what else you did, besides beat some dude up." Luci drummed her nails on her chair arm. "You know Ma is going to tear you apart when we get home. You better have a story."

He groaned. "Yeah, I figure." He rubbed his face, then winced at the pain in his knuckles. "God, sorry I fell asleep, I'm exhausted. You said Becky is all right?"

"Like I said, she's resting. They just want to make sure she's over the worst of it." She turned toward him. "Now quit avoiding the question. What did you get up to in Barbados?" She gestured at his hand. "And what's the whole story with that?"

Ty wasn't sure he wanted to tell her. He was a mixed-up mess of emotions—good and bad. Half of his mind was with Grace, and the other half was with his daughter in that room a few feet away.

"The woman I was with,"—he gazed down at his injured hand—"this guy had his hands on her, threatening her. I got there just in time. I'd come back from the airport after finding out I couldn't get a flight out until morning. I just saw red, I didn't think. I went at the guy and I put him down."

He didn't want to imagine what might have happened if he had gotten a flight and didn't return to the resort.

"Damn, Ty. I didn't know you had it in you."

"I didn't either." He shrugged. "The guy was a total asshole the entire time we were there. I'm kind of glad he gave me a reason to punch him." He wouldn't mention the foot on his neck. That was completely uncharacteristic of him, he hadn't even been thinking in the moment, just blind with rage and the need to get even with that smug bastard. His sister might think it was awesome, but she would inevitably tell their mother, and she wouldn't be inclined to praise or forgive him for such rash, violent behavior.

"You had quite an adventure." Luci smirked. "Was the girl worth it?"

Ty took a sip of coffee to hide his smile. "She's a very interesting woman. Maybe you'll get to meet her."

Luci arched an eyebrow. "You're bringing one of your tricks home?"

"She's not a trick." He scowled. "And I'm not a man whore. I just provide companionship for lonely women, at a small fee."

Luci slumped toward him, a devious look on her face. "Tell me about her. What's her name?"

"Grace. And before you ask a million questions, she lives in Manhattan, she runs a clothing boutique, she's a brunette with brown eyes, and yes, she's hot."

"And..." She leaned in closer.

He rolled his eyes. "And yes, I slept with her."

Luci sat back and let out a triumphant laugh. "I knew it. You *are* a man whore."

"I am not. I honestly don't usually sleep with my dates." He raised his right, swollen hand. "On Dad's grave, I swear it. I just usually take them out and have some fun. Good, clean, wholesome fun."

"So what made you sleep with this one?"

He was still trying to figure that out. Maybe because Grace was more complex than the other women? Because he felt a connection with her? Because she was irresistible and he had to have her?

"I don't know." He took another drink. "I just did, and I think I'm going to see her again. For free this time."

"Oh my God, seriously?" She nudged him. "You found a girlfriend?"

"It's a little early for that. I like her, I want to see her again, that's all I'm saying."

"How does that work?" Luci titled her head. "It is awkward because she paid for you the first time, or are you going to refund her, or what?"

"I don't know. I haven't done this before." He would give Grace her money back, gladly, if she requested it, no matter how much he needed it. She'd had one hell of a weekend and it wasn't exactly the sort of date he usually took women on.

Luci smiled, sweet and genuine. "I'm happy for

you actually. I've been hoping this day would come. You've not been with it since Cassie passed away."

"What do you mean by 'not with it'? I've had the store to worry about, in case you haven't noticed. Dad died not too long after her. I've been up to my neck with responsibilities."

"I know, and you deserve a break." She touched his arm. "What I mean is, I'm glad to see you smile like that again. I'm glad to hear you being happy about something. Even if it is some woman you whored yourself out to."

He smirked. "Hey, I gave her every penny's worth." He winked. "She's a satisfied customer."

"Gross." Luci scrunched up her face. "I didn't say I wanted *those* frickin' details."

He grinned. "Let's go in and see the munchkin."

They got up. Ty slung his jacket over his shoulder. He was still in a dress shirt and nice pants, which was what he'd flown home in—he hadn't taken anything overly casual, per Grace's request. He felt weirdly out of place in that informal setting, and also very unkempt and un-showered.

"She runs a boutique," Luci said over her shoulder as she led him into the room. "Think she can hook me up with some clothes? I haven't bought a new dress in ages."

"She designs them herself. She might give you a discount."

"Well, she better, since she's going to be my sister-in-law and all."

Ty poked her in the back. "Shut up."

Becky was asleep in her bed, an IV line still in her arm. Luci said she was a bit dehydrated when they brought her in, as she didn't want to drink anything. She looked peaceful now, her chubby cheeks back to their normal color, her eyelashes falling soft against them as she slept. She was curled on her side, clutching her Hello Kitty. Ty stroked her hair.

"I feel so guilty for being away," he whispered. "I should have been home."

"It was just bad timing, it's not your fault." Luci kept her voice down, too. "Don't feel bad, you were out trying to pay our bills."

Ty looked up at her, surprised to hear her say that, and it didn't sound sarcastic.

"I know you only want what's best for her. You're not going to give her a future at the store. And I know you don't want it to be her only option in the future." She shrugged. "You're a hot enough guy, you might as well work it while you got it. You're not gonna make that kind of money doing anything else. And besides, it sounds kind of exciting. Dad is probably rolling over in his grave, but let him spin."

Ty squinted. "Did you just call me hot?"

She grimaced. "*I* don't think you're hot, okay? But I've seen the way girls react to you. And my friends think you're hot, too." She mimicked gagging herself with her finger. "They have no taste, obviously."

He grinned and looked back down at his daughter. He sifted the silky strands of her hair through his fingers, the color lighter than his. "She looks so much like Cassie," he said softly. "I wish she could have seen her grow up."

"She has you in her, too. Especially when she gets whiny."

Footsteps sounded at the door, the click of heels. Someone cleared their throat, a delicate sound.

Ty looked over his shoulder and widened his eyes. He turned. "Grace."

She stood in the doorway, wearing the same

powder blue dress and white shoes she'd worn on the plane, but she looked considerably fresher than him. She clutched a little gift bag in front of her. Her gaze was hesitant, and she bit her lower lip.

"I'm sorry," she whispered. "I just—I wanted to make sure she was all right. I found out where you were at the admissions desk."

Ty walked over to her. "Hey, it's good to see you." He gripped her gently by the shoulders and kissed her cheek. "I'm glad you're here."

She glanced past him. "How is she doing?"

"Oh, she's fine." Ty turned back. Luci stood beside the bed, eyebrows raised. "She just has a bad case of the flu. They have her on fluids and they got her fever down. We'll be able to take her home soon."

"That's good." Grace held out the gift bag. "I got her a little something. I admit I'm not sure what little girls like these days, but I thought she might enjoy this."

Ty took the bag with a smile. "Thank you." He peeked inside. There was a little stuffed unicorn with a rainbow mane. "I was actually looking at this in the gift shop window when we walked past earlier and thinking she'd get a kick out of it. Are you psychic or something?"

Grace's cheeks turned pink. "Oh, well, I'm glad she'll enjoy it. We must have similar tastes." She tittered.

Luci strolled over, arms folded. The tight, polite smile on her face told Ty he was going to get quite the grilling after this.

"Grace, this is my sister, Luci." He patted Luci's shoulder. "Luci, this is Grace, my date." He left it at that.

"Hello." Grace fidgeted.

"Nice to meet you." Luci looked at Ty. "I'm going to give Ma a call and update her, okay?"

Ty nodded. Luci slipped out of the room, leaving

them alone apart from the sleeping child.

"I'm sorry." Grace shook her head. "I know it's much too early for meeting the family. I just wanted to stop by and make sure everything was okay. I don't want to make things awkward between you and your sister."

Ty smiled. "She knows what I do. My mother does, too. They knew I was on a date with you."

"Well, you must be a very close family, then." She looked over at the bed. "She's a pretty little girl, by the way."

"She's a lot cuter without all the needles and tubes."

"I can imagine." Grace smirked faintly.

He took her by the arm and led her out of the room, so they didn't have to keep whispering. "No need to apologize. I'm glad you stopped by." He looked her over in the light of the hallway. She wasn't as bedraggled as him, but her eyes were tired. "How are you doing?"

"I'm fine." She sighed. "I'll be fine, anyway. I suppose." She looked down at his hand. "And how are your knuckles?"

He smirked and flexed his fingers. "They'll be fine, too. It was worth it."

She toyed with her earring. "I must admit, as traumatic as it was at the time, it was rather lovely seeing Carl hit the ground like that. He's had it coming for a long time. In fact, I don't think he's even close to the quota of fists-to-the-jaw that he deserves."

"Let my hand heal up first, and then I'll work on that."

She took his hand and gently rubbed her thumb over his reddened knuckles. "No one, not even my ex-husband, has ever come to my aid like that." Her eyes sparkled. "I feel a bit like a rescued damsel."

"I think you're much stronger than a damsel in

distress. You're not going to see any of those people again, are you? They're not good for your mental health."

She huffed. "God, no. I have no real ties with any of them, and as far as I'm concerned, they no longer exist." She drew herself up, squaring her shoulders. "It's time to make new friends and live my life the way I want to. And that means not trying to impress anyone. I don't come from money, I never did, and I'll never be able to pretend again."

"Money isn't everything, you know."

"Unless you don't have much and you're struggling every day to make ends meet."

"Tell me about it."

She gazed into his eyes. "I can't thank you enough, Ty, for everything you've done. I needed that kick in the face, to get away from those people, to take back control of my life. It won't happen overnight, I've got a lot of adjusting to do, but I'm willing to do it now. I was blinded by the things my ex heaped on me, and I think that's what he wanted. He wanted me dazzled and suppressed so he could go on being his terrible self. I've let his legacy haunt my life for too long."

"I told you, you're a smart broad."

She smiled widely. "I certainly got my money's worth out of this trip."

Ty hesitated. "Do you want the money back? I don't feel quite right taking it now."

She shook her head. "No, I think I got more than I paid for, and you did the job you were supposed to. Above and beyond." She squeezed his hand, but lower, away from his knuckles. "Besides, hopefully the courts will soon give me what I deserve. If not, I'll keep fighting with all I have. I'll get another job and pay for more lawyers. I might get rid of the boutique and start over. I can go back to working in bars and save up money to open again on my own. Something that's all mine this time."

"Don't make any hasty decisions just yet." He sighed. "Trust me, I've been considering selling the store, too, but I need a good plan in place. I don't want it to go to just anyone, and I still want to be able to support my daughter and family. It's a lot more complicated than what we want for ourselves, you know?"

"Well, you could keep working your other job." She looked down. "I'm sure you wouldn't be lacking business."

He took her hand in both of his and drew her closer.

"The problem with that," he murmured, his face close to hers, "is that I met this girl, and I'd like to see where it goes with her. I don't think dating other women for money would really be healthy for a possible future relationship."

He could smell her perfume, soft and flowery, and even right there in the hospital hallway he wanted to devour her.

She glanced up at him. "Maybe this girl completely understands what it's like to need money, and that you're doing it to try to keep your daughter from having to struggle like you do." She looked into his eyes. "She would just have some stipulations, of course. She doesn't want you to treat your other clients quite the way you treated her..."

He grinned. "I don't know, I couldn't keep my mind on other women and show them a good time. They would be disappointed with my services. I'd be too distracted."

"It's not even an issue, is it?" She waved her other hand. "I mean, you haven't even asked me out yet."

He wrapped his arm around her waist and pulled her against him. "You wanna go out on a date? One you don't have to pay for? In fact, I'll pay this time."

She draped her arms over his shoulders. "As long as we don't go anywhere fancy, and I don't have to dress up."

"You don't have to dress at all, if you don't want to." He smoothed his hand over her hip.

"Behave."

He kissed her, slow and deep. His head spun when he did, not from the lack of sleep, or the rush of caffeine, but the thrill of knowing he'd found something good, finally. Even if the rest of his life was a juggling act, this might be the one thing that worked out.

Though he wanted to keep kissing her forever, and even longer, they were in a hospital, right outside his daughter's room, and he regretfully broke it off after a minute. Grace was breathing quickly, her heart pounding against his chest. His mind flitted to thoughts of nearby empty rooms with locks on the doors. No, he had to *behave*.

"Are you free on Friday?" She smiled. "Because I am."

He squeezed her. "I'll have to check my calendar. You know my life is so fast-paced and full of engagements."

Luci returned then, a coffee in hand—Ty realized he'd left his in Becky's room—and they quickly stepped away from each other.

"Ma says she'll make Becky's favorite dinner when she comes home. I told her she might need something a little easier on the stomach, though." She looked at Grace. "So I hear you own a boutique and make your own designs?"

Ty titled his head and gave her a "no you don't"

look. "Luci."

"What? I like fashion!" Luci shrugged. "I'm tired of wearing crap from the thrift store."

Grace looked her over. "You know, I need a model for my fall collection. You've got a nice figure. I usually give my models the clothes I dress them in."

Luci gaped at Ty. "You're keeping her."

Ty draped his arm around Grace's shoulders. "Sorry. Just wait until you meet my mother, you'll see where she gets it from."

Grace slipped her arm around his waist and chuckled. "I can't wait."

Chapter Nineteen

The July afternoon burned like a furnace, but Grace barely noticed as she jumped out of her car. She looked up at the windows above the store in front of her. They were all open, curtains fluttering in the breeze. She slammed the car door shut and cupped her hands around her mouth.

"Ty!"

Parked cars lined the narrow, cracked street. People sat out on stoops, fanning themselves and drinking from dripping bottles and glasses. Kids ran down the uneven sidewalks, shouting and oblivious to the woes of summer. The street reminded her of where she used to live when she was struggling to get through school—rundown but full of life.

"Ty!" she yelled again. She stepped up on the sidewalk, careful of her heels. She didn't dress up much anymore. These days she was back to being a jeans, t-shirts, and flip-flops kind of girl, but today's event called for her to look professional.

The curtains moved across one of the windows and Ty pushed his bare torso out. His hair was loose and fell around his face.

"Hey, beautiful." He waved. "You can come inside, you know."

She grinned up at him. Even shirtless—especially shirtless—and looking like he just rolled out of bed, he was gorgeous. She gawked at him. Sometimes she had to pinch herself to believe they were a couple.

"I have news." She spread her arms wide, purse dangling from one hand. "The hearing was today."

He pushed his hair back from his face, frowning. "It was?"

"Yes!"

He stared down at her a moment. "Yes?"

"Yes!" she shrieked. "Finally."

Ty's face bloomed into an expression of surprise and giddy joy. "Oh my God, I'll be right down!"

Grace hurried to the door of the grocery store. She yanked it open and stepped into the cool air inside. This place had become like a second home to her.

"Oh, hey, Grace." Luci sat behind the counter, flipping through a magazine. "I thought that was your car."

The place was empty of customers. That was good, because she planned to do a lot of yelling and squealing.

"Hello, Luci." Grace bounced in her heels. "I have a new dress for you, I'll bring it over tonight."

Luci's eyes lit up. "Just in time, I have a date on Saturday." She grinned. "This guy I met at school."

"Oh?" Grace wanted details, but she had other things on her mind right now.

Ty thundered down the back stairs. He appeared, still shirtless, wearing a loose pair of athletic shorts. His skin turned even darker in the summer, and he looked scrumptious.

Luci glowered at him. "Jesus, put some clothes on, huh?"

He ignored his sister and rushed over to Grace, flung his arms around her, and lifted her off her feet. She shrieked and giggled and kicked her legs.

"I can't believe I finally got the money!" she crowed as he spun her around. "I won!"

Luci yelped. "Oh my God, Grace! They gave you your money?" She jumped out from behind the counter and ran over to them. As Ty put her down, Luci hugged her.

"I felt like this day would never come." Grace

trembled with both excitement and the great release of anxiety she was experiencing.

Luci drew back. "I'm so happy for you. How much did you get?"

Ty scowled. "So not appropriate to ask!"

Grace chuckled. She didn't mind bragging a little, especially since she wasn't planning on keeping it all for herself. "The full amount my lawyer originally suggested." She took a deep breath. "Three hundred thousand. It's what my boutiques earned while we were married."

Ty and Luci's eyes popped wide. They gaped at her. She could hardly believe the number herself.

"That's a lot of money," Luci said. "Oh my God, Grace, you're rich!"

Grace tittered. She wasn't rich, but she could breathe easy for a while.

"I'm going to pay off my debts and re-open the boutique." She clasped her hands together. "My investor is still interested, and this one will be all mine, and I'll make it thrive."

She'd been working two jobs—a receptionist during the day, and a few nights a week and weekends at a bar, trying to save all she could. Her plan, if she didn't get the money, was to struggle and make her dreams come true the hard way instead.

Ty hugged her tight. She wrapped her arms around him but resisted the urge to run her hands all over his bare flesh, since his sister was standing there. She'd put her hands on him later, when they celebrated properly.

"You should have told me the hearing was today." He drew back and gazed at her. "Why did you keep it a secret? I could have gone with you for moral support."

She stroked his hair back from his face. "I wanted to do this on my own. I needed to prove I could. Also, if I lost I didn't want you to see me have a meltdown."

He gave her a firm, hard kiss. "We're partying tonight. We'll go to The Cantina and live it up."

The Cantina was a bar down the street, where they'd been spending their summer nights when they weren't at work. It wasn't a glamorous place, but she felt comfortable there, and they had an old-fashioned jukebox with good music.

"I'm coming with you." Luci hurried back behind the counter. "I'll call a babysitter so Ma can come, too. We're all going to celebrate with you, Grace." She grabbed her phone.

Grace laughed. "Drinks are on me, obviously."

Just then, someone walked past the front windows of the store, and Grace perked in surprise. A flash of blond hair, a woman walking briskly and easily. Grace blinked. "Is that…" The woman seemed familiar, and if it was who it looked like, it was astounding timing.

She hurried to the door and flung it open. The summer heat blasted her in the face.

Ty followed her. "Grace?"

Grace stared down the street, after the woman. She wore a sundress and sandals, a purse swinging at her hip. "Hey!" Grace called out. "Miss!"

The woman stopped and turned. She wore a big floppy sun hat, but her face was clear.

Grace instantly felt like a fool. She turned sheepish. "Oh, goodness. I'm sorry. You looked like someone I know. My mistake!"

The woman stared at her a moment, then she smiled and waved, and went on her way.

Grace started to close the door, feeling lame.

Ty arched an eyebrow. "Who was that?"

Grace swore, for a split second, that the woman had been Monica—the director of SASS, the woman responsible for bringing them together. What a merry coincidence that would have been, given how well her relationship with Ty had worked out.

She shook her head. "No one, I—just thought it was a friend of mine."

"Grace?"

Grace stopped short in closing the door and looked around to the voice. She gasped. This time it wasn't a mistake—the woman who stood on the sidewalk in a slinky white dress and heels, her hair loose and shimmering on her bronzed shoulders and holding her designer clutch in front of her—Grace definitely recognized her.

"Amelia?" Grace stared at her, both shocked and concerned. "What on earth are you doing here?"

Ty stepped up beside her, and his gaze darkened. He slipped a protective arm around Grace's waist. "Yeah, what *are* you doing here?"

"Hello, Tybalt," Amelia said.

He glared at her. "I thought I made it clear we didn't want to see you guys again."

"Please." Amelia held up a hand. Her nails flashed in the sunlight. Her expression was reticent, despite the fact her eyes were obscured by huge sunglasses, and she had a sort of meekness about her that Grace had never seen before. "I'm not here to cause trouble." She lowered her hand and drew a deep breath. "I stopped by your new apartment, Grace, but you weren't there. I thought you might be here."

"How do you know where my new apartment is?" Grace spoke dryly. "Or for that matter, where this place is?" It wasn't the kind of neighborhood Amelia would just visit on a lark. Grace was cautious.

"I've—been keeping up on what you're doing. I'm sorry." Amelia wrung her clutch between her hands. "I've wanted so badly to reach out and talk to you for the past several months. I just couldn't get the guts to do it. I thought now, maybe, would be a good time."

Grace was puzzled, and still worried. Was this the blowback they'd been waiting for since Ty manhandled Carl?

"What do you want?" Grace squinted.

Amelia pulled in another breath. "Carl and I are getting divorced. We've been separated since shortly after we came back from the trip. It'll be finalized soon."

Grace's mouth dropped open.

"And my father fired him." A tiny smile crossed her lips. "After he found out how abusive and controlling he is, not to mention all the affairs he had. He's rather destitute these days. Daddy will make sure I get everything I want in the divorce—the house, the cars, and plenty of alimony." Her smile widened. "Oh, and he's being investigated, because it seems a little birdie told someone that Carl just might have known about Brent's embezzlement schemes..."

Grace didn't know what to say. She was stunned, mostly, that Amelia would make such a move.

"I..." Grace still stared at her. "That's all ... good?"

"I wanted to apologize." She strolled closer. "For everything that happened, for the way I treated you." She stopped in front of them. "I know it's a little thing, but ... I'm in therapy now, and I went to rehab." She stroked her fingers through her hair. "I'm trying to be a better person. I even got Carl's 'gifts' taken out." She looked down at her chest.

Grace noted, for the first time, they weren't quite as ample as she remembered them.

"I know saying I'm sorry hardly covers it." Amelia gripped her clutch again. "But I do want to apologize, from the bottom of my heart. Even if you don't accept it, and you have no reason to." She sounded positively sincere, and that was another thing Grace had never known to come from her. "If there's anything I can do to make up for it, I'll be happy to."

Grace looked at Ty. He also seemed stunned. They both looked back at Amelia, and Grace's heart softened a little. Especially in light of what a great day she was having, she was inclined to be open and receptive to this unexpected visit.

Ty cleared his throat. "I'm glad you got away from him, I really am, Amelia. It sounds like you're using your head. I'm happy for you. We're happy for you, right, Grace?"

Grace nodded. "We're very happy for you."

Amelia smiled. "You said you were sure I was a smart girl. I wanted to prove you right."

Luci yelled from inside the store. "Are we cooling the whole frickin' neighborhood? Get in here and close the door!"

Ty chuckled. "Uh…" He ran his fingers through his hair. "You want something to drink, Amelia? Or do you have somewhere to be? Sorry I don't have anything fancy, but we've got lemonade on sale, two for a dollar."

Amelia looked over her shoulder. A sleek white car sat at the curb, a short distance down the street. She looked back at them. "I suppose I could come in for a minute and see the business."

They all stepped inside. Ty closed the door. The air-conditioning was blissful, and Grace was suddenly self-conscious that she might be sweating through her blouse. Then, she remembered she no longer cared, and Amelia didn't seem to be scrutinizing her anyway. She wished Ty wasn't shirtless right now, though. He was quite an eyeful.

Amelia slipped her sunglasses off and looked around. "This is an artisanal bakery, huh?" She grinned. "Must be themed."

"Yeah." Ty smirked. "Ghetto corner store chic is so in these days."

While he went to fetch them some drinks, Grace just stood and boggled at Amelia. What a wonderful, strange day this was turning out to be.

Amelia kept looking around, though she wasn't being disdainful. "I wish I had reached out to you sooner, Gracie. How has your life been? We really must catch up." She looked back at her. "Maybe over coffee?"

Grace thought about all the things she had right now—Ty, new friendships, a new outlook, and now the money she deserved. The sun was shining and the future looked bright.

"Life has been wonderful." Grace smiled. "It's been absolutely marvelous. Yes, I'd love to."

Amelia smiled. "I'm glad."

* * * *

Ty's place was much bigger than Grace's new apartment, with three bedrooms, a living room, and a kitchen that vastly dwarfed her own. The place stretched over the entire top of the store, and though it was old, Ty's mother kept it clean and bright and nicely decorated. It didn't have air-conditioning, as they could only afford it in the store, but Grace didn't care.

She had just come upstairs, when Becky ran out of the living room. "Grace!"

Grace scooped her up. She wore a cute pink summer dress. Grace had been considering designing some children's clothes and wondered if Ty would agree to let his daughter model them.

"Hello there." Grace carried her into Ty's room. "I hear you're going to be in first grade this year. Are you excited?"

Ty's room was the biggest bedroom, and some nights, Becky slept in there on her little bed in the corner. Other nights, she spent in Luci's room, where she had an elaborately constructed pillow and blanket fort. Occasionally, she slept in her grandmother's big bed with her. Grace envied her, so young and innocent, her hardest choice deciding whose room she wanted to sleep in that night.

Becky nodded. "I'm going to the school where the big kids go."

Ty was in the room, pulling on a t-shirt. Grace wished he wouldn't. "Don't worry, munchkin." He came over and tickled Becky's tummy. "There will be lots of kids your size, too."

Becky giggled and squirmed. "Can I go watch TV? Cartoons are on."

"Well, goodness, why didn't you say so?" Grace put her down. "I'm keeping you from important business."

Becky ran off. Ty smiled and sifted his hands through his hair, smoothing and untangling it. She absolutely forbade him to cut it. He looked so strikingly handsome in the sunlight from the window, his jaw scruffy, his eyes dark and shining.

"I'm so happy for you." He cupped her face and gave her a gentle kiss. "You've grown so much. I've watched you take charge of your future. It's been amazing."

"I don't think I could have done it without you by my side supporting me." She gripped the front of his t-shirt and pulled him closer. "And I want to return the favor."

He frowned at her. "What do you mean?"

"I mean, your uncle Andre."

Ty had been talking about selling the store to his uncle Andre, his father's youngest brother. Andre had some interest and had recently bought another business, eager to spread his entrepreneurial wings. Ty mused after selling the store he could use some of the money to go to school. Something to get him out of running the family business, while still keeping it in the family. Andre was willing to let them continue living above the store, as well.

"What about him?" Ty shrugged. "We're still discussing things. I know this place is a dump. He's family. I don't want to swindle him."

"You should sell it."

He shook his head. "It's not that easy, you know that."

"Sell it and go to school." She spoke firmly. "You want something else for yourself. You said you're interested in computers. Go to school and get a job in the computer field."

He gave a sharp laugh. "You make it sound so simple."

"You have an opportunity." She clutched his shirt harder. "Remember all the times you gave me a kick in the ass, when I was afraid?"

He smirked. "More like a slap on the ass."

"Sell the store. Go to school."

He heaved a deep sigh. "I have to think of Becky." He clenched his jaw. "Since I'm not doing the dating thing anymore, the only money I can save for her comes from the store. If I go to school, I'll have to find some part-time thing, and that's not going to be enough. I don't want this to be her fate, too. I don't want her working for my uncle someday."

She smoothed her hands down his chest. "That's why I'm going to give you the money for Becky."

He stared at her, then blinked a few times.

"I have more than enough now. I'll give you what you need to put in a savings account for her future."

He shook his head. "No, Grace, I'm not taking your money."

"Don't worry, it's not some spur-of-the-moment decision. I decided long ago if I got the money that's what I would do." She patted his chest. "Consider it a gift, for everything you've done for me."

"I'm not taking your money." He clutched her wrists. "You need it."

She laughed. "It's three hundred thousand dollars. Trust me, I can give you what you need for Becky and still have plenty to cover my debts. I mean, what am I going to do with all the extra? Go on some tropical vacation?"

He was silent, and she knew this wouldn't be easy for him to accept, but she hoped he did.

"Grace," he said softly. "You can't give me this, it's too much."

"It's not for you, it's for Becky." She stroked his cheek. "It's to make sure she has options. I'm more than happy to do it, especially since you've been by my side through every minute of this outrageous disaster."

"Grace." His voice was still soft. "We haven't been together long enough for you to give me such a huge gift."

She tugged him closer. "Then, I guess you're going to have to stay with me for a long, long time to make up for it."

He smiled, though hesitation still showed on his face.

"Listen." She looked him in the eyes. "I spent too

much time pretending to be something I wasn't, living a life that wasn't right for me, trying to keep my head above water in a pool I had no business being in. I know how much it sucks. I know how much it strips away the person you really are."

"Grace..."

"Just listen." She gripped his shirt again. "I know you've been doing what has to be done, but you're not a store owner. You're not supposed to spend your life in the family business. You should be allowed to do what feels right and still support your daughter. The road might be difficult at times—and trust me, it will be—but you'll make it." She titled her chin down, giving him a stern look. "But only if you accept a hand when it's held out to you."

He swallowed. A tiny smile touched his lips. "I don't know what to say."

"Say yes." She smiled. "Besides, I want to see the real you. I want to see who you really are when you free yourself of the things you're not. I'm excited to find that out. Not that I don't like you as you are, but I want to see what you look like when you don't have the weight of the world on your shoulders."

He wrapped his arms around her and pulled her close. She rubbed his back. If Becky wasn't in the other room, she'd throw him down on the bed and get to celebrating. She would save that for tonight, after The Cantina.

"I love you," he murmured. "You know that, right? I love you like crazy."

"I love you, too." She gave him a quick, soft kiss on the ear. "You're more than I ever could have dreamed of having in my life."

He drew back and sighed again. "Three hundred thousand." He rubbed her hip. "That's a lot of money."

He smiled. "What are you going to do with the rest of it, after you pay things off and give Becky her cut?"

She tilted her head. "That tropical vacation does sound kind of nice. You and I could use a break, don't you think?"

"Not a resort." He looked so serious it was comical. "None of that rich crap. We'll stay in a local hotel and go to dive bars and lay around naked on the beach."

"Will you promise not to punch anybody this time?"

"I can't promise, but I'll try. I swear I'll only punch assholes who deserve it."

"We can bring your family along, too. I think your mother and sister need a break as well."

He pushed out his lower lip. "No naked on the beach, then?"

"We can be naked in our room." She slipped her hand around and squeezed the firm, tight swell of his ass. "I think we should go back to where we first met."

"The airport?"

She laughed. "Technically, the first time I saw you was in that book. And my, weren't you eye-catching." She licked her lips. "Look how much being hot has changed your life."

He groaned. "And here I am, wasting my good looks in a relationship when I could be rolling in money." He held her tighter. "And I couldn't be any damn happier about it if I tried."

She kissed him. Here she was, finally—happy, secure, with a man she adored, a man who didn't lie to her or try to blind her with promises. A man who was sincere and sweet, and a little imperfect and uncertain, just like her. A man she could grow with.

They were pulled from the moment by the sound

of a door opening, and Ty's mother hollering. "Ty! Come help me with these bags. They weigh a ton!"

Grace drew back and grinned. "Reality calls."

He gave her one last squeeze. "Come on, you have to tell Ma the good news, as long as Luci hasn't already spilled the beans with her big mouth."

Becky raced by in the hallway. "Ma-Ma! Did you get cookies?" Apparently, cookies took precedence over cartoons.

"I told you, you always deserved better." He squeezed her hand and let it go, then headed out the door to help his mother.

A warm glow filled her chest as she watched him go. "Yes, and I finally got it."

The End

www.meganmorganauthor.com

BOYFRIEND MATERIAL

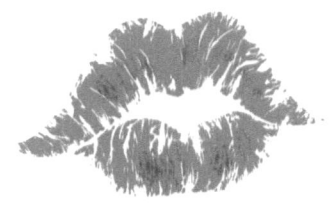

EVERNIGHT PUBLISHING ®

www.evernightpublishing.com

www.ingramcontent.com/pod-product-compliance
Lightning Source LLC
Chambersburg PA
CBHW030132180626
46812CB00002B/664